A Ward of the State

M.E. Wright

Merrywidow Publishing LLC

Names, characters, businesses, places, events, and incidents are either the product of the author's imagination or used in a fictitious manner. Any resemblance to actual persons, living or dead, or actual events is purely coincidental.

©2025 M.E. Wright. All Rights Reserved.

All rights reserved, including the right to reproduce this book or portions thereof in any form whatsoever without written permission of the publisher, except in the case of brief quotations embodied in critical articles and reviews.

Library of Congress Control Number: 2025906051

ISBN 979-8-9906996-6-3 (ebook)

ISBN 979-8-9906996-7-0 (paperback)

ISBN 979-8-9906996-8-7 (hardcover)

ISBN 979-8-9906996-9-4 (Audiobook)

To John

You gave me the space to dream, the courage to write, and the reason to keep going. I love you!

Contents

Chapter One	1
Chapter Two	17
Chapter Three	33
Chapter Four	47
Chapter Five	65
Chapter Six	79
Chapter Seven	99
Chapter Eight	115
Chapter Nine	129
Chapter Ten	143
Chapter Eleven	157
Chapter Twelve	177
Chapter Thirteen	193
Chapter Fourteen	201
Chapter Fifteen	215
Chapter Sixteen	229

Chapter Seventeen	245
Chapter Eighteen	265
Chapter Nineteen	283
Chapter Twenty	303
Chapter Twenty-One	317
Epilogue	329
The Fatherhood Mandate Preview	335
Author's Note	339
Acknowledgements	345
About the author	347
Also by M.E. Wright	349

Chapter One

The sky had faded into a mix of orange and purple, colors that meant the day was nearly over. The string lights under the pergola swayed in the cool evening breeze, their glow shifting across the table. Allison pulled her sweater tighter and curled her toes inside her fleece-lined slippers, pressing them against the wooden planks. Another gust hit, sharp and cold, and she wished she'd grabbed her jacket.

Her dad sat across from her, leaning an elbow on the table, a chess piece in his hand. The board between them blurred as Allison stared, struggling to focus on the game.

"Do you think they'll come here?" she asked, her voice barely above a whisper.

Her dad's hazel eyes flicked to her, softening as he set the knight down. He reached across the table, his hand warm against hers. "Hamburg is safe. We're a long way from the fighting."

The knot in her stomach didn't budge. She looked to the south, trying to imagine the Elbe River glowing under the bright lights as the overnight crew continued to work. Her dad said the upgrades to the current locks and dams were supposed to keep tidal flooding from spilling into cities like Hamburg and Dresden and turning streets into rivers.

It was urgent. Beyond necessary. But with storms getting stronger and the oceans rising every year, she wondered how long any of it would last.

The sudden chime of her dad's phone broke the stillness. He frowned, unfolding the slim screen and angling it so they could both see. "It's your mom," he muttered as he answered the call. "What's wrong, Rylee? Has something happened?"

Allison got up and moved closer to her dad. Her mom's face filled the screen, framed by the long black braid trailing over her shoulder. The dark blue of her shirt made her blue eyes seem darker, but there was no hiding her tension.

"The State Department issued a Do Not Travel alert for northern Germany and Poland," she began, her voice tight. "They're advising all U.S. citizens to evacuate." Her eyes darted to Allison. "It's time to come home."

Allison's chest tightened. The news was everywhere, flashing across the smart walls at school, playing on loops in public squares, and popping up in live feeds on social media. Russia had invaded Belarus, and the EU Defense Force was getting involved. She'd hoped it would stop there, but every update sounded worse. Now, the fighting had spread to Latvia and Lithuania.

Her dad rubbed his temple, glancing up at her before answering. "Rylee, the fighting is over 1,200 miles away. We're not in immediate danger."

"That's not the point," her mom shot back, her voice sharp. "The situation is escalating. Hamburg is a major port, Sam. The work you're doing will make it a target."

Her dad leaned back, the lines on his face deepening as he stared at his phone. "The upgrades aren't finished. If my crew evacuates, the work will not be completed by the time Greenland's 79 North Glacier fully disintegrates." He shook his head. "Germany isn't the only country impacted by this. Even Russia is at risk."

Allison's fingers brushed the edge of the chessboard. Her mom wasn't going to back down. The silence between her parents dragged on, broken only by the rustle of leaves overhead.

"I want you to come with us, but either way, Allison has to come back to Manhattan," her mom said, her voice quieter now.

Allison swallowed hard and nodded. She was supposed to stay with her dad for the next year. She didn't like Manhattan. Too crowded and noisy. She'd hoped that her mom would have moved somewhere quieter in the last two years, or maybe even joined them in Germany. But that didn't matter anymore.

"I've arranged for the corporate jet," her mom continued. She looked sad. "My flight leaves in about an hour. It's an eight-hour flight, so I'll be at the house by . . . "

"About 7 a.m. Hamburg time," her dad finished flatly.

Her mom nodded, then looked directly at her. "I know this isn't what you wanted," she said, her voice tight. "But it's not safe for you to stay." She hesitated, then forced a small smile. "Maybe things will settle down, and you can go back in a few weeks."

She glanced off to the side. "I need to check on the emergency travel visas. I love you both."

The screen went dark. Allison blinked, tears slipping down her face. Her dad pulled her into a hug, his flannel shirt soft against her cheek. She pressed her lips together, trying not to make a sound as she cried. His hand rested on the back of her head, steady and warm as he gently rocked her.

Allison woke, the house quiet except for the faint creak of settling wood. Her stomach felt heavy, a mix of nerves and disbelief. Mom was here. Actually here. It didn't feel real.

She laid still for a moment, staring at the ceiling, before pushing back the blankets and shuffling out of bed. The floor was cool under her feet until she slipped on her fleece-lined slippers.

She tried not to think too much about why her parents' lives were so different. Dad's world was blueprints and city planning. It was solid, structured, predictable. Mom's life was stuffed with endless emails, strategy meetings, and a business that never seemed to stop pulling her in a dozen different directions. Allison was always somewhere in between, never quite fitting into either world.

She padded into the kitchen, her slippers scuffing against the tiles. She flipped on the electric kettle and moved to the fridge. Cool air brushed her face as she pulled out Brötchen rolls, butter, jam, cheese, and cold cuts.

She hesitated over the eggs. Would they eat them? Probably not. She put them back.

The kettle began to boil as she arranged the food on the counter. Carefully, she set up the pour-over coffee drip, watching the water steam as she poured it in slow, steady circles over the grounds. The sharp scent of coffee filled the kitchen as she set the carafe on the warming pad.

She turned back to the small table, laying out plates, knives, and the small jars of jam she'd found in the back of the fridge. Something about the routine made her feel better. If she focused, she wouldn't have to think about what came next.

Satisfied, she made her way to Dad's room. She tapped lightly on the door, hoping not to wake Mom. Dad's voice, groggy but warm, came through. "Komme." *Coming.*

He emerged, rubbing a hand over his face, his hair sticking up at odd angles. "Kaffee?" he asked, already heading for the kitchen. He poured himself a cup and took a sip, hissing at the heat. "Deine Mutter schläft noch. Ihr Flug war verspätet." *Your mom's still out. Her flight got in late.*

Allison slid into a chair, grabbing a Brötchen and spreading it with butter. She hesitated, then blurted out, "Glaubst du, sie könnte bleiben?" *Do you think she could stay?*

A voice came from the doorway. "English, please?"

Mom stood there in a soft navy robe, her black hair still tousled from sleep. "My German isn't as good as yours." She crossed to the table and smiled gently. "Coffee?"

Dad poured her a cup, and she took it with a quiet thanks. She added cream, took a long sip, and sighed. For a moment, she just held the cup, letting its warmth sink in. "Now, what were you saying, sweetie?"

Allison hesitated, then blurted out what she was thinking. "You could stay in Germany with us. Maybe set up an office in Stuttgart or Munich, and I can change schools. It's not too far from here. Dad could join us on the weekends."

Mom smiled faintly, but shook her head. "We have to go back to Manhattan. The EU Defense Force needs to do their job before it's safe for you to return."

Her parents looked at each other like they knew something she didn't.

Dad reached for a Brötchen, tore it in two, and heaped strawberry jam on one piece. "Agreed," he said in a low, resigned voice. "When do you have to leave?" he asked.

Mom turned to Allison. "Would you like to spend some time with your friends before we go?"

Allison nodded.

"After breakfast, why don't you see if they're around?" she asked. "We can meet up for lunch, just the three of us. In the meantime, your dad and I can pack a few suitcases, and anything we forget, we'll replace when we get home." Mom smiled. "Including the toothbrush!"

Dad chuckled, biting into his Brötchen. He always lost his toothbrush on family vacations. It was a running joke.

Allison nodded, but saying goodbye felt wrong. She had another year in Hamburg before she was supposed to head back to the States for high school. Leaving Manhattan two years ago had been different—exciting and full of possibility. This just felt like she was losing everything.

She picked at her Brötchen, no longer hungry, and forced a smile. It'll be fine, she told herself. But it wasn't.

Allison plucked a blade of grass and twisted it between her fingers until it snapped. Her friends sat close, their voices a blur. The sun warmed her shoulders, but that uneasy feeling in her stomach wouldn't go away. She dug her heels into the grass, pressing down as if it might somehow keep her here.

Behind them, the playground was as loud as always. Kids ran around the swings, yelling and laughing. A boy kicked sand near the slide, and one of the moms yelled at him to stop. It looked like any other afternoon.

"My dad says it's not coming here," Greta said, as if she had all the answers. She leaned back on her hands and squinted at the sky. Her long blond braid hung over one shoulder. "The EU Defense Force is going to pound the snot out of them."

Allison glanced at her friends, unsure of what to say. Did they really believe that?

Lena nudged her with a shoulder. Her dark brown hair was pulled into a messy ponytail, strands escaping around her freckled face. "School's going to suck without you," she said. There were tears in her eyes, and she glanced away.

"It's not forever," Greta said with a shrug. She picked at the grass, her blue eyes flicking to Allison like she was daring her to argue. "A few weeks, maybe a month, and Russia will be forced to run back to Moscow."

Mila hugged her knees to her chest, staring at the ground. She chewed her lower lip, like she wasn't sure if she should say anything. "My parents don't think so," she finally murmured. "My dad says Russia's going to keep trying to take more and more land. They should've been stopped years ago."

"Ukraine was forever ago," Greta shot back, rolling her eyes. She flopped onto her back in the grass, arms behind her head like they were just talking about an upcoming test, not a war. "It's not like we'll never see Allison again. Even if she doesn't come back until Christmas."

"Christmas?" Clara's head snapped up, her eyes wide. Her auburn curls bounced as she faced Allison, her expression suddenly anxious. "You're coming back for fußball season, right?" She grinned, that kind of hopeful smile that made Allison's stomach twist. "It's going to be so intense! I'll have my mom record our practices so you can watch!"

Allison tried to smile back, but it felt wrong. Before she could answer, a ping told her there was an incoming call. Her fingers brushed the AR band perched on top of her head. She slid it down over her eyes, activating its sleek, dark green interface. A light pulse tapped against her temples as the system came online. White windows blinked into existence, hovering just at the edge of her vision. A notification blinked in the corner. It was her dad.

She tapped the air, and his face appeared in front of her, slightly transparent over the playground. His brow was furrowed, but his smile was warm. "Time to come home, Allie," he said.

"Okay," Allison said, barely above a whisper. She didn't want to move, didn't want to leave her friends, her neighborhood, her home. She wanted to say something—to push back—but what was the point? It wasn't her choice.

She swiped a finger through the air, shutting off the AR display. The band gave a light pulse as it powered down, and she pushed it back up onto her head.

One by one, her friends hugged her. Greta lingered just a little longer before they split up for the walk home. Clara walked with her back to the house, talking about workout routines and goals and how she was going to nail passing the ball.

When they reached the gate, Clara gave her another hug. "You'll be back," she said, her voice fierce. "You have to be."

The walk up the cobblestone driveway felt longer than it should have. The house was three stories tall, with pale brick walls and wide windows that reflected the late morning sun. A neat row of hedges lined the path to the black wrought-iron gate, and packed flower boxes jutted out from the small balconies on the upper floors.

Allison glanced at the tree-lined street, the houses standing almost shoulder to shoulder. *Spielplatz Parkallee*, just a few blocks away, had been the center of her world since she moved here. She didn't want to leave.

Inside, she sank onto the couch, staring at the room without really seeing it. Her parents' voices carried from down the hall.

"We have to leave by 3," her mom was saying. "It's a nine-hour flight, so we'll be back in New York by early evening with the time change."

"So soon?" her dad asked. "We should at least get one night together as a family."

"It's The Firm's private jet," her mom replied. The way she said it, Allison could almost see her fingers hooking around the words. "It took a lot of convincing for me to use it. Commercial flights are booked solid, and the State Department says she has to go home. You know that James only got an agreement for her to be here because of your work. Otherwise, she'd only have been allowed brief visits."

Allison sat up straighter. James. That was the lawyer they saw every year. He was nice enough, but the conversations he had with her parents were always kind of weird. Sometimes, it felt like he was some kind of counselor or social worker. How was Allison's school? What kind of vacation did they have planned for the coming year? How were both of her parents' businesses doing? Most times, she just ignored it.

But now she wondered if the U.S. had rules about kids leaving the country. Maybe that's why they had to see James. They traveled as a family a couple of times a year.

"I'm tired of other people deciding how we raise our kid," her dad said, his voice sharp. "You could've incorporated anywhere. Why does she have to be tethered to the U.S. until she's of age? We should be able to move wherever we want!"

Her mom sighed. "I know, Sam. But this is how it is."

Tethered?

Allison slipped off the couch and walked to her room. The word stuck in her head. What did her dad mean by that?

The door was open, but neither of her parents noticed her standing in the doorway. Her mom was sorting clothes while her dad folded a thick sweater, pressing it neatly into the suitcase on the bed.

Her stomach clenched. The room felt smaller, like it wasn't hers anymore. It felt like everything was being packed away, piece by piece, until there'd be nothing left of her here.

Her mom turned when she saw her. "Good, you're back." She grabbed a stack of folded clothes and shoved them into the suitcase. "We're leaving after lunch. Pack what you want to take. I grabbed some things for cooler weather, but you'll need enough for at least a few weeks."

Allison nodded and squeezed past her to the dresser. She pulled open the top drawer, her hands moving automatically until she saw what her mom had packed. Thick sweaters. Heavy jeans. Stuff she wouldn't need. Her mom was packing like she'd be there all winter.

Wasn't she paying attention? Or was this Mom's way of saying she wasn't coming back?

Allison swallowed hard. How long was she going to stay in Manhattan? Would she even be allowed to come back?

Behind her, her mom said, "I need you to look over the SkyHaven purchase, Sam. A few signatures and your 'approval' on the funding so that we can take the company private."

Her dad sighed. "It's your company, Rylee. I wish people would let you run it."

"Legally, they can't stop me," her mom replied. "But most U.S. companies won't work with me because I'm a woman. You know, because all women need a strong man to watch over them." She paused to take a deep breath. "They will, however, let me play COO while you—the CEO—approve everything."

Her dad's laugh was bitter. "Tell me where to sign and who to yell at."

Her mom didn't reply. Instead, she turned back to Allison. "Are you okay packing by yourself? I can help after lunch if you want."

Allison glanced at the suitcase on the bed. She'd have to redo everything, anyway. Mom had packed all the wrong clothes. "I've got it," she said quietly.

Her mom nodded and gave her a quick hug. "We'll be in the kitchen. Once we're done, we'll grab lunch at your favorite place, okay?"

"Okay," Allison said, not looking up. As the door clicked shut behind them, she sank onto the bed and started pulling the clothes out of the suitcase. Just a few weeks, she thought. It wasn't the end of the world. She could do this.

Before she knew it, they were racing across the tarmac. Her mom gripped her hand like she was a little kid. Allison wanted to pull away, but her mom held on tight. Her dad was right behind them.

The private terminal was nothing like the crowded airports Allison was used to. It was too quiet. No endless lines, no voices crackling over the loudspeakers—just the distant roar of a jet and the occasional clank of metal.

A uniformed officer at the customs desk had barely looked up as he stamped their passports and waved them through. No long security lines, no metal detectors. Just a quick check of the emergency visas and passports, like it was routine.

Outside, the heat from the tarmac hit first, radiating up through her thin loafers. The sleek, white jet waited a short distance away, its stairs already lowered. A crew member stood at the base, checking something on a tablet, while another loaded the last of their luggage. The air smelled like fuel mixed with hot pavement.

Her mom walked ahead, her heels clicking against the concrete. Dad's steady footsteps made her want to turn around, grab his arm, and refuse to let go.

Her mom climbed the stairs first, barely pausing as she stepped inside. Allison followed, gripping the metal handrail. The steps felt solid under her feet, but she hesitated at the top, glancing back at the terminal. This was it. No going back.

She took a breath and stepped inside.

Her mom moved down the aisle and placed her purse on a seat. Allison hesitated, glancing back.

Then her dad pulled her into a hug. Tight, like he didn't want to let her go. She pressed her face against his jacket, the fabric rough against her cheek. His cologne lingered.

"Dad, come with us," she whispered, gripping his coat. "Please."

"I can't, Allie." His voice was steady but worn. He pulled back just enough to meet her eyes, his hands firm on her shoulders. "The upgrades along the Elbe are at a critical phase. If we stop now, flooding will be worse."

"But what if—" She swallowed hard. "What if you can't leave in time?"

He exhaled and leaned in slightly. "Listen to me," he said firmly. "This is just temporary. If anything changes, I'm on the first plane out of here. This evacuation is just a precaution, Allie." He squeezed her shoulders. "Trust me on this."

Allison nodded, but she didn't believe him. She could hardly breathe.

He gave her a light hug, like he was already letting go.

Before she could say anything else, her mom swooped in, wrapping her arms around both of them. For a second, it felt like everything was okay. Allison squeezed her eyes shut, gripping the back of her dad's jacket, willing time to stop.

But it didn't.

Her dad was the first to let go. "I'll see you soon."

"Promise?" she asked, blinking fast to hold back the tears.

"I promise," he said, glancing at her mom. Then, he looked down at her and gestured deeper into the cabin. "Time to get going."

Her mom's hands slipped from Allison's shoulders as her dad guided her forward, his hand brushing lightly against her back. His presence was comforting.

He helped her into a seat on the left side of the plane, adjusting her seat belt after she fumbled with it.

Once she was buckled in, he stepped back, his expression unreadable. "Call me as soon as you land," he told her mom, his voice steady despite the tension around his eyes.

Her mom nodded. "I will."

Then, he leaned in and kissed her mom. Allison rolled her eyes, a bit embarrassed.

She watched as he stepped through the cabin door and onto the stairs. At the top, he paused and glanced back at her. For a second, she thought he might say something, but he just gave her a small nod, then slowly walked down the stairs.

The door hissed shut behind him, sealing them in. The air felt heavier now, as if the plane was already dragging her away. Her ears popped, and she swallowed hard, trying to ignore the strange, weightless feeling settling in her chest.

A flight attendant appeared, her blue uniform crisp. "Welcome, Mrs. Maxwell, Miss Maxwell," she said with a polite nod. "May I secure your bag?" She gestured to Allison's backpack.

Her mom nodded silently. Allison watched as the attendant picked up her backpack and placed it in a wall bin toward the rear of the cabin. The leather of the seat felt cold against her fingers as she gripped the armrest, her whole body tense.

The pilot's voice came over the intercom. "Mrs. Maxwell, we are ready for departure. Estimated flight time to New York is nine hours, twenty-two minutes. Please remain seated as we prepare for takeoff."

The engines whined, growing louder as the plane rolled forward, heading toward the runway. Allison kept her eyes on her dad, standing on the tarmac with his hands in his pockets, shoulders squared like he was trying to be brave for her.

She lost sight of him as the plane turned; the motion jarring enough that she squeezed her eyes shut, tears slipping down her cheeks.

When the plane lifted into the air, Hamburg began to shrink beneath them, its familiar streets and rooftops blurring into the distance. She sank into her seat, gripping the cold leather armrest as the cabin vibrated around her.

Chapter Two

Allison slouched back into the limo's leather seat, her fingers tracing the edge of the armrest. The interior reminded her of an old-fashioned car from the movies—soft lights, polished wood—but the pod itself felt strange.

In Hamburg, electric cars looked normal, with wheels and drivers, moving through streets filled with people walking or biking. But this? This was something else.

Instead of a freeway, the pod was sealed in a transparent tube, gliding smoothly above the landscape. She watched the city grow closer through the curved windows, its towering buildings rising in the distance. The pod barely made a sound, no tires skimming pavement, no rush of wind. Only a faint hum of motion, like it was floating.

She pressed her face against the window, staring out at Manhattan. She'd only been gone a few years, but after Hamburg, it felt different. Colder. A bit harsher. The buildings stretched impossibly high, crammed together like they were fighting for space.

Back home, everything felt closer to the ground; row houses with sloped roofs and narrow streets filled with bikes and shopfronts. Hamburg was built for people. Here, it felt like the city had kept growing, stretching taller and taller, until it barely noticed the people at all.

She hadn't slept much on the flight, just a few restless naps between pockets of turbulence. Now, her whole body ached, her head felt heavy, and her stomach was unsettled from exhaustion.

Mom sat across from her, scrolling through emails on her tablet, her long braid draped over one shoulder. She'd rebraided it before landing, fingers moving fast like she needed to stay busy.

On the plane, the aisle had been between them, but that hadn't stopped Mom from watching her. Every few minutes, she'd glance up or lean forward just enough to check if Allison was okay. She never said anything, but Allison felt it—the way Mom noticed her picking at breakfast, like skipping a meal was some kind of crisis.

It was annoying. She wasn't a baby.

Now, in the pod, there was no space between them. Just Mom, too close, pretending to focus on her screen.

"Almost home," she said. Her voice was calm. Too calm. Her eyes stayed on the tablet, but her fingers gripped it tightly.

Allison shifted, pressing her forehead against the window. She didn't answer.

Home. That word didn't fit Manhattan anymore.

Allison looked out the window, her forehead pressed against the cool glass. The city seemed to unfold around her, a maze of elevated streets weaving between gleaming high-rises. Their upper floors glowed against the dark sky, familiar yet distant, like a place she used to know but had somehow outgrown.

A WARD OF THE STATE

She looked down. The water hadn't been there before. Not like this.

It flowed in the streets below the freeway, creeping up doorways, swallowing sidewalks. It wasn't deep, but it didn't have to be. It was everywhere, turning roads into canals, distorting the old neighborhoods she remembered. Small boats floated between buildings, their lights skimming the rippling surface like restless fireflies.

She tried to picture herself here again, walking the streets, riding the subway, slipping back into the life she'd left behind. But all she could see was the water, swallowing up the past, one foot at a time.

Mom sighed. "You should try to sleep tonight. You'll feel better in the morning."

Allison didn't answer. She pressed her hand against the glass, leaving faint smudges as she stared out.

The pod slid out of the enclosed transit tube and onto the elevated streets. Rain spattered against the windows, loud now without the barrier shielding them. City lights streaked across the wet glass, blurring into smears of gold, green, violet and red.

The streets hadn't always been like this. When she'd left, construction had already started, raising the roads higher, replacing intersections with ramps and automated lanes. But even then, there'd been sidewalks, crosswalks, and places for people to walk around. Now, she only caught glimpses of them, narrow and intermittent, wedged between towering pylons that held the monorails up.

Farther away, floodlights illuminated the skeletal frameworks of new extensions. It was like the city had decided people didn't belong on the ground anymore. Mass transit ruled now with sealed pods, skybridges, and monorails gliding overhead. The streets below, the ones that hadn't been lifted yet, looked forgotten, abandoned to the rising water.

The pod slowed as they approached their building, a towering high-rise with its main entrance now several floors above the old street level. When Allison lived here before, construction crews had been reinforcing the foundation and raising the entryway. Now, it was elevated above the flood zone, just in case.

It didn't feel like the same place.

The pod stopped with a hiss, and the double doors slid open, letting in the steady patter of rain against the bridge that connected the road to the building entrance. Cool, damp air drifted in. The front seats of the pod had swiveled to face forward, ready for a driver if needed.

A security guard stepped out from under the awning, a large black umbrella in hand. He nodded at Mom before moving to cover her as she stepped out. Another guard followed, flipping open a second umbrella just in time to block most of the rain from Allison as she followed. She clutched the straps of her backpack, the damp air brushing her face as she followed her mom toward the tall glass doors.

Everything was so quiet, so automatic. Her luggage had been unloaded at the airport and sent here through some automated system. In Hamburg, someone would have pulled her bags from the car with a quick smile or asked if they needed anything. Here, the guards and doormen barely acknowledged them.

The lobby had been recreated just as she remembered with tall ceilings, stone floors, potted trees and neatly arranged plants with waxy, perfect leaves. A few sleek benches lined one wall, the kind no one actually sat on. The lighting cast a warm glow, elegant but cold.

Before, it had felt like something out of a movie. Now, it just felt empty.

She followed her mom toward the private elevator, her footsteps swallowed by the polished floor. Mom's heels clicked softly, the only sound in the empty lobby.

The elevator doors slid open, revealing a sleek, mirror-lined interior. Their tired faces reflected back at them. Allison stepped inside, adjusting the weight of her backpack as the doors quietly closed.

Mom pressed the button for the penthouse without a word, rolling her shoulders as the elevator began to rise. Allison leaned against the wall, her forehead resting against the cool metal. The elevator was silent except for the faint whir of movement. She glanced at her mom, who had closed her eyes for just a moment. She looked exhausted.

When the doors finally opened, Maria was waiting. Her familiar smile was calm and reassuring, like nothing had changed.

"Welcome back, Miss Allison," Maria said gently.

Allison managed a small nod, too tired to speak, as she stepped into the apartment behind her mom.

The living room looked different, but not in a way that made it feel more like home.

She could still picture how it used to be. A conference table in place of the coffee table. Gray chairs instead of couches. Monitors where paintings now hung. Back then, it felt like an office. Now, it was supposed to feel cozy.

The warm earth tones and soft lighting tried to make the space inviting, but to Allison, it just felt staged. The overstuffed couches, the carefully arranged throw pillows, the old-fashioned wooden coffee table were all too perfect. It looked like no one actually lived here.

It was nothing like her dad's place, where books piled up on side tables, jackets were draped over chairs, and nothing was ever quite in its place. His house felt lived in. This felt like a showroom.

"Allison, sweetheart," Mom said, setting her tablet on the sideboard near the couch as she walked over. She rested a hand on Allison's shoulder and gave her a small smile. "You didn't eat much on the plane. Let me have Maria make you something."

"I'm not hungry." Her voice was quiet, even to her own ears. She slipped out from under Mom's hand, dropped her backpack on the floor, and walked to the glass wall overlooking the garden.

The rain had stopped, leaving the double doors to the garden streaked with faint trails of water. Through the heavy glass, she could see the neatly trimmed greenery outside, still glistening from the rain. Beyond the garden, the city stretched out in glittering lines of light.

Maria cleared her throat softly, drawing Allison's attention. She stood near the couch, her hands folded neatly in front of her. "Miss Allison, would you like a grilled cheese sandwich? It used to be your favorite," she offered, her voice warm but tentative, as if she wasn't sure Allison still liked the sandwich.

"No, thank you, Maria," she muttered.

Allison turned back to the glass, her reflection barely visible against the city lights. Her pale, tired face blurred into the glittering skyline beyond. Manhattan might have been beautiful once, but now it felt like a city just pretending to be alive. And she was stuck in the middle of it.

Her mom crossed the room, her heels sinking into the plush carpet as she came to stand beside Allison. "Why don't you get some sleep?" she gently asked. "You've had a long couple of days, and we can get a fresh start tomorrow."

Allison hesitated, then leaned in and gave her a quick hug. Mom's arms wrapped around her, holding her close for a moment. "Sounds good, Mom," she whispered. She was too old for bedtime hugs. But tonight, it felt right. She picked up her backpack and headed upstairs to find her old bedroom.

She flopped onto her back, staring at the canopy above her bed. The sheer fabric let the glow-in-the-dark stars shine through.

"Jeeves, what time is it?" she asked the household AI.

"It's 12:33 a.m.," the AI answered in his usual British butler voice.

Great. Her body still insisted it was time to get up for school in Hamburg, even though it was the middle of the night here.

She groaned and rolled onto her side, then back again. The bed was too soft, the room too quiet. With a sigh, she sat up and flicked on the lamp beside her bed. The warm light chased away some of the shadows.

The walls were still the same deep blue she'd begged for when she was seven, with pink clouds and sparkly rainbows that had once felt magical, like she was floating in some dream world. Now, it all just felt embarrassing.

From her bed, she could see her desk, its glossy white surface spotless. Maria must have cleaned everything up after she moved to Germany. Everything was perfectly lined up. The rocket-shaped lamp. Her old solar system model. A few notebooks stacked neatly in the corner.

Her shelves were crammed with books, their spines gleaming under the lamp's glow. In Hamburg, she didn't had anything like this. Most were limited editions, embossed with her name; gifts from her grandparents and her mom. But squeezed between the fancy hardcovers were her sketchbooks and notebooks, filled with space exploration plans.

She spotted her favorite drone, sitting on a lower shelf. It was painted with glow-in-the-dark swirls and covered in stickers. She used to fly it through the apartment, weaving around furniture, until Mom made her take it outside.

Everything was exactly where she'd left it. And yet, none of it felt the same.

The carpet was soft under her bare feet as she pushed herself up and crossed the room to the shelves. She ran her fingers along the spines of the books before pulling out a sketchbook labeled: Mars Habitat Project. The cover was covered in little rockets she'd drawn years ago.

She flipped it open and stopped on a detailed drawing of a residential habitat. Each module was labeled: Sleeping Quarters, Hydroponic Gardens, Communal Spaces, Storage. She'd spent hours designing it, making sure people could actually live on Mars, not just survive. She'd even added tiny plants and furniture, imagining what it would feel like when it was built.

Her mom had encouraged her to submit the design to a SpaceX contest. She never did, but she used to daydream about it. The engineers would study her sketches. They'd pause, nod, and realize her design might actually work.

She set the sketchbook down and turned to the holographic globe on the shelf. It flickered faintly, the Earth's rotation glitching like an old game. She tapped it. The glow brightened, the continents sharpened—but the movement was still jerky. She frowned and hit it again. Nothing.

"Broken," she muttered as she turned it off.

Her eyes drifted to the photos on the wall and all the places they'd traveled as a family. Venice. Argentina. Hong Kong. South Africa. These were the same pictures she had in her room in Hamburg, but here they looked different. Brighter. Sharper.

She stopped at the one from Venice. Her dad's arm was slung over her shoulders, pointing at the old buildings by the water. Her mom stood next to him, grinning, sunglasses in hand. She could almost hear her dad explaining how the city was sinking and her mom rolling her eyes, telling him to stop being such a downer.

In another photo, she was laughing on the back of her dad's scooter in Argentina, her arms wrapped tightly around his waist as they zipped through the streets. Next to it was the picture from Hong Kong. Her mom was showing her how to hold chopsticks properly while her dad made faces at her.

She swallowed hard and looked away. Vacations were really the only time she'd felt they were a family.

She wandered back to her desk. What had she been thinking when she begged for that rocket-shaped lamp? Its sleek, modern design had seemed so cool back then. Now, it just looked like something meant for a little kid. She sighed and shook her head.

She pulled open a random drawer, and the sharp, familiar smell of dried paint hit her. Inside were crusty brushes, cracked paint tubes, and notebooks filled with half-finished doodles and forgotten projects. One by one, she tossed them into the white wicker trash can next to her desk. Each thud felt weirdly satisfying, like she was clearing out more than just junk.

When the drawer was empty, she flopped onto the bed and grabbed her tablet. Opening her notes app, she typed: sketchpads, her art pack, the tech kit. Stuff she'd left behind in Hamburg that her dad could send. She stared at the list for a long moment before adding one more thing: my life.

Her chest tightened. She deleted that last piece and set the tablet aside, pulling the quilt up to her chin. The fabric was soft but unfamiliar, like everything else in this place.

Her eyes drifted back to the photos on the wall. Venice. Argentina. Hong Kong. Hamburg. The places where she felt like herself. She tried to hold on to those memories, to the feeling of who she was, but it all seemed to slip further away.

She reached over and switched off the light. Darkness swallowed the room, and she closed her eyes, too tired to think anymore.

She lay there, her mind drifting between memories and the emptiness of the room around her. But eventually, exhaustion won.

Allison groaned and rolled onto her side, wincing as the sharp morning light stabbed through her eyelids. She yanked the quilt over her face, but light still seeped around the edges, relentless and unyielding. With a frustrated sigh, she grabbed her pillow and buried her face in it.

A WARD OF THE STATE

It didn't help. The sun had already won.

With another sigh, this one more dramatic, she pulled the pillow away. Sunlight hit her like a spotlight. She squinted, shielding her eyes with one hand. The windows faced east. Of course, it did. Mornings here were always like this. Bright, blinding, and way too early.

"Jeeves, dim the windows to fifty percent," she mumbled.

"At once, Miss Allison," the AI replied crisply, his British accent making him sound far too awake. The windows darkened to a more bearable glow. Finally, she could open her eyes without feeling like a vampire.

She sat up slowly, rubbing her face, then flopped back against the pillows.

"Jeeves, what time is it?" she finally asked.

"The time is 8:22 a.m.," Jeeves announced. "Would you care for an update on today's weather?"

Allison groaned.

"Today is Tuesday, September 16th. The current temperature is—"

"Hör auf!" she growled. "Stop. Be quiet. That's enough."

Jeeves fell silent.

Allison stretched her arms as far as they could go, her shoulders still stiff from the plane trip. The bed was soft, but it didn't help. Her head felt fuzzy. Jet lag was the worst.

Lying there wasn't going to fix anything.

Before she forgot, Allison reached for her nightstand, fumbling past the lamp until she found her tablet. She blinked at the screen, her brain still foggy, and typed quickly: *Hi Dad, can you send my sketchbooks, art supplies, and maybe my tech kit? Thanks.*

She hit send and let the tablet drop onto the bed. Only then did she rub her eyes, trying to shake off the last bits of sleep. With a groan, she pushed herself up, kicking off the tangled blankets.

One step at a time, she thought. Dad told her that often enough! Her lips twitched into a faint smile. Breakfast could at least fix one thing.

She headed to the closet. Maria had hung everything up last night. She grabbed a fresh pair of jeans and her favorite T-shirt, then reached for her security card on the nightstand.

Without it, she couldn't go anywhere. The elevator, the front entrance, even the small movie theater required a scan. She hated how locked-down everything was. Back in Hamburg, she just needed a key to get into the house and she could walk anywhere.

On her way to the door, she paused, glancing up at the canopy over her bed. The sheer fabric was tied neatly to the bed frame at the corners and was easy enough to take down. Maybe getting rid of it would make the room feel less like it belonged to her seven-year-old self.

Her stomach growled, reminding her she hadn't eaten last night. Time to get breakfast and find out what her mom was up to.

Allison opened her bedroom door slowly, her hand still on the handle as her mom's voice floated down the hallway. "Lithuania's military . . . " Her mom sounded tense. " . . . repelling the Russian invasion."

She froze. Another voice. Softer, harder to make out. Dad.

She let go of the door and stepped into the hallway. As she got close to the library, she could make out what her dad was saying. "The headmaster at Kaiserhof was very firm. No virtual attendance is permitted."

"That's ridiculous," her mom snapped. "There's a war going on. Are you sure that they won't allow an exception?"

Allison edged closer, her fingers brushing the smooth wall as she crept closer to the open door.

"Kaiserhof only allows ten days of absence within the school year," her dad replied, his voice calm, like he was trying to smooth things over. "Some students have transferred temporarily, but Kaiserhof requires that they stay on track and meet academic requirements."

Allison bit her lip and leaned against the wall. Inside, she could hear her mom pacing, her movements quick and restless.

"I'll find a school here," her mom said, her voice quieter now. "Someplace that will work with us until she can move back."

Allison edged closer, just enough to see around the door. Her dad was on the video screen, scrubbing a hand through his hair, leaving it even more of a mess.

"She deserves some stability," he said, his voice low.

Stability? That wasn't what this was about. This was about the stupid war. The State Department had forced her to leave, and now her parents were acting as if it had been a choice.

She'd been happy in Hamburg. She had her school, her friends, her life. Now she was stuck here, trapped in Manhattan, because of a war that she had nothing to do with.

Allison swallowed hard and backed away, her hands balled into fists. She didn't want to hear anymore. She turned and hurried down the stairs, gripping the banister to steady herself.

The faint smell of coffee and something sweet hit Allison as she headed to the dining room. Her stomach growled, and she scowled. Really? She'd just found out she probably wasn't going home anytime soon, and her body still wanted food?

Maria appeared almost instantly, her apron crisp, her warm smile steady and familiar.

"Good morning, Miss Allison," she said, setting a small carafe of orange juice and a glass on the table. "What can I make you for breakfast?"

Allison hesitated, trying to remember what she used to eat here. "Pancakes," she mumbled. "And bacon. Maybe yogurt? And some fruit, too."

Maria nodded, unfazed by her flat tone. "Of course," she said, pouring the juice with practiced ease. "It's good to see you hungry."

Allison sat down, dragging her fingers along the table's edge. She poked at the fruit salad that Maria had brought out first, wincing at the sharp sweetness of the pineapple chunks. She stabbed a strawberry with her fork, chewing without really tasting it.

Her mom walked in, moving with the same effortless grace she always had. Her heels tapped against the tile, each step precise. Maria didn't miss a beat, handing her a latte before she even sat down.

"Thank you, Maria," her mom said, taking a sip. "This tastes amazing."

"The pancakes and bacon will be ready soon," Maria said, before disappearing into the kitchen.

Allison kept her eyes down, pushing a piece of melon around her bowl. She didn't really want to eat it. She could feel her mom watching her.

"We need to talk, sweetie," her mom said, her voice gentler than it had been upstairs. "Kaiserhof won't allow virtual attendance."

Allison kept her gaze on her bowl, gripping her fork tighter. She already knew this, but hearing it from her mom made it feel more real.

Her fork scraped against the bowl as she forced herself to speak. "So . . . what am I supposed to do now?" she asked.

Her mom folded her hands on the table, her expression softer now. "I'll find a local school for you. Just temporarily. You'll be able to transfer back once it's safe to return."

Allison swallowed hard. "A new school?" she asked quietly. She hated how small her voice sounded.

"It'll only be for a little while," her mom said, offering a faint smile. "I promise."

Allison nodded. She poked at her fruit salad, no longer hungry.

Maria reappeared with a plate of pancakes and bacon, smoothly swapping it for the bowl of fruit. "Here you are, Miss Allison." Then, she brought Mom a small vegetable omelet.

Her mom took another sip of her latte. "Why don't you explore the building while I work on it?" she said, her tone lighter. "It's changed a lot since you were here. If you can find your old security card, you'll have access to the gym, lounges, restaurants, and the library. There's even a new shopping center downstairs. Just don't leave the building. Security is tighter now, and we're still waiting on your updated link."

Allison nodded again, more out of habit than agreement. Her mom had already moved on and was focused on her breakfast.

Allison pushed her chair back, wincing at the scrape of wood against the floor. Wandering the building didn't sound great, but it was better than sitting here, waiting for more decisions to be made about her life.

Chapter Three

Allison leaned back in the poolside chair, letting her head rest against the cushion. She stared up at the high, curved ceiling, its smooth surface broken by recessed lights that cast a warm glow over the pool. The warm air smelled like chlorine, with a hint of eucalyptus drifting in from the nearby spa.

Allison reached up and tapped the side of her AR band, feeling a quick pulse against her temples as it unlocked. Then, she slid it down until it rested lightly on the bridge of her nose. Another pulse followed, so light she almost didn't notice it.

"Send a message to my squad," she murmured. A virtual chat window popped up in front of her. At the top, the name My Squad glowed in soft white letters. She could still see the water gently moving around the pool, the lounge chairs, and the light coming in through the windows. She flicked her fingers through the air, and the window shifted to the left. Sometimes, it felt a bit like magic, even though she knew it was just smart programming.

"Hey, everyone," she said, keeping her voice steady. The words appeared as she spoke, forming line by line. "I'm back in New York for a while. Let's catch up." She paused, then added, "Miss you guys."

With a flick of her hand, the message was sent. The chat window closed, leaving her alone with the quiet ripple of the pool.

Before she could push the band back up, a light pulse tapped against her temples, and the chat window popped up.

Marjani: Where are you?

Allison hesitated before responding. Shouldn't Marjani be in school? "I'm at the pool in our building," she said quietly.

Marjani: Stay there! I'm coming!

Just a few minutes later, the glass doors slid open, and Marjani burst in. Allison sat up as her friend strode toward her, the beads in her long, braided hair clicking against each other. Marjani always looked like a burst of color, and today was no different. Her deep red and gold dress shimmered with every step. Her dark skin, rich and warm like polished mahogany, seemed to glow under the lights.

"Allison!" Marjani's voice filled the space, warm and full of energy. She hurried across the tiled floor.

Allison smiled. She couldn't help herself. She hadn't realized how much she'd missed this: Marjani's loud voice, her bold colors, the way she made everything feel like a celebration.

"Why didn't you tell me you were coming back?" Marjani demanded, stopping just short of her chair.

"I wasn't sure how long I'd be here," Allison said, deactivating the AR band and pushing it back up on her head. Her fingers fidgeted with the edge of the chair as she looked down. "Things were kind of . . . sudden."

Marjani nodded knowingly, then pulled a chair over and plopped down beside her. "Eh, my mum says Europe is a mess now. She talks and talks and talks about it like she's a professor."

Marjani shrugged, the beads in her braids clicking softly. "But you're here now and that's what matters."

Allison didn't reply. The only sound was the faint splash of water lapping against the pool's edge.

"Anyway," Marjani said, her voice lifting, "I missed you! It's been forever since Christmas, right? We have so much to catch up on. You're not just sitting here all day, are you?"

When Allison just smiled at her, Marjani stood up and pulled her away from the pool and into the quiet hall. Her sandals slapped against the smooth tiles, while Allison followed without a word.

They passed the spa entrance, its sleek glass doors reflecting the soft hallway lights. Allison barely glanced at the signs by the doorway. Everything here felt too clean, too perfect. Like no one who came to this spa ever spilled a drink or had a bad hair day.

When the elevator arrived, Marjani pressed a button without hesitation. "You're gonna love this," she said as the doors slid shut.

Allison fidgeted with the edge of her shirt. "Where are we going?"

"The greenhouse. The big one."

The elevator ride was short. The moment the doors opened, Allison gasped.

A massive glass-walled atrium stretched in all directions, the floor-to-ceiling windows wrapping the entire space in a panoramic view of the city skyline. Sunlight poured in from the transparent ceiling, filtering through hanging vines and the leafy canopies of full-sized trees. The air was warm and thick with the scent of damp earth and fresh greenery. It was nothing like the manicured perfection of her mother's penthouse garden.

"This wasn't here before," Allison said, stepping onto the raised stone walkway.

"Nope. They finished it last year," Marjani said. "Took, like, three floors to build it. Now it's a 'controlled ecosystem' or something."

Allison scanned the space. It felt alive. The towering trees with thick, twisting roots rose between winding paths, their branches stretching toward the glass ceiling. A small waterfall fed a pond stocked with brightly colored fish. Planters overflowed with flowers and edible greens, while sleek hydroponic columns sprouted vegetables in perfect, floating symmetry.

At the far end, a lounge area was set into the greenery, half-hidden behind a wall of ferns. Allison could see a few residents sitting there, talking. A nearby panel displayed live data on the greenhouse's conditions—humidity, temperature, oxygen levels—all fine-tuned to maintain its artificial paradise.

"And let me guess," Allison said, "the people who live here don't take care of any of this."

Marjani smirked. "Of course not. They've got a team of botanists and automated drones." She pointed at a sleek, white drone hovering near a lemon tree, its robotic arm snipping a ripe fruit before gliding away. "They even have an integrated AI system that decides when to harvest stuff."

Allison snorted as she looked up into the tree canopy. "Because it would be too hard to pick your own lemons," she said.

Marjani laughed. "Obviously. We don't pick. We point."

A WARD OF THE STATE

Allison shook her head. This place was different from anything she'd ever seen before. Unlike her mom's controlled, private terrace, this wasn't just for show. It felt like its own world, hidden inside the city.

Marjani nudged her. "Come on, there's more."

They walked deeper into the greenhouse, past rows of exotic plants, orchids blooming in temperature-controlled glass cases, and herbs growing in neatly labeled sections. The sound of water trickled from a stone fountain, and for the first time since landing in New York, Allison felt like she could breathe again.

But the moment Marjani turned toward the exit, that feeling faded. "Come on," Marjani said, already heading for the doors. "There's more."

Allison hesitated for half a second before following her, stepping out of the humid warmth and into the temperature-controlled hallway. The shift was immediate. The fresh, earthy air of the greenhouse was replaced by something cooler, more sterile. The glass doors slid shut behind them with a soft hiss, sealing off the only place in the building that had felt even remotely real.

She followed Marjani reluctantly down the hallway, watching as her long braids swayed gently as she walked. They rounded a corner, and a gold and silver escalator came into view, its rails gleaming under the overhead lights.

Marjani hopped on without hesitation, and Allison followed, gripping the handrail. As the escalator carried them down, soft music, the murmur of conversation, and the distant clink of glassware shifted the atmosphere.

The first floor unfolded below them. It was a sleek, high-end shopping pavilion designed more like a private showroom than a mall. Each boutique was an enclosed glass space, the interiors visible but untouchable, like exhibits in a museum. There were no bright sale signs, no crowded displays. Just curated selections with each piece meticulously presented.

Luxury brands lined the walkways, their entrances flanked by security that scanned residents' IDs before allowing them inside. Some stores had personal AI concierges, sleek humanoid figures standing motionless until a guest approached. There was very little foot traffic. No browsing. Everything looked to be by appointment or invitation.

Marjani led the way past storefronts showcasing clothing draped on lifelike mannequins, jewelry displayed in floating glass cases, and technology that looked more like art than anything practical. Even the security guard movements seemed choreographed.

"This place really has changed," Allison muttered.

"Right?" Marjani shot her a grin. "They rebranded it a few months ago. No more regular shopping. Everything's custom now. You don't just buy clothes; you get the 'full curated experience'." She mimicked the bored tone of a luxury concierge, "'Allow our stylists to craft a wardrobe tailored to your lifestyle and legacy.'"

Allison snorted. "Legacy?"

"I know, right?" Marjani rolled her eyes. "Like, just say 'You're too rich to shop like a normal person' and move on."

They stopped in front of a café encased in frosted glass, its name subtly etched in gold. The doors slid open as they approached, the air inside cooler than the mall. A few guests sat in plush chairs, their drinks served in crystal glasses.

Allison's sandals tapped lightly against the glossy floor as they stepped up to the counter. There was no cashier, just a curved display screen that lit up as they stepped closer.

Marjani didn't hesitate. "Two fruit smoothies. One strawberry, one mango passion fruit."

A chime acknowledged the order, and behind the counter, a robotic arm whirred to life. It moved with clinical precision, measuring, pouring, and blending, with every motion smooth and efficient. Not a single drop spilled.

Allison stared, unable to look away. Back in Germany, automation stayed behind the scenes. Here? It felt like watching a performance, polished, controlled, and just detached enough to feel unsettling.

They found a small table overlooking the main mall. Marjani twirled her straw between her fingers before lowering her voice. "So, have you noticed all the security?"

Allison nodded. "Yeah, it's hard to miss."

"It's because of some scares," Marjani told her. "Last year, someone tried to break into one of the residences. And over Christmas vacation, some crazy guy snuck into the mall level and started screaming about class warfare."

Allison's eyebrows shot up. "Seriously?"

Marjani nodded. "Yeah," she said with a frown. He didn't even get past the first floor. Security took him down in, like, two seconds. But after that, they upgraded everything." She lifted her wrist, showing Allison a gold and blue bracelet. "Everyone has to wear these now. My father told me it will track us if anything happens."

"Like what?" Allison asked.

Marjani shrugged. "Break-ins, protestors, people trying to sneak in. It's never been anything serious, though." She tapped her bracelet again. "Honestly, I think they just like reminding everyone how 'protected' we are. Makes people feel important."

Allison glanced around, her eyes landing on one of the security agents patrolling the walkways. His expression was unreadable, his gaze sharp as he scanned the first floor. She wasn't sure what to feel. It was strange, being watched so closely.

"Anyway," Marjani said, brightening. "There's still more to see. You have to check out the new game lounge. It's got immersive gaming pods that make you feel like you're right there. Oh, and they upgraded the theater, too!"

Allison smiled faintly. Marjani's excitement was contagious. For the first time since she'd arrived, she didn't feel so out of place. The fruity tang of her strawberry smoothie lingered on her tongue, the coldness a welcome contrast to the warm air in the mall.

Her AR band vibrated with an alert. She held up a finger to Marjani, then slid the thin band down over her eyes. A chat window opened.

Mom: Ready to come back yet?

Allison tapped the respond icon, watching her words appear in real time as she spoke. "I'm at the mall with Marjani, Mom." She flicked at the window to send. The message hovered briefly before disappearing.

Mom: I'm glad to hear that. Dinner is in about a half-hour.

"Okay," Allison replied aloud and sent the message. The screen faded as she pushed the band back up.

Marjani raised an eyebrow. "Everything okay?"

"Yeah." Allison shrugged. "My mom was checking in."

Marjani smirked. "Moms are like that." She crumpled the wrapper of her straw and tossed it into the café's automated trash bin. It responded with a quiet, "Thank you."

"Wanna check what movies are playing?" Marjani asked, standing up. "Maybe we can plan something for the weekend."

Allison grinned. "I'd love that. Let's take a look, then head back before both of our moms come looking for us."

Marjani laughed, her voice blending with the gentle murmur of the sparse crowd as they walked toward the theater. The brightly lit storefronts reflected off the mall's floors.

They stopped at the digital kiosk, its screen flickering on to display movie times as they approached. Allison scanned the listings. For the first time since coming back, things felt almost normal. Maybe it was the familiar rhythm of Marjani's chatter or the quiet buzz of life around them. Either way, she was grateful.

The elevator doors slid open with a chime, and Allison stepped into the penthouse. The familiar smell of roasted chicken and warm spices made her stomach growl. Her sandals scuffed lightly against the floor as she walked into the entrance hall.

Her mom stood by the tall windows, one hand resting on the back of the couch, the other cradling a glass of wine. The glow of the city skyline cast her silhouette in sharp relief, the light catching the edges of the rooftop garden beyond the glass.

"That smells amazing," Allison said with a small smile.

"It does, doesn't it?" Her mom turned from the window with a small smile and sank into the couch. "I asked Maria to make your favorite dinner tonight."

"Thanks," Allison said, unsure of what else to say.

Her mom nodded. "It's been a day," she sighed. "Between finding a school that will accept you as a temporary transfer and finalizing SkyHaven Aviation's move to private ownership, I haven't had a minute to myself!"

Allison sank onto the wide armchair and tucked her legs underneath her. She glanced around the living room, trying to see it as it was now, not as the place where her mom used to hold endless business meetings. Back then, it had never really felt like a place where she belonged. Her mom's business always seemed to come first. Allison had learned to sit quietly in the corner, doing her homework or reading a book while her mom ran meetings as if she wasn't even there. Sometimes it felt like she was just another task to manage.

But now, it was just the two of them. No meetings. No assistants. No back-to-back calls.

She blinked, turning back to her mom. "Do you like it here?" she asked, breaking the silence.

Her mom glanced over, raising an eyebrow. "Here? The family room?"

Allison shrugged. "I mean, it's different now. Not like before, when it was all business."

Her mom chuckled. "That's true. It was just a bit much, wasn't it?" She sighed, swirling her wine. "I thought I was showing you how the world works. How to handle things. But I guess it wasn't exactly fun for you."

Allison hesitated. She couldn't remember her mom ever admitting something like that. "It wasn't all bad," she quickly replied. "Sometimes, it was interesting. Like when you had those big meetings over there." She pointed toward the smart wall. "I couldn't tell who was winning the argument half the time. Because it always seemed to start with an argument."

Her mom smiled, but there was something softer in her expression. Something that almost looked like regret.

"I wanted you to learn how the world works, sweetie," she said after a pause. "Spending time with my dad taught me a lot about business." She leaned forward slightly. "My nana once told me that princesses shouldn't wait for a knight to save them. They can slay their own dragons. Your grandpa taught me how to do just that."

Allison gave a small nod. Her mom was trying, but it still felt like they were miles apart.

She turned toward the rooftop garden, watching the city lights stretch out toward the horizon. The colors in the sky deepened, the last rays of sunlight casting long shadows across the skyline.

"Dinner is ready, ma'am," Maria announced, standing at the threshold of the dining room.

They made their way to the table. White plates gleamed under the warm overhead lights, and the steam rising from the dishes made Allison's mouth water. Golden-brown grilled chicken sat next to a creamy pile of mac and cheese. Another bowl had bright green broccolini, slick with butter and ready to eat.

Allison slid into her chair, the cool leather pressing against her legs as she reached her hand out to her mom. They shared a brief smile before bowing their heads.

"Come, Lord Jesus, be our guest and let these gifts to us be blessed," Allison murmured, reciting the familiar words with her mom. "Oh, give thanks unto the Lord, for He is good. For His mercy endures forever."

"In Jesus' name, we pray. Amen," her mom finished.

"Amen," Allison echoed softly.

Her mom gave her hand a gentle squeeze before reaching for the roasted chicken. She took a few slices and then passed the dish to Allison.

"I found a nearby school that will accept you as a temporary transfer," her mom said as she spooned some mac and cheese onto her plate. "We'll go shopping tomorrow morning for appropriate school clothes, and in the afternoon, we have an appointment at Vanguard Preparatory Academy."

Allison paused mid-bite, her fork hovering over her plate. "Vanguard? That sounds like a school for superheroes."

Her mom smiled. "I'm told it's the best school in the tri-state region. Families send their kids there not just for academics but for the connections they make," she explained. "By the time you're ready for an internship or a job, you'll already know the people who can help you. Three of my friends' kids work for me right now."

Allison frowned and set her fork down. "So, people go there just to get fancy jobs?" she asked.

Her mom nodded. "In part, yes. It's not just about being smart. It's about making sure the right people know you. That's why Vanguard's setup works so well." She paused to take a bite of chicken. "I've been warned that boys and girls are taught on separate floors, but advanced courses are coed if there aren't enough students to split them. It keeps things competitive."

Allison wrinkled her nose. "Separate floors? Why?"

Her mom gave a small shrug. "It's just how they do things. Keeps distractions to a minimum, I guess."

That was weird. She was used to being one of the smartest kids in her class, but now it sounded like her last name might matter more than her grades.

"So, this is where the kids of CEOs and senators hang out?"

"Exactly," her mom said, looking pleased. "And now, you'll be one of them. At least for a few weeks."

Allison pushed a piece of chicken around her plate. She liked her old school in Germany. People cared about how well you did, not who your parents were.

She didn't know how to push back without sounding ungrateful. So, she nodded. "Okay, I guess. Can Marjani come shopping with us?"

Her mom's smile widened. "Of course. I'm glad you're reconnecting with her. It's important to keep good friends close."

Allison nodded slowly, her shoulders relaxing just a little. "I was thinking about redoing my room," she blurted out. She glanced up, meeting her mother's sharp blue eyes. "I'm not a baby anymore."

"I didn't want to redecorate without you here to make the decisions," her mom told her.

"So, I can paint and pick out new furniture?" Allison asked, a spark of excitement creeping into her voice.

"Absolutely," her mom said. "Come up with some ideas, and we'll work out a budget tomorrow evening."

Allison dug into her dinner, feeling relieved. Maybe she wouldn't be here long enough to finish redecorating, but at least her room would finally feel like hers.

Chapter Four

The boutique's doors slid open with a whoosh, and Allison followed her mom inside, blinking at the sudden brightness. It was quiet, like a library for rich people's clothes. No loud background music or colorful displays. Just rows of perfectly spaced clothing under soft lights, as if they were meant to be admired, not touched. Even the air smelled expensive, like leather and perfume had been mixed into some sort of exotic, faintly metallic scent.

Her loafers barely made a sound, but her mom's heels clicked sharply against the marble floor. The sound carried through the stillness.

"This place is cool," Marjani whispered, her bangles jangling as she moved.

Cool wasn't the word Allison would use. Weird, maybe.

She was about to say something when her mom slowed. Allison felt the change before she even saw it.

Her mom's steps grew more deliberate, her back straighter. Even the way she tucked her purse into her elbow felt different, as if she had morphed into a completely different person.

Allison wasn't sure why, but she suddenly wanted to step back.

Then, as her mom turned toward the counter, Allison caught a glimpse of her face. Her expression was smooth and unreadable, her sharp blue eyes sweeping over the boutique as if she owned it.

It was almost like watching someone put on armor. No flashing metal. No dramatic moment. Just a shift, subtle, but complete. For a second, Allison barely recognized her.

Her mom wasn't just Rylee Williams, the woman who had mentored her Little League robotics team. This was Rylee Williams, entrepreneur and business owner. And everyone shopping in the boutique knew it.

A tall woman in a black and silver retro jumpsuit popped out of the room behind the counter. "Welcome back, Mrs. Maxwell," she said with a warm smile. "Everything is ready for you."

"Thank you, Maxine," her mom smoothly said, her gaze already sweeping the room. "This is my daughter, Allison, and her friend, Marjani."

Maxine's eyes flicked briefly to Allison, then to Marjani, who stood nearby, looking around with interest. Marjani's vibrantly colored blouse and flowing kanga wrap skirt, with bold patterns and delicate beadwork, looked completely out of place here. But if Maxine noticed, she didn't show it. If anything, she looked intrigued.

The woman stepped out from behind the counter. "Why don't we get started?" she said, gesturing to a glowing platform near the center of the boutique. "Just step onto the scanner and we'll update your measurements, Miss Maxwell."

Allison hesitated. The platform pulsed gently in front of her, its glow shifting like liquid light under the surface. The edges rippled, almost like it was breathing. Carefully, she stepped onto it.

The instant her loafers touched the surface, a tingling sensation crawled up her legs. Warm, weightless, and slightly electric.

A low, steady hum vibrated beneath her feet, like the muted thrum of a spaceship engine in the movies. Lines of soft blue light flickered to life, rising from the platform like glowing strands of thread. They moved too fast to follow, tracing along her arms, shoulders, and legs, wrapping her in a shimmering web. It felt like ghost fingers were brushing over her skin.

Then, just as fast as it started, the lights vanished. The platform dimmed, returning to its original faint glow. Allison quickly stepped off, rubbing her arms as though she could brush off the strange sensation.

"Her measurements have been updated," Maxine said, checking over a slim tablet in her hands.

Maxine turned to Allison's mom. "Everything set aside should fit within the guidelines you gave us, Mrs. Maxwell," she said, leading them deeper into the store.

As they approached the dressing area, another boutique assistant, a tall woman with sleek hair and a precise smile, emerged from a side room, pushing a rack of clothing. The hangers clicked as she adjusted the lineup, smoothing out a jacket sleeve here and tucking in a blouse there.

"Most of these are already in her size, but a few pieces will need minor adjustments after she tries things on," the woman said.

Allison stared at the sheer number of clothes. "Isn't this . . . a lot?" she asked, looking at her mom. "I mean, you said I'd only be here for a few weeks."

Her mom's voice was calm but firm. "You'll be back for the holidays, and then there's high school next year." She ran a practiced eye over the clothes, brushing a sleeve between her fingers. "Ciel Noir can make adjustments as needed."

She glanced at Allison, her expression softening just slightly. "Besides, you're going to look amazing. Trust me, okay?"

Allison shrugged, not really convinced, but too tired to argue. "I guess."

She inspected the rack. The clothes were perfectly arranged. Formal wear for events, weekend outfits that still somehow looked expensive, and after-school pieces that were supposed to feel 'relaxed' but still had an intimidating level of polish.

Her mom gestured toward the first set Maxine was offering, a soft gray blouse and a pair of tailored trousers. "Let's start with the basics and build from there."

Allison took the clothes and stepped into the dressing room, except 'room' didn't seem like the right word. It was bigger than her bedroom in Germany. It felt more like a private lounge than a place to try on clothes. The walls were lined with gold-lit panels that gave off a warm glow, and the floor was covered in a thick, cloud-like rug that sank under her feet.

A plush chaise lounge sat in the corner, draped with a cashmere throw. A full-length smart mirror stretched across one wall, its surface displaying subtle menus at the edges. There were lighting controls, fabric details, and even styling suggestions. Next to it, a sleek vanity table held a tray of glass bottles filled with perfume samples, along with a crystal dish of delicate chocolates.

Allison blinked. Did they seriously expect people to eat chocolate while trying on expensive clothes?

She changed quickly, eyeing herself in the full-length mirror. The trousers fit better than expected, and the blouse wasn't as stiff as it looked. But as she smoothed her fingers over the perfectly pressed fabric, she couldn't help but think about her old jeans and hoodies back in Germany.

When she stepped out, her mom beamed. "You look great! Doesn't she look great, Marjani?"

Marjani gave her a thumbs-up. "You look like a movie star!"

Allison smirked, the comment making her feel a bit awkward. "Yay . . . " she muttered, but Marjani still grinned.

Maxine approached with a sleek, hand-held scanner, no bigger than a remote. "Let's check the fit."

She ran the scanner over the tag on the trousers, and it beeped in acknowledgment. Then, with the press of a button, a miniature blue grid unfolded in the air around Allison, shimmering like a cocoon of light.

The grid rippled, its lines moving in precise, sharp patterns, tracing the outline of her clothes with a futuristic glow. Allison stood still, watching as the light crawled over her like a swarm of digital fireflies, mapping every seam, every stitch.

"The scanner detects any adjustments needed for the perfect fit," Maxine explained. "It will also account for movement, posture, even fabric flexibility."

After a moment, the grid dissolved as if it had never been there. "All set," Maxine said, glancing at the tablet in her hand.

"Next outfit," her mom said with a smile, handing her a dress this time.

The process repeated over and over. Each item fit like it had been designed just for her.

Even the shoes were perfect. Too perfect. Simple loafers, ankle boots, and plain white sneakers that looked ordinary but probably cost more than a normal person's rent.

"Ciel Noir used data from your wardrobe in Hamburg and past family holidays to curate this collection," her mom said, casually scrolling through something on her tablet. "But the final choice is yours."

Allison sighed, looking at the racks of clothes as Maxine ran a small brush over each item, smoothing out wrinkles that weren't even there. "I guess this is fine."

Her mom smiled, satisfied. "Good. Why don't you pick something to wear for our appointment?" She turned to Maxine. "Please have the rest delivered."

Allison grabbed a pair of jeans and a dark green tunic before heading back to the dressing room.

She changed quickly, but then just sat there, her old clothes folded neatly on her lap. The mirror reflected a girl she barely recognized.

What the hell is happening? she thought. It was like she'd stepped into another life. Instead of her usual bohemian tops and skinny jeans, she was suddenly wrapped in designer labels, being waited on by boutique staff as if she was some VIP.

What's next? Diamond earrings? A closet full of handbags I'd never use? She shook her head, frustrated.

There was a soft knock on the door. "Is everything alright, Miss Maxwell?" Maxine's voice was polite, but there was a hint of expectation behind it.

Allison exhaled slowly. "I'll be out in a minute." She glanced at the mirror one last time.

Yes, she kind of liked how the clothes fit. Yes, they would probably help her blend in. And yeah . . . maybe she'd take a few pieces back to Hamburg. But none of it felt like her.

She squared her shoulders, picked up her old clothes, and stepped out. Her mom was waiting with two tall bottles of neon-pink liquid. "Here," she said, handing one to Allison as Maxine quietly folded her old clothes into a store bag.

Allison took it and stared at the drink. Tiny bubbles rushed to the surface, popping in soft bursts that tickled her nose. The liquid seemed to glow faintly.

"What is this?" she asked.

Marjani grabbed her own bottle eagerly. "Fizz," she said. "You're gonna love it."

Allison sniffed cautiously. The scent was sickly sweet, like a mix of bubblegum and melted candy.

She took a small sip. The liquid exploded on her tongue, tingling like tiny fireworks. It was overwhelmingly sweet, as if someone had liquefied cotton candy and added extra sugar just for fun.

Marjani slurped hers loudly, her bangles jingling as she tipped the bottle back. "Isn't it amazing?" she asked.

Allison pulled the drink away from her lips. "It's different," she said, then took another hesitant sip. She wasn't sure if she liked it, but the fizz popping against her lips was strangely addictive.

Marjani was already halfway through hers, practically bouncing. "This place is amazing. I'm so jealous."

Maxine approached with her tablet. "We'll send everything directly to your home once the final tailoring is complete," she said, scrolling through the order details. "Shoes, socks, and all accessories are included. If there's anything else you'd like to add, let me know."

"Thank you, Maxine," her mom said, already guiding Allison and Marjani toward the exit.

As they left, Maxine's gaze flicked toward Allison, her expression unreadable. Maybe curiosity. Maybe envy. Or maybe Allison was just imagining it.

She clutched her drink, letting the bubbles tickle her nose, and followed her mom to the waiting pod.

"Thanks for coming," Allison said quietly as they walked.

"Are you kidding?" Marjani grinned. "This was amazing! Those jeans look so good on you."

Allison smiled back, but she still felt unsettled.

This was her life for now. Designer clothes, glowing platforms, and pink drinks that fizzed like soda but tasted like candy. She just hoped she wouldn't lose herself in all the fuss.

The headmaster's office smelled faintly of bitter coffee, the kind adults drank when they were exhausted but refused to admit it. Allison sat stiffly in the sleek guest chair, her loafers barely brushing the plush carpet. The room felt too quiet. It made her want to fidget, but she forced herself to stay still.

She glanced at the large windows behind Mr. Brice. The sunlight outside should have been bright. Instead, the LED panels washed it into a cold, bluish-white glow. The whole room felt artificial, like a place where rules mattered more than people. Her stomach churned with frustration.

Her mom's voice, cool and sharp, sliced through the silence. "Mr. Brice, there seems to be some fundamental misunderstanding. My daughter's transcripts from the *Kaiserhof Gymnasium* clearly demonstrate her academic abilities."

The headmaster grunted, his eyes skimming over the screen in front of him like he hadn't really bothered to read it. "Vanguard Preparatory Academy prides itself on maintaining rigorous academic standards," he said, his voice thick with condescension. "It's my responsibility to ensure that students are appropriately challenged, including your daughter."

Her mom's eyebrow arched. "By having her retake pre-Algebra?"

Allison's fingers tightened around the chair's armrests. If Russia hadn't started another war in Europe, she wouldn't even be here. She'd be in Hamburg, hanging out with her friends as they worked through their homework. Not being treated like she didn't belong.

Mr. Brice sighed, his tone dripping with patience he didn't appear to have. "Ones across the board don't demonstrate the level of excellence we expect from Vanguard students."

The knot in Allison's chest snapped. "Ones are the highest grades in Germany!" she burst out.

Mr. Brice barely reacted. He didn't even look at her, almost as if she wasn't worth acknowledging.

"Allison," her mom said sharply, brushing her fingers against Allison's knee. Her tone softened, but the warning was there. "Let me handle this."

Allison slumped back in her chair, her jaw tight, her pulse pounding in her ears.Mr. Brice folded his hands, his thin smile barely masking his disapproval. "If your husband were here—"

Her mom's posture went rigid. Wrong move.

Without a word, she reached into her handbag, pulled out her thin tablet, and stabbed at the screen with precise, practiced movements.

The screen lit up, and her dad appeared. He was still at the construction site, even though the sun had already set. Floodlights cast long shadows over the towering barriers and steel scaffolding behind him, their harsh glow making the deep lines of exhaustion on his face even more pronounced. The faint clang of machinery echoed through the tiny speaker.

But the moment his hazel eyes landed on Allison and her mom, they softened. "Wie läuft das Meeting mit Vanguard?" he asked, his voice steady but edged with curiosity. *How is the meeting with Vanguard going?*

The auto-translator on the headmaster's desk repeated the words in English, its gentle, mechanical voice making the room feel even more unnatural.

Her mom's jaw tightened. "We've hit a bit of a roadblock," she said in clipped English, the words grinding out between her teeth. Allison had never seen her this angry before.

With a sharp flick of her fingers, her mom transferred the call to the office wall screen. Her dad's expression shifted instantly as he took in the room, his gaze flicking between Allison, her mom, and the headmaster. The construction site noise faded into the background.

"Was ist das Problem?" he asked, his voice sharper now. "Sind deine Schulunterlagen nicht angekommen?" *What's the problem? Didn't your school records arrive?*

Allison sat up straighter. "Doch, Papa," she said hesitantly, shooting a quick glance at the headmaster. "Aber Herr Brice glaubt nicht, dass ich eine gute Schülerin bin!" *They did, Dad. But Mr. Brice doesn't believe I'm a good student!*

Her dad's face hardened as he turned his full attention to the headmaster. "Why don't you believe that my daughter is a good student?" he asked, switching to English, his Midwest accent crisp and direct.

Mr. Brice blinked, clearly thrown by the sudden language shift. He straightened in his chair, adjusting his tie like it would help him regain control of the conversation. "She received all ones in her classes," he said, exhaling in clear exasperation. "Surely you understand that's a failing grade."

Allison felt a rush of heat crawl up her neck. He hadn't even bothered to check.

Her dad's voice was cold and firm. "In Germany, that's a top grade." He didn't raise his voice, but there was no mistaking the edge of frustration beneath it. "A five is failing. If you'd contacted her school, you'd know that."

Mr. Brice blinked, his face reddening slightly as he adjusted his glasses. He cleared his throat, unsettled by the rebuke.

Her mom leaned back, crossing her arms. "And this misunderstanding is why she's been placed in remedial classes?"

Mr. Brice gave a sharp nod, avoiding her gaze. "I'll review this with the academic advisor and the dean of women, and we'll adjust her schedule accordingly."

Her dad frowned. "We'll deal with it now," he growled. "Rylee, send me the class schedule."

Her mom's fingers danced over the tablet. The main screen split, displaying Allison's schedule alongside her transcripts.

Her dad's frown deepened as he scanned the list. "Longer school days than she's used to," he muttered. "That's to be expected. Hmm . . . Civics, Language Arts, Pre-Algebra, Introduction to Social Studies, Life Science Overview, Painting, and Mandarin." He paused and looked up. "That's it?" His tone was flat, but the disbelief was obvious. "I expected more from Vanguard."

He turned to Mom. "This is the school that came highly recommended?" he asked.

Mr. Brice bristled. "Our students have the highest test scores in the Upper Northeast," he said stiffly.

Her dad was unimpressed. "Her math class at Kaiserhof covers algebra, geometry, probability, and logical reasoning." His voice stayed calm, but Allison knew he was done playing nice. "They also rotate science subjects, including introductory biology, physics, and Earth science. That's in addition to history, English, geography, ethics, Mandarin, and two electives."

Her mom nodded. "That's why I called."

Her dad turned back to Mr. Brice, his hazel eyes like steel. "Allison starts Monday. I need this fixed." He let the word hang for a moment before adding, "Immediately."

Allison watched Mr. Brice carefully. Her dad rarely used that tone around her, but she knew what it meant: He wasn't going anywhere until this was done.

She remembered how hard it had been to catch up when she first moved to Germany. It wasn't just the language. She'd been fluent enough in German, thanks to her dad and her tutor. But, it had been like she'd skipped an entire grade just by moving.

It took a lot of effort, but the next year, her grades had been good enough for her to move on to a Gymnasium, a place for high-achieving, university-bound students. Kaiserhof was highly competitive, but the classes were interactive and fun. Now it sounded like she was falling back a grade just by coming back to the States.

Mr. Brice exhaled sharply, shifting in his chair. "Let me bring our academic advisor and the dean of women into this discussion so we can correct the error."

Allison hid a small smirk behind her hand.

Her dad nodded. "Let's make this quick. I have an inspection coming up."

Mr. Brice's lips pressed into a thin line. "This shouldn't take long," he said, his voice clipped. Then he turned to Allison, his tone drenched in false politeness. "I've arranged for a student navigator to give you a tour while we finalize your schedule."

Allison's stomach tightened. She didn't like the way he said it. Like she was some inconvenient problem that needed to be pushed out of the way.

"Our vertical campus takes some getting used to," he added with a thin smile. "It's easy to get turned around. Is that acceptable, Mrs. Maxwell?"

Her mom gave a gracious nod. "Of course."

Mr. Brice barely acknowledged her before turning back to his screen. "Why don't you wait outside, Allison? Denise will be along shortly."

Allison hesitated. She glanced at her mom, who gave a small nod, her expression softening for the first time since they'd arrived.

With a sigh, Allison stood and grabbed her bag.

Mr. Brice barely looked up. "Thank you," he said curtly, already dismissing her. "This won't take long."

The door automatically closed behind Allison, and she found herself in a quiet hallway. The faint murmur of her dad's voice faded away. She stood still for a moment, her hands hanging awkwardly at her sides. Shouldn't a school have noise? Footsteps, lockers slamming, even people talking? Instead, it felt empty.

A door at the end of the hall opened, and a girl stepped in. "Allison Maxwell?" she asked.

Allison nodded, shifting her weight. "Yeah."

The girl smiled, polite but practiced. "I'm Denise, your navigator," she said. "Let's get started. Vanguard takes some getting used to."

As they walked down the hallway, Allison smoothed the sides of her tunic, suddenly aware of how casual it looked compared to Denise's uniform. The girl's gray blazer had a shiny gold crest on the pocket, her white blouse buttoned up neatly, and her pleated skirt almost reached her ankles. The uniform fit her perfectly, right down to the polished black loafers. Even her hair, with its long, dark blonde waves, looked like it belonged in a school brochure.

"Welcome to Vanguard," Denise said, her tone light but practiced. "We're technically coed, but boys and girls have separate classes."

Her mom had mentioned that. Allison frowned. "Why?"

Denise shrugged like it was obvious. "Because boys and girls learn differently."

Allison raised an eyebrow. "We do?"

Denise nodded. "Yes, we do," she assured Allison. "Boys need more hands-on stuff to really understand things, and girls . . . " She smiled. "We're smarter, but we can be too emotional. So, it's better to keep things structured for us."

Allison opened her mouth to argue, but stopped. That didn't sound right. Boys in her old school could be loud, sure, but so could the girls. And since when did girls need 'structure' to learn?

Denise didn't seem to notice her hesitation. She gestured toward the elevators. "Vanguard is a vertical campus, so our classes aren't based on grade level. You change floors based on your academic track."

"So, if you're ahead, you just move to the next floor?" Allison asked.

"Pretty much," Denise said. The hallway was lined with framed paintings, each with a tiny plaque underneath. Some were labeled On Loan from famous collections. Allison vaguely wondered if her extended family had donated one.

Denise pressed the button with a green fork-and-knife icon. Two others showed blue and pink figures, one in a suit, the other in a dress.

"We don't get a lot of transfers," Denise said, glancing at Allison. "Where did you live before moving to Manhattan?"

"Hamburg, Germany."

Denise's eyebrows lifted. "Huh. Europe, right?" Her voice took on a slightly dismissive tone. "Manhattan is much safer than Europe right now. Things are getting really bad over there." She tilted her head. "Honestly, I don't know why any American families would stay."

Allison stiffened, pursing her lips. Hamburg was a great place to live.

Denise stepped into the elevator and tapped her gray bracelet against the scanner. "Vanguard's one of the best prep schools in the republic," she added as the doors slid shut. "You'll see."

Allison didn't feel lucky. Safe wasn't the word she'd use for Manhattan, not with security guards on every street like they were expecting an attack at any moment. Since when did people even call the U.S. a republic?

By the time the elevator reached the 20th floor, Denise had slipped back into tour guide mode. "This is the coed floor," she said as the doors slid open. "It has the student lounge, library, and dining hall."

The space was huge, open, and bright. Floor-to-ceiling windows stretched along one side, letting in a flood of sunlight.

To the right, the dining hall looked more like a high-end restaurant than a school cafeteria with rows of polished tables and cushy chairs, all perfectly arranged. A few servers were still clearing away dishes from lunch.

To the left, the library was quieter, more serious. Shelves of books lined the walls, and students sat at sleek desks, scrolling through digital textbooks or flipping through print books.

Straight ahead, the carpet gave way to smooth tiles. Chess tables, a small theater, and a glass case holding what looked like an old gaming console sat near the back. A group of boys clustered around a gaming setup, their AR bands lit up, laughing as one of them tripped over nothing.

"Hey, Denise!" a voice called. "Giving the full tour?"

Denise stiffened for a moment, then forced a bright smile. A tall boy with black hair strolled over, hands stuffed into his pockets like he had all the time in the world. His uniform was similar to Denise's, but his blazer had a patch on the sleeve—a gold gear with a lightning bolt stitched through it.

"This must be the new girl," he said, glancing at Allison. His eyes flicked over her, quick and measuring. "Welcome to the Tower."

"The Tower?" Allison asked, shifting slightly to look up at him.

His grin widened. "That's what we call it," he said in a teasing voice. "It's a fortress."

"A fortress . . . ?"

"Of learning," he told her, leaning in slightly like he was letting her in on some kind of joke. "I'm Tomas. And you are?"

Allison hesitated. Something about him made her uneasy. Maybe the way he looked at her like he already had her figured out. Maybe it was the way he stood, just a little too relaxed, like nothing could touch him.

"Allison Maxwell," she said finally, keeping her voice neutral.

He smirked, reaching out his hand, palm up. It wasn't quite a handshake, and she didn't know what to do. When she didn't take his hand, he reached for hers instead, lifting it with a flourish as if to kiss it.

"Don't," Allison said sharply, yanking her hand away. What the hell? she thought.

Tomas's smirk faltered for a moment, his dark eyes narrowing slightly. "Hǎo qiángshì." *Feisty.*

Allison felt her expression harden, almost as if her entire face had become a mask. She barely noticed that he had switched from English to Mandarin. "Bié pèng wǒ!" *Keep your hands to yourself!*

Tomas froze, clearly surprised, before his smirk deepened into something colder. "Interesting," he said, switching back to English.

"Leave her alone, Tomas," Denise said, her voice sharper now.

He shrugged, backing away with a lazy wave. "Enjoy the tour," he said as he sauntered off.

Allison clenched her fists, her nails digging into her palms as she stared after him. "Does he always act like that?" she asked, her voice tight.

Denise sighed, her cheerful tone slipping for a moment. "Pretty much. Best advice? Avoid him. Guys like Tomas aren't worth the trouble."

Allison didn't answer, but her stomach churned. Something about Tomas's smirk stayed with her. What made him think it was okay to touch her like that?

Chapter Five

Allison stretched out on her bed, running her fingers over the soft quilt, its antique stitching fraying slightly at the edges. Over the last few days, the room had been rearranged completely. Her bed, minus the canopy, was now tucked against the wall nearest the bathroom and closets, and a larger worktable with two adjustable computer chairs replaced the old desk. The monitor that had hugged the far wall had been replaced by a new smart wall, and a small couch now nestled under the window wall between two end tables.

The light gray-blue walls, freshly painted, caught the late afternoon light streaming through the windows, offering a sweeping view of the Manhattan skyline. It was better than before. More grown-up.

The wall around her bed was now a sleek display with built-in shelves, a mix of wood and glass with soft lighting. Framed photos from her favorite family vacations—Venice, Ushuaia, and Lantau Island—were carefully spaced out. Some hung flat against the wall, while others leaned casually on the shelves.

Underneath, a few shelves held small souvenirs: a seashell from Greece, a wooden 'Gelato' sign from Venice, a set of wristbands from Argentina, and a glacier rock from Ushuaia with a tiny brass plate that read Glaciar Martial. She remembered picking it up on a hike with her dad, the cold wind stinging her nose while he talked about how glaciers were disappearing.

Her Ngong Ping 360 cable car model sat off to one side, next to a couple of books, its tiny windows reflecting the light. It wasn't crowded or messy, but it felt like her stuff instead of just decoration.

She smiled. It was really coming together. She'd make sure to bring more small items when she moved back for high school.

A gentle knock pulled Allison from her thoughts. She sat up, glancing toward the door. "Come in!"

Marjani pushed it open, grinning. "Allison! Finally, I get to see your new Manhattan lair."

Allison got up as Marjani stepped in, her colorful skirt catching the light. The gold threads in her blouse shimmered as she flopped onto the small couch under the windows. "This place is serious," she said, looking around. "Way better."

"Yeah, well, I outgrew pink clouds," Allison said with a smirk.

Marjani tilted her head, scanning the room. "It's nice. Grown-up. Except . . . " She pointed at the lowest shelf of the display case, where a neat row of stuffed animals sat.

"Don't even start," Allison warned with a laugh.

Before Marjani could say anything, Mom poked her head in. "Beatrice, Charlotte, and Victoria are here."

Allison grinned. The whole crew was back.

She barely had time to step toward the door before Beatrice walked in, giving the room a once-over like she was critiquing a fashion show. Her sleek orange dress looked straight off a runway. Typical Beatrice. Her honey-brown hair was smooth and glossy, not a strand out of place. She looked taller. More put-together.

Beatrice gave Allison a quick hug, then dropped onto the couch next to Marjani. "This is different," she said, waving a hand at the space. "Didn't you used to have a canopy bed?"

"Gone," Allison said flatly. "It was time."

Charlotte and Victoria stood in the doorway. "Admiring the view?" Allison asked with a smirk.

Charlotte nodded, then sauntered into the room as if she owned it. "I like what you've done with the place," she remarked. She had a seat on the floor.

Victoria leaned against the doorframe, her dark ponytail so sleek she could have been a model. "Well, look at you, back in the city," Victoria said, her voice teasing. "Love it." She strolled over to the project table, spinning one of the chairs before sitting down.

"Thanks, I guess," Allison said. "Still doesn't feel like mine yet."

"Speaking of which," Marjani said, kicking off her sandals and tucking her legs under her. "Are you here for good, or just for now?"

Allison sank onto the floor, running her fingers over the thick carpet. "I'm leaving as soon as it's safe," she said. "But Kaiserhof has strict attendance rules. They completely drop you if you miss more than ten days. I had to enroll at Vanguard." She paused. "I'm allowed to transfer back after the fighting's over."

"Vanguard? Ugh," Victoria said, making a face. "That place is intense."

"Tell me about it," Beatrice muttered. "At least St. Agnes has some freedom. No uniforms, no boys, no nonsense."

Victoria scoffed. "No nonsense? Please. There's still drama. It's just quieter. And don't even get me started on the dress code. You might as well wear a uniform."

Beatrice shrugged. "It's better than wearing the same thing every single day," she stated.

"St. Agnes sounds awful," Marjani shot back. "Hybrid's the way to go. Tutors in the morning, real-world experience in the afternoon. Way better."

"Maybe," Beatrice admitted, "but at least at Vanguard, people have a sense of style."

"Do they, though?" Victoria smirked. "You've seen their uniforms, right?" She turned to Allison. "What's it like? Please tell me it's not as bad as I've heard."

Allison sighed. "Gray blazer, white shirt, matching long pleated skirt. It's fine, I guess. Not hideous, but not exactly fun."

Beatrice snorted. "So, basically a prep school factory for hedge-fund heirs."

"Or future politicians," Marjani added, grinning. "But it's just for a little while, right?"

"Yeah," Allison said softly, glancing at the window. "I'm going back as soon as I can."

"For your sake, I hope it's soon," Victoria said with a small nod. "Manhattan isn't what it used to be."

"And you have to go to Vanguard?" Beatrice groaned dramatically. "I'd die if I had to wear a uniform every day."

"Could be worse," Marjani said, throwing a pillow at her. "At least it's not a public school."

That set them all off laughing, and for a moment, Allison let herself relax. It felt normal sitting around, talking about school, and glitching at dress codes.

The conversation shifted to gossip. Charlotte's latest run-in with the St. Agnes dress code police. Some guy sneaking into a friend's building after curfew. A long conversation about families that Allison didn't even know who planned to winter abroad. Allison let their voices blur together, just happy to have them here.

When they left, the room felt weirdly quiet. Allison sat on the floor for a minute, staring at the door. It used to be different. Sleepovers, movie marathons, sneaking snacks from the kitchen. Back then, they didn't talk about schools, security, or when they'd have to leave.

She glanced at the shelves with her little souvenirs, then out at the city skyline. Things weren't the same, but at least her friends hadn't changed.

The rooftop garden was Allison's favorite part of the penthouse. Up here, the city noise felt far away, like it belonged to a different world. She curled into the corner of a deep couch under the canopy, tucking her feet beneath her. Her khaki shorts bunched at the edges as she shifted, trying to get comfortable. The air smelled fresh and green, with roses, lavender, and something earthy that reminded her of the park near her dad's place.

She held her glass of Spezi in both hands. Condensation gathered along the sides, cool against her fingers. The fizz tingled on her tongue, sharp and familiar. It tasted like summer afternoons at the café back home, where she and her dad would sit outside, watching boats drift along the Elbe. It was a real drink, not like the sickly sweet Fizz everyone here seemed obsessed with.

Her tablet rested on the arm of the couch, still open to *Das Schattenprotokoll*. The German thriller had her hooked with hidden codes, narrow escapes, and a detective who always seemed to be one step behind the criminals. It was easier to focus on spies and secret messages than on how weird everything felt here.

Then, the tablet chimed.

Allison groaned and set her glass down. Ugh. Another school alert. It was the third one today. She'd ignored the others, but this one flashed like it actually mattered. Reluctantly, she swiped open the notification, her nose wrinkling as a new calendar loaded.

At first, she thought it was a mistake. She scrolled back up and read it again.

A designer fashion preview. Private art showings. A charity gala for some nonprofit she'd never heard of. A biweekly Saturday luncheon. Weekend theater performances.

This wasn't a school calendar. This was her mom's idea of a social networking season.

Her stomach sank. She swiped to her class schedule, hoping those events weren't mandatory. The headmaster had promised her parents that her course load would be like Kaiserhof's.

Monday/Wednesday/Friday Schedule
8:00 am: Arrival/Prep
8:30 am: Daily assembly
8:45 am: Language Arts
9:30 am: Life Science
10:15 am: Wellness Break
10:30 am: Social Studies

11:15 am: Mandarin
12:00 pm: Lunch
1:30 pm: Algebra I (individual instruction)
2:15 pm: Civics
3:00 pm: Wellness Break
3:15 pm: After School Women's Chess Club
4:15 pm: Pickup

Allison frowned and scrolled back to the top of the list, scanning it again. Something wasn't right. Her legs twitched, and she stretched one foot out, brushing her heel against the cool fabric of the couch.

She tapped on Language Arts, hoping for a normal course description, but the words on the screen made her stomach drop:

The Craft of Eloquence: Students will refine their ability to express themselves with poise and grace, focusing on storytelling, persuasive communication, and the art of correspondence.

"What does that even mean?" she muttered. She clicked on Algebra I next, hoping for something better.

Algebra I: An individualized introduction to algebraic fundamentals, emphasizing logical thinking, structure, and problem-solving to support confidence in everyday tasks and social endeavors.

Allison covered her eyes, shaking her head. Are they serious? It was like they assumed she didn't have two brain cells to rub together.

She scrolled through the rest of the list. Mandarin was a step back since Vanguard insisted on testing before placing her in a higher-level class. But wellness breaks? And how had language arts turned into something called *The Craft of Eloquence?*

A cool breeze swept through the garden. Allison barely noticed. She shoved her hair back, irritated. "This is so stupid," she muttered.

How was this supposed to prepare her for high school? Did Vanguard even have real academics and real challenges? What was she even learning here?

She flopped back against the couch, staring up at the sunlight as it lit up the canopy above her. The rooftop had always felt like a quiet escape. But now? It felt different.

A thick glass barrier ran along the edge of the garden. It was supposed to give her an amazing view of the city, but all it did was remind her how far away everything was. She wasn't in Manhattan. She was above it, separated from it, looking out like a guest behind a velvet rope at an exclusive restaurant or show.

A breeze stirred the trees, cool against her arms. She used to love that sound, the way the leaves whispered in the wind. Now, it barely reached her. The wind hit the glass and changed direction, scattering instead of flowing through.

She sat up, grabbed her drink, and frowned. The Spezi had gone flat. Figured.

She let her head drop back, turning her head to look at the sky beyond the glass. Open, endless. But down here? She was closed in.

Not trapped. But not free, either.

Allison slid the AR band down over her eyes, feeling the familiar pulse against her temples as it activated. She hesitated for a second before opening the messaging app.

The words came out before she could second-guess them. "I just got my class schedule. I think we need to talk, Mom."

She flicked at the window and pushed the band back up, not even waiting for a confirmed the message was sent.

Her hands clenched the fabric of her shorts as she pulled her knees to her chest. The sun dipped lower, stretching long shadows across the garden. The golden light flickered against the glass barriers, but she barely noticed. Her thoughts churned, looping back to the same thing over and over again.

This isn't going to work, she thought. I can't stay here.

Allison curled into the corner of the deep leather couch, her arms wrapped around her legs. Her tablet lay face down and forgotten on the antique mahogany coffee table. Across the room, her dad was perched on the edge of his desk, his expression tense. The floor in his office seemed to merge seamlessly with the plush carpet beneath her feet.

He looked exhausted, she thought.

The smart wall made it feel like he was sitting across the room from her. It was so realistic that she almost forgot he was thousands of miles away in Hamburg. Almost.

But the faint shimmer of the screen at the edges gave it away. The connection lagged just enough to remind her that he wasn't really in Manhattan.

Her mom sat stiffly on the opposite couch, her tablet still open in her lap, the school syllabus glowing on the screen. Her fingers curled around the device, tightening and loosening as if she were trying to keep herself from gripping it too hard. After a long moment, she exhaled sharply through her nose and set the tablet aside.

Her dad's voice cut through the silence, sharper than usual. "So this is the best they can do, even after an in-depth conversation with Kaiserhof?" His frustration was barely contained. "This isn't education. It's a finishing school!"

Her mom pressed her fingers against her forehead before answering. "I know," she admitted. But she hesitated, just for a second, before lowering her hands to her lap. "This is what they're selling as 'the best'. And it's not just Vanguard, Sam. Every school in Manhattan has adjusted to fit the new guidelines."

His frown deepened. His fingers drummed against his desk before he rubbed the side of his face, sighing heavily. "So, no other options?"

Mom slowly shook her head. "I reached out to my network again, and they all told me the same thing. Vanguard is the best in the state," she told him. "If she stays here for the entire school year, she'll have her pick of high schools next year, even out of state."

Her dad scoffed. "Really?" His voice was edged with disbelief. He ran a hand through his already messy hair. "That doesn't add up."

"Just to test the theory, I called a few high schools in other states," her mom said, glancing at him. "The admissions offices practically drooled over the idea of getting a Vanguard student."

His lips pressed into a thin line. "Let me guess," he said. "Academic excellence. Prestigious connections. Competitive."

Her mom exhaled. "Exactly."

Allison barely heard them. At Kaiserhof, she'd taken real classes. Math had been more than just basic equations. History was global, covering the political shifts in Europe, South

America, Africa, and beyond, not just whatever version of history the government approved here. And science? Rotations through biology, physics, and Earth sciences.

Now, she was supposed to spend an entire year learning how to write thank-you notes and hold polite conversations. It was a joke. A bad one.

Her AR band buzzed again. She clenched her fists. Another school notification. She ignored it.

Her mom looked at her, something sad flickering in her expression, before she turned back to her dad. "I made a few more calls," she quietly told him. She exhaled and straightened her shoulders, but her voice stayed tight. "I thought maybe Vanguard was missing paperwork or something. But Kaiserhof assured me they'd provided Vanguard with complete access to all of Allison's records. There's nothing more they can do."

She lowered her gaze, pressing her lips together for a moment before continuing. "They also told me they're going to start reaching out to the parents of students who transferred out. They recommend those students finish out the academic year where they are." She hesitated, her voice soft with regret. "They said they'll welcome everyone back next fall. But they're worried. If the fighting moves west into Poland, more evacuations could be coming."

Allison pressed her back against the couch, staring at the ceiling.

Next fall. That wasn't the plan. She was supposed to come back to the U.S. for high school.

She sat up suddenly, turning to her mom. "Why can't we just move to southern Germany or western France?" she asked, the words rushing out. "Even if it's just for the rest of the school year? That way, we're close enough to Dad for him to visit!"

Her mom looked away for just for a second. Her hands smoothed the fabric of her skirt.

"I wish we could, sweetie," Mom finally told her. She looked like she was holding back tears. "The SkyHaven deal is at a critical phase. If I leave the state now, the whole transaction will collapse. It's not just the company's reputation on the line—it's the employees, the shareholders, the regulators. They're all counting on me to move the company private."

"And if I leave the Elbe project," her dad added, picking up where her mom left off, "Germany will have to rebid the entire contract. The locks won't get upgraded in time, and if we get another spring storm season, like last year . . . " he trailed off, shaking his head. "It could be catastrophic."

He stepped closer to the screen. It felt like she could just reach out and touch him. "If I could bring you back, Allie, I would. In a heartbeat," he said, his voice low and steady. "But it's not safe here for you. Things could shift fast, and I don't want to risk you or your mom. As soon as this project is done, I'm on a plane back home."

Her mom reached out, brushing a hand over Allison's knee, but she didn't move. "The Vanguard academic advisor suggested hiring a tutor," her mom said softly. "Math and science. That way, you won't fall behind."

Allison's head snapped up. "A tutor?" Her voice was sharp. "So I go to school, waste my time in dumb classes, then come home and do actual work with a tutor? How does that make sense?"

Her dad sighed. "I know you're frustrated, Allie."

She shook her head, her throat tightening. "I don't want a tutor," she said, her voice cracking. "I want a real school. I want to go home."

"I know," he told her, "But for now, this is the best we can do."

Allison pressed her lips together. It wasn't an option. It was a way to keep her quiet. She shifted her gaze back to the smart wall. It looked like she could just step through. But Dad was thousands of miles away. And he wasn't coming back anytime soon.

Her AR band buzzed against her temple. Probably just another school notification about an upcoming art show or something. She dismissed it with a tap of her fingers, but the haptic pulse lingered against her skin, like an itch she couldn't scratch.

"Can't I just take classes online?" she asked after a long pause. "Or transfer somewhere else? Marjani does hybrid classes. Why can't I do that?"

Her mom shook her head. "New York's Board of Education grandfathered that program last year. No new enrollments are allowed."

Allison let out a frustrated noise. "So what? I go to Vanguard, take their stupid etiquette classes, and pretend this is normal?" She threw up her hands. "Because it's not! This is not normal!"

Her mom slowly exhaled through her nose before looking at her. "No, it's not normal," she admitted. "But it's where we are. And the best thing we can do is figure out how to make it work."

Her dad nodded. "For now, we get you a tutor. We make sure you're still learning what you need for high school. And in the meantime, we keep looking for other options."

The idea of a tutor still felt like slapping a pain patch on a compound fracture. It was just wrong.

Her mom squeezed her knee. "This isn't forever," she said. "We can start looking at high schools that are a better match for you."

Allison didn't respond. She stared out the window at the Manhattan skyline, its glittering lights cold and distant. It felt like another world. One she didn't want to be a part of.

Chapter Six

"Good morning, Miss Allison," a clipped, too-cheerful voice announced, slicing through the haze of sleep. "The time is 7:02 a.m. The weather in Manhattan is currently 72 degrees, with a forecast high of 79. Shall I adjust the lighting?"

Allison groaned and yanked a pillow over her head. "Go away, Jeeves."

"I'm afraid I cannot comply," the AI responded in its usual too-polite, ultra-smug British accent. "You have a full schedule today, including breakfast at 7:30 and departure for Vanguard at 8. Adjusting lighting now."

The windows brightened automatically, the amber glow creeping across the room like an unwelcome guest.

"Ugh." Allison peeled the pillow off her face, blinking against the artificial sunrise. "You're evil, Jeeves."

"Duly noted, Miss Allison," the AI replied smoothly. "Shall I inform your mother that you are awake?"

"No!" Allison sat up, already regretting the outburst. The last thing she needed was her mom checking in.

Then came the knock, soft and deliberate. "Allison, are you up?"

She barely smothered a sigh. "I'm up."

The door cracked open, just enough for her mom to peek in. "Good," she said with a smile. "Don't take too long, sweetie. Breakfast is in a half an hour."

"Yeah, yeah," Allison muttered, rubbing the sleep from her eyes as the door clicked shut.

She padded over to the closet and slid it open. There they were. A whole row of identical uniforms, perfectly pressed and waiting. The long gray skirt. The stiff white shirt. The tailored blazer. It looked more like something a business executive would wear than something for school.

Allison sighed and grabbed the closest one. No point in stalling.

In the bathroom, she turned the shower on full blast, letting the near-scalding water wake her up. Steam fogged up the mirror, curling around her like a thick cloud. She probably stood under the spray longer than she should have, letting the heat pound against her back.

When she finally got out, she yanked the brush through the worst of the tangles before quickly blow-drying her hair, then twisting it into a ponytail. It wasn't perfect, but whatever.

She pulled on the stiff white shirt, buttoning it up. The starched collar felt tight against her neck like it was trying to keep her posture in check. Next came the long wool skirt, the fabric brushing against her calves in a way that felt weird and too proper. Finally, she shrugged into the blazer. It fit snugly across her shoulders, the silver crest on the pocket standing out like a tiny shield, heavy and serious.

She stared at herself in the mirror, tugging at the hem of the blazer.

It fit. But she didn't feel like herself at all.

Allison flicked off the bathroom light and stepped into the hallway. The cool air hit her skin, sharp and annoying. The day was officially starting, whether she liked it or not.

She trudged downstairs, following the smell of coffee and something buttery. Hopefully, that meant croissants. Or at least something equally good.

Sunlight streamed through the oversized windows. It was almost too bright. Allison stood there for a moment to let her eyes adjust.

The oval table was already set with a basket of fresh bread, neat little dishes of butter and jam, and a chilled pod of yogurt. Maria bustled in from the kitchen, smiling when she saw her. "Good morning, Miss Allison," she said warmly. "I hope you're hungry."

Allison slid into one of the leather chairs, glancing at the table. "Morning, Maria," she said, reaching for the yogurt.

Maria set down a tall glass of orange juice in front of her. "Let me know if you'd like eggs or bacon," she added. "I can have it ready in minutes."

Allison peeled back the lid on the yogurt container. Too much work this early. "This is fine."

Maria lingered nearby, hands on her hips. "I'll have coffee and . . . cushion . . . ready for when you get home."

Allison froze, the yogurt spoon halfway to her mouth. She blinked. "Wait. Do you mean *Kuchen*?"

Maria frowned. "Coo-kwin? That's 'cake', right?"

Allison set the spoon back into the container and smiled. "Yeah. That's right."

Maria grinned. "I'm trying my hand at Butter Cake today. It should be ready by the time you're back from school."

"Sounds great," Allison said automatically. She scooped up a spoonful of yogurt and immediately regretted it. The texture was all wrong, like jelly pretending to be fruit. Too sweet. Way too sweet.

She swallowed fast and shoved the container away. Maybe she should ask Maria to have some cereal delivered from the grocery store. Something that didn't taste like fake sugar and regret.

Her mom walked in, heels clicking on the tile. Sharp, precise—just like her. "Almost ready?"

"Yes, Mom." Allison pushed her chair back, placing her spoon next to the yogurt container.

Her mom held out a bracelet. It was sleek, with silver and navy bands tightly woven together. "This is your security bracelet. You'll need to wear it from now on."

Allison slipped it on. The metal was cold, adjusting itself automatically to fit her wrist. It wasn't tight, but it wasn't loose either. It felt weird.

"Why do I need this?" she asked, turning the bracelet over to study the clasp. "I already have my security card."

"Things have changed a bit," her mom said, holding up her wrist. She was wearing an identical bracelet. "Access IDs are now required in Manhattan proper."

Allison frowned, but followed her mom through the penthouse toward the private elevator. More security. Because apparently, Manhattan wasn't locked down enough.

A tall woman with short silver hair was waiting at the elevator. "Allison," her mom said, motioning toward her. "This is Omega. She'll be taking you to school."

Omega gave Allison a small nod. "Good morning, Miss Maxwell. Are you ready?"

Allison hesitated. Something about her gave off bodyguard vibes. Like she could snap someone's leg without breaking a sweat.

"Yeah," Allison said finally.

Her mom smoothed a hand over her blazer, adjusting the fabric even though it wasn't wrinkled. It was her version of a goodbye hug. "Let me know if you need anything. And remember, first impressions matter."

Allison stepped into the elevator with Omega, the doors sliding shut behind them. The ride down was quiet, except for the faint vibration of the machinery. Allison glanced at Omega, but she didn't move. Didn't fidget. Just stood there, unreadable. It felt less like she was getting a ride to school and more like a mission briefing.

The elevator doors slid open, revealing the underground garage. Cool air rushed in, carrying the faint hum of charging stations. The space was spotless, lined with sleek electric vehicles docked in their bays, silent except for the occasional beep of status updates.

The limo pod waited just ahead, its black surface gleaming under the bluish overhead lights. Polished. Perfect. A mirror of the world around it.

Omega moved first, opening the door with practiced ease.

Allison hesitated for half a second before stepping inside. The leather was smooth and cold against the backs of her calves, where her legs peeked out from under the long skirt.

Omega slid in after her, closing the door with a quiet click. The pod pulled smoothly into traffic, slipping effortlessly into the flow of sleek, autonomous vehicles. Above them, the towering skyline loomed, all glass and steel, flashing in the morning sunlight. The buildings seemed to be stacked one on top of the other, almost like a maze of glass and steel pressing against the sky like they were fighting for space.

Allison tightened her grip on her bag's strap. It's just one day, she told herself. How bad could it be? She slumped against the seat, half-reading, half-scrolling through the Vanguard student handbook. White-on-black text. Formal. Wordy. Boring. The handbook didn't even explain things. It just talked down to her like a lecture, with no room for questions.

"We've arrived, Miss Maxwell," Omega said smoothly as the pod eased to a stop.

Allison's fingers automatically tapped off her screen, shoving the tablet into her pack. She exhaled, pressing her palm against the cool leather seat for a second. Through the window, Vanguard loomed just as she remembered: Sleek and polished, reflecting the morning sun like a giant mirror.

Clusters of students streamed toward the entrance, walking in pairs or small groups. Not rushed. Orderly. Like they'd done this a thousand times before.

Omega stepped out first, scanning the area with a practiced glance before opening the door for Allison. "Have a good day, ma'am."

"Thanks, Omega," Allison muttered, adjusting her bag as she slid out.

The double doors opened with a familiar, quiet hum. The moment she stepped inside, the Vanguard entry hall stretched around her, wide open. Skylights beamed sunlight onto the glossy floors.

A buzz tickled her wrist. She glanced down at her security bracelet. A tiny light pulsed faintly. Attendance tracker, she guessed. Clever, she thought, but kinda invasive.

Some students stopped at a kiosk, grabbing juice or a muffin. Nothing unusual. Except—

Allison blinked. There were actual people were working behind the counter. Not self-serve stations. Real people, handing over food, like this was a café from a hundred years ago.

Her bag slipped off her shoulder as she pulled out her tablet. Her schedule flickered onto the screen: *Women's Conclave Pavilion – Morning Assembly*

"Allison!"

She turned just as Denise weaved through the crowd of students, her bright smile cutting through Allison's confusion.

"There you are!" Denise said, stopping beside her. She gestured to the girl next to her. "This is Michelle."

Michelle was taller, maybe by a couple of inches, with wavy black hair and kind brown eyes. Her uniform was just as crisp as everyone else's, but the way she smiled felt different. Warmer. Less formal.

"You'll be sticking with us today," Denise continued, her tone brisk but friendly. "We'll grab lunch together, and I'll walk you to your math class later. Just wait for me, okay? It's on the 20th floor and may be hard to find."

"Okay," Allison said with a nod.

They moved through the hall together, passing three massive doorways. Each of them was labeled in large, gleaming letters: Young Men, Administration, and Young Women.

As they approached the Young Women entrance, Denise gestured toward the doors. "Come on," she said. "Assembly's this way."

Allison followed them through the doors, her bracelet lightly vibrating as they stepped inside.

The hallway narrowed slightly, the ceiling arching overhead. The tile gleamed beneath recessed lighting, and a few framed portraits of historical women lined the walls. The hallway opened into a bank of elevators.

Her bracelet buzzed again as they approached, and one of the doors slid open just for them.

"Your security bracelet is synced to your schedule," Denise explained. "The elevator will automatically take you to the correct floor."

The ride was smooth, a faint vibration the only sign of movement. Allison adjusted the strap of her bag and exhaled slowly. When they stepped out, the Pavilion stretched before them.

A grand lecture hall, curved seating rising in neat tiers, all angled toward a raised stage with a gleaming lectern. Behind it, a massive wall glowed with scrolling announcements and a bold quote in elegant script: Success is measured not by what you accomplish but by the elegance with which you meet challenges.

They found seats near the back. More students filed in, the air buzzing with laughter and whispers. There was a sense of camaraderie that Allison envied.

A chime rang out. Silence fell like a curtain.

A tall, severe-looking woman stepped onto the stage, her gray hair pulled into a bun so tight it looked painful. Her blazer was crisp, her pleated skirt precise. Everything about her felt sharp.

Allison straightened her back before she even realized she was doing it.

"Good morning," the woman said, her voice cutting through the air without a microphone. "Before we begin, I'd like to welcome a new student to the Vanguard family: Allison Maxwell."

Every head turned.

Heat crawled up Allison's neck. She stood stiffly, smoothing the front of her skirt. A sea of polite smiles met her. No waves, no whispers, just the same practiced expression. She barely had time to nod before sinking back into her seat.

"That's Mrs. Branson," Denise whispered. "Dean of Women."

Mrs. Branson's gaze swept the room. "Success is not just about achieving your goals," she said. "It's about how you carry yourself," she said in a flat voice. "True refinement lies in how you handle obstacles." She paused. "Elegance in the face of adversity reflects strength of character."

Allison's shoulders tightened under her blazer. The quote had appeared on the smart wall at the back of the stage. It was glowing as if to catch everyone's attention. It didn't feel inspirational. It felt like a law.

"And now," Mrs. Branson continued, "let us bow our heads."

A rustle of fabric moved through the room as every girl lowered their head in unison.

Allison hesitated, her hands clasped awkwardly, fingers pressing together as she followed along. No one looked up. No one shifted in their seats.

Mrs. Branson's voice dropped into a solemn, practiced rhythm. "Heavenly Father, we thank You for the divine order You have set in creation and for the roles You have ordained for men and women. Help these young women embrace humility and obedience, learning in quietness and submission as they honor You in their homes, schools, and communities.

"May they resist the temptations of pride and independence, and instead reflect Your grace through their modesty, purity, and dedication to serving others."

Allison's fingers twitched.

"Grant them the wisdom to trust in Your plan, the strength to submit to authority, and the courage to live righteously in a world that often strays from Your teachings."

Submit to authority? Allison kept her eyes squeezed shut, her hands pressed together. The words rolled over her, heavy and unfamiliar.

"May their lives be a beacon of Your truth and their hearts be steadfast in faith. Guide them as they strive to embody the virtues of a godly woman, bringing glory to Your name. In Jesus' name, Amen."

A quiet, perfectly synchronized 'Amen' swept the room, and she cautiously opened her eyes.

Submission? Quietness? This didn't sound like the same faith she'd grown up with. It was more like an order than a reflection of faith. What about Ephesians? The verse where it said believers were supposed to submit to one another out of reverence for Christ?

Was it a different Bible translation? Or just Mrs. Branson's version of it? She made a mental note to ask Dad on their next call.

Mrs. Branson smiled thinly. "Now, ladies, please rise for the Pledge of Allegiance." Hundreds of girls stood tall and still, their hands moving in perfect synchronization to rest over their hearts. She mirrored them, a half-second behind, sneaking a glance at Michelle, who already looked at ease, her lips forming the familiar words.

"I pledge allegiance to the flag of the United States of America . . . " The voices around her were low and reverent. Allison stumbled over the words, her mouth half-moving as she tried to catch up. It had been several years since she'd said the Pledge.

" . . . and to the Republic for which it stands . . . "

She glanced around the room, careful not to turn her head too much. *Why does this feel so different?* she wondered.

" . . . one nation . . . "

Mrs. Branson's voice cut through the calm rhythm like a blade. "UNDER GOD." The girls echoed her without hesitation, their voices rising in unison.

Allison flinched. The swell of voices sent a prickle down her spine.

Then, as fast as it had built, the intensity vanished. " . . . indivisible, with liberty and justice for all."

As soon as the last word faded, hands were lowered and skirts smoothed as they returned to their seats in unison.

Allison sat down, her heart thudding in her chest. The other girls looked completely at ease, like nothing had happened. She pressed her palm against her blazer. Was it always like this?

She remembered saying the Pledge in middle school. Half the class mumbled it, some didn't say it at all. It was just a thing you went through. But here, it felt like something else.

Mrs. Branson's voice pulled her back. "Thank you for your attention today." She gestured toward the glowing wall behind her. "This week's announcements and inspirational quote have been transferred to your schedule."

The room stirred as students gathered their belongings. Denise nudged Allison's arm gently, pulling her back to the moment.

"Our first class is Language Arts," Michelle said in a soft voice with a hint of an Italian accent.

Allison nodded, slinging her pack over one shoulder. But as they stepped into the next available elevator, the echo of 'Under God' stayed with her. She couldn't shake the feeling. It didn't sound like they had been reciting the Pledge of Allegiance. It felt she'd accidentally participated in some sort of ritual. Something they considered sacred, even. More than just a prayer.

Allison followed Michelle into the classroom, her steps slowing as she entered the room. It didn't look anything like the classrooms in Germany or even what she remembered from just a few years ago, for that matter. It was so fancy.

The soft blue chairs were set out in a semicircle, facing the smart wall at the front of the room. They looked like they had been taken out of a luxury hotel. The overhead lighting was warm, not the harsh, fluorescent kind that usually made her squint.

She hesitated. The other girls were already seated, their desks folded neatly to the side of their chairs. They sat straight, their ankles either crossed or tucked to the side, their skirts falling perfectly around their ankles.

Allison hesitated, suddenly aware of every movement she made.

Michelle touched her shoulder. "Here, sit next to me." She guided Allison to an empty chair.

The chair gave slightly under her weight, its fabric softer than expected. She ran her fingers over the smooth armrest, stealing a glance at the other girls as she awkwardly tried to copy the way they sat. She crossed her ankles, but it felt forced and unnatural.

She nudged the attached desk, and it swiveled up silently, the cool surface feeling almost too polished under her fingers.

At the front of the room, the teacher stood, waiting. Mrs. Taylor looked like someone from an ancient black-and-white movie. Silver hair, styled perfectly. A black skirt and white blouse pressed so sharply they could've been ironed moments ago. She smiled, but her watchful eyes made Allison sit up straighter.

"Good morning, ladies," Mrs. Taylor said. Her voice silenced the murmur of conversation. "Before we begin, let's welcome our newest member. Allison Maxwell has joined us this semester."

She smiled at Allison. "Ladies, please introduce yourselves." She gestured to a redheaded girl on the far left side of the circle. "Why don't you begin, Elinor?"

The first girl spoke with the kind of confidence that made Allison feel like she'd been rehearsing this moment for years. "Elinor Alden. My father is James Alden, CEO of Alden Enterprises." She looked to the next girl on her right.

"Margot Hastings," the blonde said with a slight smile. "My father, Robert Hastings, is an investment banker." She said it smoothly, effortlessly, as if her father's name alone should mean something. The names rolled on, one after another. Each girl sat a little straighter when she spoke. Each introduction felt like a performance.

Allison fidgeted, her ankles slipped uncrossed for a second. She quickly fixed them.

Then it was her turn. She swallowed hard. No big deal. Just say it.

"I'm Allison Maxwell," she said, her voice hoarse with anxiety. "My father, Sam Maxwell, is a civil engineer. He works in Germany."

She caught a flicker of something, maybe surprise, in a few faces before Mrs. Taylor nodded and moved on.

Allison looked down, frustrated. She shouldn't have said that. *Stick to the script,* she thought. *Dad owns his own business and does important work around the globe.*

She slouched just a little. Her ankles uncrossed again, and this time, she didn't bother fixing them. She felt destitute compared to them.

Mrs. Taylor nodded, smoothing over the awkward moment. "Now, does anyone have questions about last week's assignment on storytelling?"

Silence.

Allison glanced around. The girls sat perfectly still, hands folded, their attention locked on Mrs. Taylor. No shifting in their seats, no scribbling notes, no whispered side conversations. It felt so scripted.

Mrs. Taylor turned to her. "Last week, we read excerpts from *Little Women* and worked in small groups to outline a story based on a moral lesson. Each student wrote an opening scene, focusing on vivid imagery and character introduction."

Allison frowned. Excerpts? Why not just read the whole book? Taking pieces felt weird, like skipping to the end of a movie and pretending you understood everything.

"Since there are no questions," Mrs. Taylor continued, "we'll move on to this week's lesson: The Elegance of Persuasion."

Behind her, words appeared on the wall: Logos. Pathos. Ethos.

"Persuasion," Mrs. Taylor began, pacing slowly, her heels tapping against the wooden floor, "is the art of influencing others. It has shaped societies, sparked revolutions, and forged alliances." She paused, letting the words hang for effect. "To persuade effectively, you must understand the three pillars: Logos, Pathos, and Ethos."

Allison glanced at Michelle. Her stylus hovered over her tablet. Was she supposed to write this down? Or was it being recorded for later? Allison shrugged and jotted a quick note, just in case.

"Logos," Mrs. Taylor said, "is logic. Facts, data, and reasoning. It's the backbone of your argument."

That made sense. It sounded like math. Solid and structured.

"Pathos is emotion," she continued. "It's how you connect to your audience's heart. Stories, vivid language, and personal anecdotes help to bring your message to life."

Emotion. Allison hesitated, tapping her stylus against the desk. This was different from the way they had discussed rhetoric at Kaiserhof. Less philosophy, more personal.

"And finally, Ethos," Mrs. Taylor said, her voice softening. "This is your credibility. It's about trust. If your audience believes you are honest and ethical, they will follow you."

Allison's pen hovered over her tablet. *So, persuasion is about weaving all three together?*

Mrs. Taylor turned back to the front. "Tomorrow, we'll analyze how Mary Wollstonecraft uses these techniques in *A Vindication of the Rights of Woman*. Excerpts and today's lecture notes have been sent to your tablets. Please review the first section before class."

There it was again. Excerpts.

A chime rang, signaling the end of the period.

Allison fumbled, closing her tablet and shoving it into her bag. Her desk swung down with a click louder than everyone else's. She winced. How did they all move so silently?

Michelle caught her eye. "*A Vindication of the Rights of Woman*! I can't wait to start reading," she said with a grin.

"Yeah," Allison mumbled, forcing a smile. But the word *excerpts* lingered. Why not read the whole book? What were they skipping?

Allison followed Michelle through the morning in a daze. She was deeply disappointed. Their last class, Life Science, had sounded like it would cover DNA, plant life, maybe even evolution. Not the art of homemaking!

Mrs. Langford's cheerful voice still echoed in her head: "*Meal planning is the cornerstone of a harmonious household!*" Harmonious household? Was this 2042 or 1942?

She gritted her teeth. This wasn't just weird. It was wrong.

Allison leaned against the smooth, cold elevator railing, gripping it a little too tightly. "Are the classes always like this?" she muttered, trying to keep her voice steady.

"Pretty much," Michelle replied with a shrug, like it was completely normal. Then, her face lit up. "Are you hungry? Chef makes the most amazing truffle mac and cheese!"

Seriously? Allison blinked. *We just sat through an entire class about how to plan meals, and the first thing you talk about is food?* But she bit her tongue, stuffing her frustration down. What was the point of arguing?

The elevator doors slid open onto the coed floor, and warm bread and something herbal filled the air. Rosemary, maybe? The murmur of conversation drifted over the quiet clink of silverware against china.

Allison hesitated, scanning the room for Denise. She'd barely been at Vanguard for half a day, and already it felt like she'd been moved into a completely different world.

"Allison! Michelle!" Denise's voice cut through the dining room.

Allison looked around and saw her waving from a table near the windows. Michelle immediately started walking in her direction. Allison followed, but her brain was still stuck on Life Science. Cooking? Household harmony? How was that considered a science?

The dining hall was way too fancy. Each of the fancy white tablecloths had a small crystal vase with fresh daisies that must have been grown in a nearby hydroponics farm. The wooden floors were shiny enough to see her reflection, and the sunlight pouring in from the tall windows made everything look extra perfect, like a movie set.

She pulled out a chair and ran her fingers over the tablecloth as she sat down. It was too soft. The chairs were too comfortable.

"How was class?" Denise asked, all smiles as she poured herself some water.

Allison frowned, trying to find the right words. "It's... really different from my classes in Hamburg."

"How so?"

Allison looked at Michelle, then back to Denise. "I thought Vanguard was an academic academy," she finally told them.

Denise waved a hand to get a server's attention. "Vanguard is much more than that," she told them in a firm voice. "Let's order first," Denise added, still smiling. "Then we'll talk."

Allison glanced up as the servers moved between tables, balancing trays of food like this was some high-end restaurant instead of a school cafeteria. At Kaiserhof, students grabbed their meals from automated kiosks, the kind that dispensed the food on trays with a whirr and a satisfying click. Done.

"Don't worry, meals are included in tuition," Denise said, watching her look at the menu. "Just pick what you want. They'll bring it to you."

An actual paper menu. Not a touchscreen. The kind with fancy fonts listing stuff like grilled salmon with asparagus and lemon herb chicken.

This wasn't lunch. It was a five-star dining experience.

A server stopped at their table, her uniform crisp as her smile. When it was her turn, Allison hesitated, then mumbled, "Veggie wrap and water." The words felt awkward.

As soon as the server walked away, Denise leaned in. "So, how were your morning classes different from those in Germany?"

Allison wasn't sure how to answer that. "It wasn't just the emphasis on lectures," she finally told them. "It's the classes themselves. For example, Life Science wasn't really what I expected."

"What were you expecting?" Denise asked, tilting her head.

"Plants. Animals. DNA." *Science.* She tapped her fork against the table. "Not meal planning. Or, I don't know, homemaking."

"That's how it is at Vanguard," Michelle said with a shrug. "It's about preparing you for your role in society."

Allison frowned. "What role?" she asked. "This is supposed to be an academic academy. Shouldn't the focus be on learning?"

Denise rested her elbows on the table for a moment. "Technically, that's correct," Denise told her. "But, the difference between Vanguard and other academies is that the focus is on training the republic's future leaders and their wives."

Allison blinked, leaning back in her chair as she glanced out the window. The city stretched endlessly below them, a maze of buildings and streets that felt so far removed from this insulated world.

"That's ridiculous," she muttered. "In Germany, I was taking classes that fit my academic track. The focus was on understanding the material, not fitting into some mold."

"Men and women are meant to complement each other," Denise said evenly. "Not compete."

Allison gritted her teeth. "That's insane."

Denise arched an elegant brow, unimpressed. "Insane or not, that's how it works. This isn't Europe."

The server returned with their food, setting each plate down with smooth, quiet precision. The smell of warm grilled veggies drifted up from Allison's wrap, but her appetite was gone.

The tension settled between them, thick and unmoving. Allison could almost feel Denise watching her, waiting to see how she'd react.

Michelle clapped her hands lightly, breaking the moment. "Okay, but more importantly," she said, flashing a bright smile, "you have to try the desserts here. The lemon tarts? Life-changing!"

Denise let out a small, knowing laugh like she understood what Michelle was doing but didn't mind playing along. "Agreed," she said, finally looking away from Allison. "And the crème brûlée? Almost as good as the one at my father's social club."

Michelle nudged Allison's arm. "Trust me, you'll want to leave room for it."

Allison forced a small smile but barely touched her food as the conversation shifted to weekend plans, favorite music, afternoon classes. Normal stuff.

She didn't belong here. Not in Manhattan. Not in a school that treated girls like supporting characters in someone else's story.

She needed to change schools. Anything would be better than this. Even public school.

Chapter Seven

Allison shifted in her seat, the smooth leather cool beneath her as she stared at the chessboard. The glossy walnut surface reflected the soft, ambient light overhead, making the pieces look almost like they were floating. Chess club hadn't been her idea. Her parents thought it would be a good way to meet people, and Michelle had encouraged her to come, too. So, here she was, looking over the board and debating her next move.

Michelle moved a pawn forward, her black nail polish chipped at the edges—a tiny imperfection in a school where everything else felt controlled, polished, and intentional.

"So," Michelle said, her voice low and casual, "what do you really think of this place?"

Allison hesitated, eyes flicking to Michelle's before returning to the board. This place.

Michelle was studying the board. They could have been talking about next week's mandatory Bible Study Seminar or next week's dining menu.

Vanguard didn't feel like a school. It felt like a training ground, where students followed invisible rules without question. No choice. No questions.

Her fingers brushed against the knight, the smooth piece warming under her touch. "It's . . . different," she finally said.

Michelle tilted her head, her dark waves slipping over her shoulder. "That's one way to put it." She smiled, but her eyes flickered toward the other tables before she refocused on the board.

Allison studied the pieces, but she wasn't really thinking about the game. It wasn't just the rules that made her uneasy. It was how easily everyone else followed them.

Only five tables were in use, even though the room had space for twice that. The whole place felt too quiet with just the sound of pieces clicking against boards and the occasional whisper. Even the way the other girls sat, backs straight, hands folded neatly between moves, felt off. It was like they were actors waiting to say their line.

Allison shifted in her chair. "It doesn't feel like a school," she muttered, moving her rook forward. The piece scraped against the board, louder than she expected. "It's like . . . I don't know, a stage. Everyone's playing a part."

Michelle didn't answer right away. Her gaze flicked across the room before she moved her knight, putting Allison's bishop in danger. "You just need to learn how to blend in," she murmured. "Or you transfer."

Allison frowned, her fingers hovering over her knight. "Blend in?" She pushed the piece forward and to the left, setting up a counterattack that put Michelle's queen in danger.

Michelle shrugged. "Smile when you're supposed to," she whispered. "Agree with the teachers, even when they're wrong. Don't ask too many questions." She leaned back in her chair, her gaze flicking to the other tables. "It's easier."

Easier, maybe, but not better. Michelle hesitated, then moved her queen out of harm's way, landing it in a spot that now threatened Allison's rook. A small, knowing smile tugged at her lips.

"You're good at this," Michelle said, voice quieter now. "Did your dad teach you?"

Allison ignored the rook and pushed a pawn forward instead, blocking Michelle's queen's path and setting up a counterplay. It wasn't the obvious move, but it sent a message. She wasn't easy to push around.

"He says it's all about seeing the whole board," she said.

Michelle tapped the table lightly, considering that. "Smart guy."

After a moment, Allison moved her bishop diagonally, capturing the pawn. "Bold move," Michelle said with a smirk. "But you left it unprotected."

Allison finally looked up, meeting Michelle's eyes. The move had been calculated, but so was the conversation. Was Michelle trying to be helpful, or was she just another piece in this game?

Michelle didn't look away. Instead, she studied Allison the way she studied the board. Calm, assessing, waiting to see what she'd do next. She was very different here than she had been in class.

Allison exhaled quietly, fingers hovering over another rook. "Do you like it here?" she asked. She slid her rook across the board, capturing Michelle's exposed bishop. The piece clattered softly against the table as she set it aside.

"Interesting move," Michelle said. She looked up, her brown eyes concerned. "It's fine," she said after a moment. "You just need to know how the game is played." She reached for her queen. With a deliberate movement, she slid it across the board, putting Allison's rook in immediate danger.

Allison's eyes narrowed as she studied the board. "Huh," she said as she considered her options. "How do you play if no one has shared the rulebook?" She smiled, spotting the perfect play. "Or even worse: The rules seem to change with very little notice."

With a careful hand, she moved her knight to threaten both Michelle's queen and one of her rooks at the same time. It was a clever move, forcing Michelle to choose which piece to save and letting Allison take the other. A flicker of satisfaction crossed her face as she glanced up, meeting Michelle's gaze.

Michelle shook her head and smiled. "Nice," she said. "And that's how you have to play it here. Pick your friends carefully. Some people will act nice to your face and sell you out the second it benefits them." She let out a soft laugh, more amused than annoyed, and reached for her queen. With a quick movement, she pulled it out of danger to threaten one of Allison's pawns.

Allison didn't hesitate. Her knight leaped across the board, capturing Michelle's rook and landing firmly in its place. She set the captured piece aside with a quiet but deliberate motion, her eyes flicking up to gauge Michelle's reaction.

"What else?" she asked.

Michelle studied the board, her fingers hovering over her remaining pieces. "Know who's important. The kids from political dynasties can get away with everything—especially the boys," she said, moving a pawn forward. "The girls are princesses. And if you ever need to push back, do it quietly.

People here respect power plays, not the drama they assume that automatically comes from being a girl."

Her hand hovered for a moment before she moved her queen with a quiet but deliberate motion. The piece now threatened Allison's knight, forcing her to decide whether to protect it or risk losing it.

Allison stared at the pieces. Letting her knight go wasn't an option, not yet. She moved her bishop into position, blocking the queen's path and setting up an attack on Michelle's king. The move gave her a small opening to keep the pressure on.

"Anything else?" she asked.

Michelle slid her king across the board, her queen still close to Allison's defenses. "Don't let this place get to you."

Allison leaned in, trying to adjust her strategy. There was a gap in her defenses and she'd missed it.

"Vanguard is just a game, like chess. The difference is they're training our generation to lead the fight for Christian Nationalism." Michelle's queen moved with a sharp tap, cutting across the board. "Checkmate." She leaned back in her chair with a satisfied smile.

"You're lucky I'm so out of practice," Allison told her.

Michelle laughed, a soft, genuine sound that cut through the tension. "Sure, let's go with that."

Allison exhaled slowly. "And if I don't want to play?" she asked.

Michelle gave her a knowing look, tilting her head slightly. "Then you lose."

"Good morning, Miss Allison," Jeeves' clipped voice broke through the fog in her brain. "Today is Saturday, and you have a call scheduled with your father in ten minutes. The weather in Manhattan is currently 54 degrees, with a forecast high of 76. Shall I adjust the lighting?"

Allison groaned and flopped onto her side, pulling the pillow over her head. "Nooo . . . "

Jeeves ignored her. The windows brightened, letting golden light seep into the room.

"Jeeves, reduce illumination to thirty percent," she mumbled from under the pillow.

"Reducing illumination," Jeeves replied smoothly. The bright glow outside dimmed until the sun looked like it was stuck in a weird solar eclipse, creating an artificial twilight.

Much better.

Ten minutes, she thought. *I can do this.* When she was little, she'd be up early, practically vibrating with excitement. Now? Just rolling out of bed felt impossible. Maybe being thirteen made mornings harder.

She dragged herself up, grabbed her robe, and shuffled downstairs for a glass of orange juice. By the time she got back to her room, she barely had time left. Her room was a disaster. She scooped up her hoodie, socks, tablet, and AR band and dumped them on her bed. Then she rushed to tidy the rest so her dad wouldn't see the mess.

She had a seat on the couch just as the smart wall lit up. Her dad's office filled the screen, looking as cluttered as ever. There were blueprints everywhere, coffee mugs stacked on top of each other, and random notes scribbled on whatever paper he could find. Rain was pattering against his office window, making Hamburg look gray. He was leaning back in his chair, his sleeves rolled up and his shirt slightly rumpled.

"Guten Morgen, Kleines," he said with a smile. *Good morning, kiddo.*

Allison smiled faintly. "Guten Tag, Papa." *Good afternoon, Dad.*

"How are you doing?" he asked. "Are you settling in?"

Allison hesitated, picking at a loose thread on her sleeve. "I guess."

Her dad frowned. "You guess?"

She shrugged.

"How's school? Making any new friends?" he asked.

Allison blew out a breath and slumped against the back of the couch. "Yeah. Kind of."

Her dad raised an eyebrow.

"It's fine," she said, carefully choosing her words. "Vanguard is just . . . different."

He nodded slowly, leaning forward until his elbows rested on his cluttered desk. "I know, Allie," he told her. "It's a big change from what you're used to. But you've got this, kid. You're tougher than you think."

"I don't feel tough," she admitted, her voice barely above a whisper.

Her dad's expression softened. "You don't have to feel it all the time. Being tough isn't about not struggling. It's about showing up anyway, even though you're scared."

She looked down, fingers picking at the hem of her pajama sleeve. "Dad, the classes don't make any sense. It's like they're teaching us to be . . . perfect little wives."

"I know," her dad said after a pause. "But we're close to finalizing your tutor. Your mom has narrowed it down to two candidates. One's even from Germany. Both of them can start in the next few weeks."

Allison blinked. "Really? That soon?"

"Yup." He managed a small smile. "They both have EU teaching certificates, so you'll have someone to help keep you on track."

Her shoulders eased just a little. "So, I don't have to worry so much about Vanguard?" Hope crept into her voice. The school had a simple pass/fail grading system. If she just turned in the assignments, who cared?

Her dad studied her for a second, his hazel eyes steady. "Focus on what's important, Allie," he told her.

Allison nodded slowly, the tight feeling in her chest loosening just a bit. "Okay. I can do that."

"And don't forget," he added, his tone lighter now, "it's Saturday. That means two whole days of freedom."

Allison managed a small laugh. "You make it sound so easy."

"Sometimes," he said, his voice softer, "it's not easy to relax." He glanced at the mess on his desk, then back at her. "Take the time, Allie. Try for me, okay?"

"I will," she told him.

They drifted to easier topics after that: the weird pigeons outside her window, her first chess club meeting, his latest project. By the time they finally said goodbye, she felt something she hadn't in days: A little bit of peace.

When her dad's image faded from the smart wall, the room felt quieter. Allison sat there for a moment, staring at the blank screen before whispering. "Danke, Papa." *Thank you, Dad.*

A WARD OF THE STATE

Allison dragged her feet down the stairs, still tired even after the conversation with her dad. The smell of coffee and something delicious cooking wafted up from the kitchen, making her stomach growl. She wandered into the dining room to find her mom already sitting at the table, a coffee mug in one hand and her tablet resting next to her plate.

Mom looked up as Allison entered. Her hair was in a messy French braid, with a few strands hanging loose, and she was wearing her usual comfy weekend cardigan and leggings. "Good morning," she said with a small smile.

"Morning," Allison mumbled, sliding into her usual seat. She yawned and leaned her elbows on the table, waiting for Maria to bring breakfast.

Maria appeared a moment later, carrying a pitcher of orange juice. "Good morning, Miss Allison," she said cheerfully, pouring the juice into Allison's glass. "I made sticky buns, and they should be ready in about five minutes. Would you like me to get your omelet started or would you prefer oatmeal?"

"Definitely the omelet," Allison told her. "I love your spinach and goat cheese recipe!"

Maria nodded with a smile and headed back into the kitchen.

Her mom sipped her coffee. "Your grandmother's birthday is next weekend," she finally said, setting her mug down. "We'll be heading to Chicago on Friday."

Allison groaned. "Do I have to?"

"Yes." Her mom didn't look annoyed, just firm. "It's important. Your grandmother will want to see you, and the whole family will be there to celebrate."

The whole family. That meant Patrick and Grayson. Patrick had been awful to her for as long as she could remember, and now that they were older, he'd just gotten sneakier about it. At least when they were little, he'd been obvious. Yanking her braids and pushing her buttons until she cried. Now? Now, he waited until no one was paying attention. Quick jabs, whispered insults, comments just low enough that the adults never caught them.

And Grayson? He followed Patrick around like a shadow.

Allison slumped in her chair. It wasn't like anyone would actually care if she showed up. These family events weren't about her. They were about networking, business, the family name. She could sit there all night, quiet as a ghost, and no one would care.

"It's not like anyone will even notice if I'm there," she muttered.

Her mom gave her a look, the kind that said, *Don't push this*. "You're going, and that's final. We'll go over what you're wearing tomorrow morning to make sure everything fits."

Allison rolled her eyes. "The store already tailored everything. It's fine."

Her mom tilted her head slightly. "Humor me," she said.

Allison didn't argue. What was the point?

Maria reappeared from the kitchen and set a plate in front of her. The rich scent of goat cheese and spinach filled the dining room. Normally, she'd have dug in without a second thought, but her stomach protested. She pushed the plate away.

Her mom picked up her tablet and started scrolling. "On another note, we've got interviews for your tutor today. There are two finalists."

Allison sat up a little. "Who are they?"

Mom flicked her finger over her tablet, and the monitor built into the wall blinked to life. Two photos appeared. On the left side of the screen was a woman about Mom's age, with cropped blond hair and sharp blue eyes. Something about her expression, curiosity mixed with calculation, made Allison hesitate. The other woman was older, her dark, wavy hair streaked with gray. Her brown eyes and dark shirt gave her a formal, no-nonsense look.

Her mom tapped her tablet. "This is Amanda Trevelyan," she said as the blonde's picture filled the screen. "She's British, highly qualified, and fluent in German, Mandarin, and English. She specializes in higher-level math, science, and writing."

She swiped the tablet again, and the older woman's image enlarged. "This is Anke Fischer," her mom continued. "She's German and works mostly with younger students. She's not as credentialed as Trevelyan, but she has more hands-on experience tutoring and knows the German school system inside and out. She's fluent in both German and English and covers writing, math, history, science, and social studies."

Allison frowned. "Does Frau Fischer normally teach *Grundschule*?" She glanced at her mom, who gave her a blank look. "I mean, younger kids or kids my age?"

"That's a good question," her mom said, tapping the screen. "I'll add it to the interview notes."

Maria brought out a platter of sticky buns dripping with melted sugar and slathered with cinnamon. "Fresh from the oven," she said with a small smile.

The sight of them made Allison's stomach tighten, but this time, with actual hunger.

"This looks great!" She grabbed a sticky bun and dropped it onto her plate beside the omelet. The glaze was still warm, pooling at the edges. She tore off a piece and popped it into her mouth, the cinnamon melting on her tongue.

Her mom took another sip of coffee and tapped her tablet, shutting off the monitor.

"So, you've got two interviews set up today," Allison said, using her fork to cut into the omelet. "How long until you decide?"

"I'm not the final decision-maker, Allison." Her mom smiled. "You are."

Allison paused mid-bite. "Wait, really?" she mumbled.

Her mom nodded. "I'll handle the interviews, but I expect you to pay attention and ask questions if you have any," she told her. "This is about finding the right fit for you, so your dad and I agree that you should be a part of the decision-making process."

Allison slowly chewed, thinking it over. What if she picked the wrong person?

Her mom watched her, waiting. After a moment, she set her coffee cup down. "Don't overthink it," she said lightly. "This is about finding someone to help you succeed. That's all." She reached for a sticky bun and pulled a piece off. "And if they aren't a good fit, we'll keep looking, okay?"

Allison nodded, though she wasn't entirely convinced. At least the sticky buns were good.

The week just flew by. Between the video interviews (which were a whole lot less stressful than Allison thought they would be), packing for Grammy's birthday weekend (which was just as stressful as she'd thought), and getting through a week of nothing classes, Allison was drained by the time school let out on Thursday afternoon.

Vanguard hadn't even cared that she was missing a day of class. No attendance warnings. No makeup assignments. Just a single message from her etiquette instructor, reminding her to take note of the dinner table settings at her grandmother's party. Next week's assignment involved comparing American and European table customs.

Allison rolled her eyes. Of all the things to focus on.

She shouldered her backpack; the straps digging in as she trudged outside. The early afternoon breeze carried the sharp tang of briny water from the south, a faint reminder of the flooded streets in Lower Manhattan. She wrinkled her nose slightly as she stepped into the sunlight. The October warmth hit her skin, gentle but clinging. The air wasn't exactly humid, but it clung to her just enough to make her want a shower.

Omega waited by the curb, motionless in her perfectly tailored black suit. Her mirrored sunglasses caught the glare of the sun, making her look even more like someone out of a spy movie. Beside her, the pod gleamed, its quiet hum almost lost beneath the city's low buzz.

"Good afternoon, Miss Maxwell," Omega said smoothly, pulling the door open with a practiced motion.

"Hi, Omega," Allison muttered as she slid into the car, her backpack landing with a dull thud beside her. She sank into the cool leather, relaxing as the air conditioner overrode the tangy salted air.

Omega took her seat, the door closing with a soft hiss. The pod glided forward, its electric motor humming beneath them.

Allison leaned her head back against the seat, watching the city blur past.

"Your new tutor has arrived," Omega said, her voice calm but deliberate. "Ms. Trevelyan is waiting for you at the condo."

"Seriously?" Allison leaned forward.

Omega met her gaze in the rearview mirror, her lips curving slightly, just enough to suggest approval. "Mrs. Maxwell expedited her visa. Ms. Trevelyan had already cleared the necessary security and background checks."

Allison took a deep breath and settled back into her seat. Finally, something was going right in her life. Her day had been a never-ending loop of boring classes.

Mandarin was the worst. This week's topic? Cultural appreciation. Except it barely scratched the surface. Today's lecture on Chinese New Year was a joke with a focus on red envelopes and dragon dances, like something out of a kiddie book. Did no one else care that there was so much more to learn about their culture?

And social studies? Ugh. Allison pressed her forehead against the cool window. Who thought reading about the Treaty of Paris was a good way to learn about diplomacy? There wasn't just one treaty. There were thirty-one different ones! Sure, the 1898 one was important because Spain handed Cuba, Puerto Rico, Guam, and the Philippines over to the U.S., marking America's rise as a global power. But shouldn't this be in a U.S. history class instead? She sighed. At this rate, her German friends were leaving her in the dust.

The car pulled into the underground garage. The moment the door unlocked, Allison hopped out, her backpack bouncing against her back.

"She's waiting for you in the family library," Omega said, steering Allison toward the elevator.

The ride to the penthouse felt like it took forever. Allison slouched against the wall, tapping her fingers against her bag strap as the glowing floor numbers crawled upward. The faint sound of the motor filled the silence. By the time the doors slid open, she was practically vibrating with anticipation.

The entryway was quiet, but the air carried the warm scent of freshly baked bread. Maria had been busy today.

Instead of dropping her bag in the hall, Allison made a beeline for the stairs and took them two at a time, heading straight for the library.

The door was slightly ajar, and she pushed it open, breathing in the familiar scent of books and leather. Sunlight streamed through the floor-to-ceiling windows, catching on the sleek glass shelves that lined the walls. Her mother's desk sat near the window, in its usual state of organized chaos. Actual paper files were stacked alongside scattered data cubes, and a half-full mug of tea sat forgotten in one corner.

Near the far bookcase, a woman stood with a book in one hand, her long fingers tracing its spine like she was memorizing every detail. The door bumped against Allison as it tried to close. The woman turned, a polite smile on her face. She was taller than Allison had expected.

"Hello, Allison," she said, each syllable clipped and deliberate. She stepped forward, extending a hand. Her grip was firm. "It's wonderful to finally meet you in person."

"Likewise," Allison replied, shaking her hand.

Amanda smiled slightly and switched smoothly to Mandarin. "Let's begin by comparing your current coursework to what you'd be studying in Germany. That way, we can prioritize where you need the most support."

Allison's eyes widened. Was this really happening? Someone who actually knew what they were doing?

"Sounds great," she answered in Mandarin, excitement bubbling in her chest. She quickly shrugged off her backpack, letting it drop onto the conference table.

Amanda picked up a tablet, her fingers flicking across the screen. A moment later, the smart wall flared to life, splitting into two sections with one side displaying her Vanguard coursework, the other listing the German syllabus.

Allison dropped into a chair, her eyes scanning the German curriculum. The content was challenging, structured, and real. Exactly what she'd been craving. A rush of relief flooded through her.

"Finally," she muttered.

Amanda clasped her hands together, glancing between the two syllabi. "Shall we get started?"

A grin tugged at Allison's lips. Maybe, just maybe, this would work.

Chapter Eight

The hum of the jet engines filled the cabin as Allison pressed her forehead against the cool window, watching clouds drift below like waves on a light blue sea. The leather seats and waxed wood gave the cabin a hotel-like feel, a stark contrast to the cramped commercial flights she was used to with Dad. With him, travel was simple. They took commercial flights, had their backpacks crammed into overhead bins, and grabbed snacks on the go. Here, everything felt orchestrated and effortless. It was like stepping into someone else's world.

Across the aisle, her mom's voice broke through the quiet. "Would you like to hear about my SkyHaven Aviation acquisition?" she asked, setting her coffee mug aside.

Allison almost said no. Business talk was so boring. So many meetings and conference calls, too many 'go-no-go' decisions, endless emails and something called white papers.

But Mom sounded so excited. Allison exhaled softly and turned to face her. "Sure."

For once, her mom's hair wasn't pulled back into the usual French braid or ponytail. Instead, loose curls framed her face, falling past her shoulders. She wore a white dress that blurred the line between business clothes and daywear, paired with sapphire earrings and a matching bracelet. Even the small silver wedding band on her finger was understated. It was a sharp contrast to her usual polished but practical look.

"I've been quietly buying up shares in a company called SkyHaven Aviation," her mom said, her voice holding that careful excitement that meant she was close to closing a deal. "They provide private flights for what's left of the middle class. Well . . . middle class by today's standards. Families with millions, not billions. People who can't afford their own planes but still want reliable private travel."

Allison nodded. She took a sip of her Spezi. The sweet mixture of cola and orange flavors tasted like home.

"SkyHaven weathered the Great Recession of 2032 because most of its stockholders refused to sell and kept using their services," her mom continued. That business voice was back. "Between furloughs and a reduced workweek, they managed to stay afloat. WM Holdings has been buying stock through a few shell companies I control."

Allison twisted the tab on her can. "Why quietly?"

"This company has potential, but it needs to go private again. It can't compete with the big airlines or smaller startups with the way that it's structured," her mom explained. "I should be able to turn it around and make it profitable again."

Allison tried to wrap her head around it. "So . . . you're going to own it?" she asked.

Her mom took another sip of coffee. "Yes. It'll take time, but it's worth it."

Allison hesitated, then asked anyway. "So that means you're going to be CEO of SkyHaven?" she asked.

Her mom's smile didn't quite reach her eyes. "No. That will be your father."

Of course. Allison looked down at her drink. It didn't matter how much work her mom put in, people wouldn't accept her as CEO. The investors, the board, whoever the men in suits were, who sat in glass towers making decisions about people they'd never meet, would never take her mom seriously, no matter how smart she was. No matter how many businesses her company owned.

She could build it, fix it, and run it. Be the second in command who did the real work. But Mom could never be the face of it.

"Sounds complicated," Allison said as she looked up. The way Mom talked about business made it seem slippery and vague. She preferred algebra. At least math had clear answers.

Her mom's smile softened. "It is. But it's exciting, too. You might find it interesting someday."

Allison wasn't so sure. "Maybe," she said noncommittally, turning back to the window.

The clouds outside shifted, and sunlight bounced off the wing. It was bright enough to make her squint. She tried to think about the weekend, but she just couldn't focus. The Firm, as her mom's family called themselves, would be there in full force. To everyone else, they probably looked like a tight-knit clan. To Allison, it felt more like an exclusive club she didn't belong to.

Her grandmother had always been kind in a quiet way, gently nudging the other grandkids to include her. But no matter how hard she tried, Patrick and the others always edged her out. It wasn't exactly mean, but it still left Allison on the outside, watching instead of belonging.

She glanced at her mom again. Her attention was back on her tablet, her perfectly manicured fingers scrolling through her email as if it was a part of who she was. For a moment, Allison wondered if this more poised version of her mother was a facade, another layer of armor for the battles ahead.

The idea of her mom trying to impress The Firm was strange. She never seemed to care about anyone's opinion but her own. Yet here she was, looking like she'd stepped out of a corporate fairy tale.

Everything about this weekend felt off, almost like the faint chirp of a home assistant stuck in a reboot loop. She pressed her forehead up against the window. Whatever was coming, she'd get through it. But deep down, she felt it. Something was about to change. And she wasn't sure if she was ready.

The butler stepped back, smoothly clearing the way as he opened the left side of the massive double doors. The heavy oak panels swung inward with a faint creak. "Mrs. Maxwell, Miss Maxwell," he said with a slight bow. "Welcome. Please, follow me."

Allison stepped inside, glancing around the familiar grand entrance hall. Her mom had insisted she wear something 'nice but not fussy', so she'd settled on a knee-length dark green dress with subtle gold embroidery along the neckline. Her low-heeled shoes clicked against the marble floor, the sound swallowed by the immense space.

She hadn't been here in years, but the house looked exactly as she remembered. The soaring ceilings, the intricate plasterwork, and the chandelier casting rainbows across the marble floor didn't surprise her. What did surprise her was that they weren't staying here for once. It was only a short visit.

After they landed, they'd stopped at the Bellevue Estate Hotel to drop off their luggage. Aunt Chloe had insisted—multiple times—that they stay at the house or, at the very least, at Grammy's. Grammy's new condo was just a few blocks away, closer now since Aunt Chloe had moved her from Wisconsin to Chicago 'just in case she needed help'. But Mom had brushed off the offers with a smooth, polite smile.

"Your aunt Chloe has enough on her plate without worrying about hosting us," she'd said as their driver pulled up to the hotel. "Besides, I'd rather not impose."

Allison hadn't missed the glint in her mother's eyes when she said it. Mom didn't have to mention that The Bellevue was one of her favorite places to stay when they visited Chicago or that WM Holdings was a major shareholder. Somehow, Allison doubted that anyone in the family knew that. Her mom didn't really talk about business with them.

"Mom," Allison had asked as the bellhop unloaded their bags. "Do you think Aunt Chloe is upset that we aren't staying with her?"

Her mom had adjusted her sleek black sunglasses, her expression cool. "Allison, my sweet, people who offer out of obligation expect you to refuse. It gives them a chance to complain about your decision later." She'd smiled faintly. "Trust me on this."

The butler led them deeper into the house. The air was warm and faintly scented with beeswax polish. She could almost hear the echoes of her childhood. Her cousins' laughter bouncing off the marble floors as they played tag. The shouts of 'Jenga!' The arguments over who won at various board games.

Back then, the mansion had felt like something out of a fairytale. Now, she noticed things she hadn't before. The curl in the carpet runner. The outdated sconces along the walls. Small things, but enough to remind her that even castles aged.

The butler stopped at the reception room, gesturing for them to enter.

Inside, the grand fireplace took up most of the wall, its carved mantle lined with porcelain figurines. Above it hung the same hunting scene that had always been there, the paint slightly cracked, the colors faded. A life-sized statue of Venus stood in the corner, its surface duller than Allison remembered. The fire crackled, mixing with the steady ticking of the grandfather clock.

Near the seating area, an antique cart held a delicate tea set. The porcelain was thin and white, scattered with tiny blue flowers. A quilted tea cozy covered the silver teapot, ivory with gold stitching. The faint scent of bergamot lingered in the air, warm and citrusy, comforting in the quiet stillness of the house.

Aunt Chloe rose from her chair by the window, a book resting on the armrest. From afar, she looked as polished as ever. But up close, Allison noticed the shadows under her eyes and the forced edge to her smile. Her bright yellow dress caught the light, but the color made her look washed out.

"Allison," Chloe said warmly, her voice smooth. Then her gaze shifted. "Rylee."

"Chloe," her mom replied, stepping forward to hug her. Her white dress shimmered under the light, understated but elegant. Even standing next to Aunt Chloe, she seemed to outshine her.

"You look . . . tired," Mom said, her voice just loud enough for Allison to catch.

Aunt Chloe waved a hand, her rings catching the light. "Don't you start too, Rylee," she said. "I'm fine."

Allison glanced back and forth. She'd seen this before, the way they talked in circles, saying everything and nothing at the same time. There was always something unspoken, like they were carefully stepping around invisible lines.

Chloe turned back to her, smiling in a way that didn't quite reach her eyes. "Darling, why don't you go find your cousins? They're in the cinema."

Allison hesitated, looking at her mom for help. The little ones would be screaming while the nannies tried to wrangle them. The older ones would be waiting to pick a fight the second she walked through the door.

"Go on," her mom said gently. "I'll join you in a few minutes."

With a reluctant nod, Allison turned and walked out of the room.

As she reached the end of the hall, the faint murmur of voices reached her. She glanced over her shoulder, realizing the door hadn't fully closed.

". . . they said it was time for the next generation to take over." Aunt Chloe's voice was bitter.

"What?" Her mother's reply was laced with disbelief.

"Do you know what they told me?" Aunt Chloe's tone didn't waver. "'Chloe, you've done so much for the company. Isn't it time to focus on your family? You've got kids at home. Surely, they need you more than the company does. Maybe you can use your experience to help a nonprofit.'"

A brief silence. Then a clink as someone set down a cup.

"They actually said that?" Mom's voice was quiet, but Allison could hear the tension.

"As if my years of running the company, of making sure we didn't go under during the Great Recession, meant nothing. All they saw was a woman who could be shoved aside. I had to walk away before they could push me out publicly."

Her mom's response was slower this time. "I'm so sorry, Chloe. I didn't know."

Allison edged forward, her heartbeat thudding in her chest. She glanced up and down the hall to make sure no one was there, then crept toward the door. Her hands tightened into fists as she shifted on her feet, uneasy.

Her mother's voice dropped. "Dad believed in us," she told Aunt Chloe. "He thought we could lead better than anyone." She paused, and Allison could imagine that she'd started pacing in frustration. "But the world doesn't agree. I can't tell you how many times I've had to bring Sam into meetings just to be taken seriously. I even had to make him CEO of my own company, just so we'd pass muster."

Aunt Chloe let out a dry laugh. "I know, Rylee. That's the world we live in."

"Maybe," her mom finally said. "But our uncles and their boys don't know the business like you do." She paused. "I didn't know, Chloe."

Aunt Chloe's voice turned sharp again. "Why would you? Mackenzie left the country. You have your own life on the East Coast. I'm the one who stayed behind and tried to keep the family businesses afloat with absolutely no help from anyone!"

The door slammed.

Allison flinched. She turned and hurried down the hall to the cinema, her pulse still racing. She used to think this house was strong and The Firm had it all together. But now it felt like everything was falling apart, and no one seemed to notice.

The dining room was warm with the glow of the chandelier, casting golden light over the long mahogany table. Polished silverware and crystal glasses caught the reflections, making everything look sharp and expensive. The second course had just been served. It was some kind of fancy duck with delicate sides that looked too pretty to eat.

Allison sat stiffly in her chair, careful to keep her back straight. She'd been drilled on formal dining since she could hold a fork—how to eat what was served, how to place her utensils just so, how to keep up polite conversation.

Something about the gathering bothered her. Conversations were polite, careful, like no one wanted to say the wrong thing. Even the soft clink of silverware against china sounded too precise, as if everyone was making sure not to draw attention to themselves.

Patrick sat farther down the table near Aunt Chloe, but he kept shooting sharp looks her way. She ignored him, sipping her water from a huge crystal goblet.

At the far end of the table, Aunt Chloe shifted, her jewelry catching the light. She wore a dress that felt way too formal for a family dinner. It shimmered under the chandelier as if she were attending a gala instead. But it didn't make her look glamorous. It made her look tired. Her makeup was perfectly applied, but up close, Allison could see the way it settled into the lines around her mouth. She seemed so worn out.

Great-Uncle Phillip cleared his throat, the deep rumble silencing side conversations. "The company's recovery from the Great Recession was no small feat," he said with a slight nod to Aunt Chloe. "But we've stagnated since then. It's time for the family to return to its roots: real estate development, import/export, and providing essential services. That's where the money is."

One of the older cousins leaned forward. "Why not focus on light manufacturing? It's an industry we haven't seriously explored yet."

Uncle Phillip sighed, shaking his head like the idea wasn't even worth considering. "Manufacturing in this country? It's nearly impossible. Labor shortages. The cost of importing raw materials. It's a mess. Canada, Mexico, and South America are better bets. The stuff we do make here? It's either outrageously expensive or low-quality junk."

"You don't agree, Rylee." Uncle Phillip's gaze slid toward her mother, his tone sharp.

Allison turned, watching her mom carefully. She sat composed as always, her fork resting neatly on her plate. She tilted her head slightly before responding. "Manufacturing in the U.S. is challenging, Uncle. There are ways around it, but they can be costly to implement."

Phillip grunted, leaning back in his chair. "Costly solutions don't always yield profitable results."

"Agreed," she replied.

Wait. What?

Allison put her fork down. That wasn't true. Her mom had bought a small electric motor engine plant that was entirely automated a few years back. Mom had practically gushed about how having the heavy lifting done by robotics was making American manufacturing competitive again. *Focus on training your people on things that robotics can't do*, she'd said.

Allison glanced between her mom and her great-uncle. Mom was always five steps ahead when it came to business. So why wasn't she pushing back?

She stole another glance at her mom, but her face was calm and unreadable. Allison pressed her lips together and poked at the food on her plate. Something wasn't right.

For the rest of dinner, she stayed quiet, listening. The adults spoke like they were playing a game that only they knew the rules to. But the way they looked at each other—the silences between their words—said more than anything they might have said.

The sitting room in Aunt Chloe's mansion was suffocatingly perfect. Everything gleamed. The floors, the crystal lamps, the stupid silk curtains that probably cost more than an entire apartment in Lower Manhattan. Even the thick white carpet looked untouched, like nobody was allowed to walk on it except company. Allison eyed the dessert trays scattered across the pristine coffee table, half expecting someone to drop something or spill a drink and ruin it forever.

Lemon tarts, chocolates with gold leaf wraps, tiny éclairs. It was too much. They just had dessert after dinner, and now this? Overkill.

Her youngest cousins lounged across the couches and armchairs, sleepy. Bennett and Sebastian were hunched over their tablets, elbows jabbing at each other as they played some stupid game. Alistair was perched on the arm of a chair, pretending to read while sneaking glances in their direction.

On the opposite couch, Penelope and Vivienne whispered behind their hands. Their giggles slipped out anyway as they kept glancing at Margot, who sat cross-legged on the floor. Margot's blond curls bounced with every nod, her smile so practiced it looked like she was posing for a photo shoot.

Allison pressed her palms against the edge of the table, resisting the urge to grab another tart just to give her hands something to do.

Patrick slouched in an armchair across from her, slowly turning his glass of sparkling water between his fingers. His tie hung loose, and he'd tossed his jacket over the chair like he thought it made him look older.

"Bet you're happy to be back," Patrick said suddenly, cutting through the background conversation in the other room.

Allison glanced up, brushing crumbs off her fingers. "Back where?"

Patrick smirked. "Here. You know, where people have roots. Must be weird for you. You've been dragged all over Europe. Where was it this time? Hong Kong? Madrid? Oh, wait, wasn't it Prague last year?"

She rolled her eyes. "I wasn't dragged anywhere. I love traveling, and it's better than being stuck in one place forever." She grabbed another tart. "Besides, I loved living in Hamburg."

Patrick leaned forward, his voice dropping low. "At least I have a home."

Allison froze mid-bite.

Patrick tilted his head, eyes sharp. "What's it like, anyway? Being passed back and forth like cheap luggage?"

A WARD OF THE STATE

Sebastian looked up from his tablet, eyebrows raised, and nudged Bennett. Penelope and Vivienne stopped whispering. Even Margot's perfect smile faltered.

Allison put the tart down on her plate carefully, her stomach twisting. "What are you talking about?" she demanded. "My parents are busy. They run real companies. My dad's building infrastructure to save cities from flooding. He's smarter than anyone in this house."

Patrick's smirk widened. "And your mom? What's her excuse? Too busy being disowned to stick around?"

The words hit her like a slap. "What are you talking about?" Allison snapped.

Around her, the cousins exchanged uneasy looks. Even Bennett and Sebastian had abandoned their game.

Patrick leaned back, stretching like he had all the time in the world. "Your mom got kicked out of the family when she had you. Your parents aren't married." He shrugged like it was nothing. "That's why she's not in the family trust. You're not either. Technically, you're not even family."

Disowned? Family trust? Allison's hands curled into fists in her lap, nails digging into her palms. "You're lying," she snapped, but it didn't come out as strong as she wanted.

Patrick stood, motioning for Grayson to follow. "Ask her if you don't believe me," he told her. "Or don't. Ignorance is bliss."

Silence.

Penelope and Vivienne suddenly found their half-eaten desserts fascinating. Margot stared at Allison, wide-eyed, like she might cry.

Allison sat frozen. Patrick was lying. He had to be.

Her mom talked to Grandma almost every week. They were included in the annual trip to the Williams family ranch in Montana. They even spent holidays together. Obviously, her mom hadn't been disowned!

The sound of clinking glasses and cheerful conversation floated in from the drawing room. The cousins started talking again, almost as if it had never happened.

Patrick didn't know anything, Allison decided. He was just being cruel. He didn't know her family. He didn't know her. He was just being his usual asshole self.

Chapter Nine

Allison curled up her legs, arms wrapped around her knees. Her mom sat across the aisle, scrolling through her tablet. She'd traded her heels for flats, but she looked the same as she had at dinner the other night. Neat. Polished. The kind of person who always looked like she had a plan. Even when everything was falling apart.

Allison pressed her forehead against the window. Chicago was long gone, swallowed by darkness. She tried to think about anything else, but Patrick's words stuck in her head.

You're not even family. Her fingers curled into the hem of her sweater.

Her chest tightened. Patrick had said it like it was fact; something everyone knew but her. And no one had told him to shut up. Not even Margot, and she cried over everything.

She swallowed hard, her fingers pressing into her knee. Ask her if you don't believe me.

She didn't believe him. Couldn't believe him. Patrick was always saying stupid things to hurt people.

"Mom?" she asked, her voice barely making it past her throat. "Am I really not part of the family?"

Her mom froze. The subtle movement of her fingers scrolling through the tablet stopped as she looked up from the screen.

For a second, she didn't say anything, just studied Allison like she was trying to figure out where the question had come from.

"Allison," her mom said carefully, setting the tablet aside. "What happened?"

Allison's stomach clenched. She could just say never mind and let it go. Pretend Patrick's words hadn't clawed under her skin. But, she really needed to know.

"Patrick said I wasn't," she muttered, turning away to stare out the dark window. "That you got kicked out of the family because of me. That you and Dad aren't even married."

Her mom inhaled sharply. "He said that?" Her mom's voice was flat.

Allison nodded, gripping the hem on one side of her sweater and pulling it down and into the seat cushion. "In front of everyone."

Her mom exhaled slowly, her fingers pressing into the armrest. "And what did you say?"

Allison blinked and glanced over. That wasn't what she had expected her to ask. "I—I told him he was lying. That he didn't know anything."

Her mom let out a small breath, as if she approved. "Patrick hears things and tries to piece them together," she said, voice low. "From his mom, from other family members, from whoever was angry that day. And he doesn't always understand what he's repeating. But, he knows how to use it to hurt people."

Allison's throat felt tight. "So . . . he's lying?"

Her mom didn't answer right away. Instead, she reached for her water, took a slow sip, and set the glass back down with deliberate precision.

"It's not always about lying," she said finally. "Sometimes, people hear only a small part of the truth and they twist it enough to make it hurt. Other times, it's about saying just enough to make people doubt themselves." She took a deep breath and let it out with a sigh. "That's how my family works, Allison. They use words like weapons. Patrick's just a teenager, but he's learning from the wrong people."

Allison clenched her jaw. "Then why don't you stop them?"

Her mom's expression didn't change, but there was something harder in her eyes now.

"It's not my place," she said, quiet but firm. "They've been playing these games for a very long time. But you don't have to. You're my daughter, and you're stronger than they think. Don't let Patrick or anyone else make you feel like you don't belong."

Allison hesitated, then blurted out, "What about what happened with Aunt Chloe?"

"What do you mean?" her mom asked. She tilted her head to one side.

"She was supposed to run the company. Grandpa made her CEO. And now she's not." Allison shifted in her seat. "Why did they make her leave?"

Her mom studied her like she was deciding how much to tell her. "Chloe did everything right," she told Allison. "She kept the business afloat during the worst economic downturn in over a hundred years. She made smart investments and took risks that paid off. But the men in our family—" She paused, her fingers tapping lightly against the armrest. "They were never going to let her stay in that position forever."

Allison frowned. "But Grandpa put her in charge."

"Yes, because he believed in her," her mom said, her voice quieter now. "But when he died, there was no one left to stand up for her. And after everything she sacrificed for The Firm, the board of directors—especially our uncles—decided it was time for a 'transition'."

The ache in her mom's voice made Allison's chest tighten. "Does she blame you?" she asked quietly. "For not helping her?"

Her mom sighed, rubbing her temples briefly before meeting Allison's gaze. "Chloe believes that I abandoned her by staying in New York," she admitted. "I understand why she feels that way. But she's wrong about some things. And her anger..." she trailed off, shaking her head slightly. "Sometimes people say things they don't mean when they're hurt."

Allison pressed her nails into her palm. "She meant it."

Her mom didn't argue. She just looked down, smoothing her dark crepe pants as if brushing the conversation away. "We'll talk more tomorrow if you want," she said softly. "But for now, let's just get home."

The plane touched down without a jolt, rolling smoothly along the private airstrip. Outside the window, the darkened Manhattan skyline stretched across the horizon.

A chime, followed by the pilot's voice. "Mrs. Maxwell, Miss Maxwell, we've arrived in Manhattan. The local time is 7:13 p.m., and the temperature is 48 degrees with clear skies. Thank you for flying with us."

Allison barely moved. The lights and buildings were exactly how she'd left them, like the city had been waiting for her. Not to welcome her, but to remind her she didn't belong.

By the time they reached the private terminal, a black limo was already waiting. Its doors opened silently, the pod's interior dimly lit, like it knew they weren't in the mood to talk. Allison slid into her seat without a word, her mom following. The door sealed shut and the pod glided forward, merging seamlessly onto the main road.

The city passed in streaks of light and motion, too familiar to feel exciting but too distant to feel like home. Inside, the pod was silent except for the faint sound of her mom scrolling through messages.

Allison closed her eyes. She was tired.

When they pulled up to the building, the security guard was already at her door. "Good evening, Mrs. Maxwell. Miss Maxwell." His voice was crisp. "I hope your flight was uneventful."

Her mom gave a practiced smile. "It was, Alex. Can you have our luggage brought up?"

Alex nodded and waved to a nearby portable. "Absolutely, ma'am." The portable wheeled itself over to the pod and began to unload the few pieces of luggage they had. Allison stepped out of the pod, the cool air biting gently at her cheeks, and followed her mother into the building.

The warmth of the lobby hit her as they stepped inside. It wasn't cozy, though. It was controlled, designed to look inviting without feeling personal. They walked past the concierge desk without stopping and headed straight for the private elevator.

Allison folded her arms, staring at the sleek metal doors as they closed behind them.

Your mom got kicked out of the family when she had you. She tried to shake it off. Patrick was always saying things to get under her skin, but this time, his words felt different.

Then, there was Aunt Chloe. She acted like Mom had abandoned her, but how? They were a few states apart, not an ocean. And if family was so important to The Firm, why had they forced Aunt Chloe out?

A chime and the doors slid open. Her mom stepped out first, slipping off her shoes and placing them neatly by the door. "Allison," she said, glancing back, "don't forget your tutor starts tomorrow."

"I know," Allison muttered.

She silently followed her mom to the second floor. At the top of the stairs, her mom turned to her. "I need to make a few calls." Then, softer, "Good night, sweetie," as she pulled her in for a quick hug.

"Good night," Allison murmured, watching her mom disappear into her bedroom.

She turned left, heading for her own bedroom. She caught a glimpse of the city as she passed by the family library. It seemed to stretch beyond the penthouse windows, glowing and endless, but it felt like looking at someone else's world. Distant. Untouchable.

Inside her room, she shut the door and leaned against it, arms wrapped around herself. The noise in her head didn't stop. Patrick's accusations. Aunt Chloe's bitterness. The way every conversation this weekend felt like it was covering something up.

Patrick was lying. He had to be.

She dropped onto her bed, staring up at the dark smart wall across the room. She reached up and tapped the side of her AR band to unlock it. She quickly slid the device down and waited for the response pulse against her temples.

The main window appeared to her left. She moved through the menus with a slight flick of her fingers. She could run a search, maybe. Or message Dad. But Dad barely talked about Mom's family, and Mom's explanation earlier had been too vague. And asking Patrick for more information? Yeah, right. That would only make things worse.

Her reflection flickered in the dark window across the room, the city lights blurring behind it.

Think, Allison, she ordered herself. What do you already know?

Her eyes drifted toward the couch by the windows, the only place in the penthouse that actually felt like hers. She pushed herself off the bed and sank onto the floor, her back up against the bed frame.

Wedding photos.

Mom in a long white dress. Dad in a suit. The two of them standing in front of the church. She vaguely remembered paging through an old-fashioned photo album as a kid.

So why did Patrick's words keep nagging at her? She needed answers.

She stood up and carefully moved toward the door. She tapped the band to shift it into standby mode and pushed the device back up. Then, she flicked off the bedroom lights, cracked the door open just enough to listen, and held her breath.

The house had powered down for the night. Allison stepped carefully into the dark hallway. Her mom's bedroom door was closed, a faint sliver of light glowing underneath. She froze, holding her breath and listening. No footsteps. Just the steady hush of the apartment.

She moved past as quietly as possible, her heart pounding like she was sneaking out. At the library door, she hesitated before slipping inside, easing it shut behind her.

The room noticed her movement and the overhead light clicked on, casting long shadows across the wooden floor. Allison quietly walked to the nearest bookcase, fingers trailing over the spines. Most of the mismatched books were old, although she could tell that they were not a part of her mom's prized first-edition collection. Then, her fingers stopped.

A thick white album with gold embossing.

She slid it free, hugging the album to her chest as she crept back out. The light died behind her as she closed the door. She slipped past her mom's door, not daring to breathe until she was safely back in her own room.

Closing the door gently, she let out a slow breath and set the album on her bed. Her fingers reached up, pulling the AR band from her head. She placed it on the charging station and ran a hand through her hair. Then, she grabbed a pair of comfortable pajamas and changed, stuffing her travel clothes into the hamper before crawling under the covers.

She flicked on her bedside lamp and pulled the album onto her lap. Her fingers hesitated on the cover before she finally opened it.

The first photo was a bit of a relief. Her mom looked young and glowing, the white dress and veil making her seem softer, more elegant than Allison had ever seen her. Her dad had his hair unusually neat, his face caught between a laugh and something close to stunned, like he couldn't believe it was real.

They looked so happy. She flipped through, absorbing every detail. Aunt Mackenzie in a pale yellow bridesmaid's dress. Uncle Josh, standing beside his future wife, Aunt Elena. Both sets of grandparents.

The last picture stopped her. A full family portrait in front of the altar. Her parents were surrounded by smiling relatives. Even baby Patrick was in Aunt Mackenzie's arms, barely old enough to sit up.

Allison let out a slow breath. Just like she remembered. Patrick was just being a jerk.

She closed the album and slid it into the lower drawer of her nightstand. Then, she turned off the light and burrowed under her blankets. The tension in her chest finally dissolved and she drifted off to sleep.

Allison slipped her tablet into her bag as Civics class wrapped up. The teacher's closing remarks about their essay barely registered—some vague prompt about choosing their place in society.

The smart wall at the front of the classroom still displayed the diagram from the lesson:

Leaders: The ones in charge, make decisions.

Supporters: The people who advise them and help enforce their vision.

Contributors: Those who implement the Leader's vision.

The neat little pyramid made it sound fair, like everyone had a role to play and everything just worked. But Allison knew better. Her mom built companies, controlled investments, and made things happen. Yet no one saw her as a leader. She was an advisor at best, useful but never in charge.

And Patrick? He acted like he belonged at the top, just because he was a boy with the Williams surname. She doubted he had even a single original thought in that stupid head of his!

Allison's jaw tightened as she slung her bag over her shoulder. Did people really choose their roles or were they just assigned?

She wondered what Amanda would say about it. Amanda wouldn't dumb it down or give the usual scripted answers. She'd probably pull up historical examples to show how power really worked. Not just in theory, but in practice.

Outside, the crisp autumn air cleared her head as she walked toward Omega, who stood waiting at the curb. At least her tutoring session wouldn't be like this. Amanda wouldn't hand her pre-approved answers. Today, she'd actually get to learn something real and that made all the difference.

The library door was slightly open. Allison nudged it wider and stepped inside. Amanda was already seated at the table with multiple documents displayed on the smart wall behind her. She glanced up and gestured for Allison to join her.

Allison hesitated before sinking into the chair across from her. She wasn't nervous, exactly, but there was something about Amanda's precise movements that made her sit a little straighter.

"Well, Allison," Amanda said, folding her hands over the tablet on the table. "I've reviewed your schedule at Vanguard and compared it to what your peers at Kaiserhof would be learning at your level. I've created a study plan that will keep you on track for the *Abitur* exams, should you wish to return to Germany."

Allison nodded but kept her lips pressed together. The *Abitur* was Germany's university entrance qualification. It was rigorous, comprehensive, and not easy to pass without intense preparation. She knew she was already behind her friends in Germany.

"Here's an overview of your current academic program," Amanda continued, maximizing one document on the screen. She sat back and waited for Allison to look it over.

Allison skimmed over the document, silently wincing. "They don't even sound like real subjects," she muttered.

Amanda arched an eyebrow. "They are," she told her. "Just not ones designed for students planning to study engineering, medicine, or law."

Allison looked down. That made it worse.

Amanda continued, "Vanguard emphasizes social and cultural education, which has its benefits. However, it lacks certain academic foundations." She flicked through a few files. "That leaves us with a rather steep continuity gap. For example, your life science class."

Allison exhaled sharply. "It's mostly about nutrition and raising kids," she said. "Last week, we planned meals and talked about how to deal with food waste in larger households."

Amanda didn't laugh, but her lips twitched. "Cooking is a useful skill, but it won't prepare you for advanced coursework."

That sinking feeling in Allison's stomach got worse. "So, how far behind am I?"

Amanda flicked through more documents. "Not as much as you think," she told her. "We'll focus on bridging gaps.

For math, we'll work on your algebra skills and introduce geometry, linear functions, and probability. For science, we'll cover key topics from the German curriculum. Nothing too in-depth, but enough to keep you familiar with the material. And for languages, we'll continue Mandarin while reinforcing your German grammar and writing."

Allison frowned. "That sounds like a lot."

"Two hours a night, maximum, including instruction," Amanda said briskly. "You'll have study blocks for each subject, with specific goals for each session."

Allison slumped. "What if I fall behind?"

Amanda met her gaze. "No one expects you to be perfect," she told her in a gentle voice. "This isn't about overloading you. It's about helping you learn at your own pace." She smiled. "And I'll be here to guide you every step of the way."

Allison took a deep breath. "Okay. What's first?"

Amanda tapped her tablet. "Math," she decided. "Let's review what you've been covering in your algebra class and see how we can build on it."

Allison hesitated before pulling her tablet out of her backpack. The device's screen flickered to life as she handed it to Amanda, who swiped her hand over the tablet to throw the file up on the wall with practiced ease.

She scanned the screen. "Your calculations are mostly accurate," she said, enlarging one equation. "But here, you skipped the step where you isolate the variable. That's why your final answer is correct, but doesn't hold up when verified."

Allison grimaced. "My teacher barely covered that step," she replied. "Girls aren't supposed to really understand higher math."

Amanda didn't look surprised. "Skipping steps isn't acceptable. We'll practice breaking equations down properly."

She swiped to a blank workspace on the smart wall, her expression thoughtful. "Breaking problems into smaller steps is the backbone of problem-solving," she told Allison. "It'll help with both algebra and geometry."

For the next hour, they worked through linear equations, isolating variables and balancing each side until the patterns made sense. It wasn't easy, but Amanda's explanations made the material feel less intimidating.

Amanda finally leaned back, satisfied. "That's enough for today." She saved the file to Allison's tablet with a list of assignments displayed on the screen. "These should take about thirty minutes. Finish them tonight, and we'll review them tomorrow."

Allison glanced at the assignment, already feeling exhausted. "Great," she muttered.

Amanda's expression softened. "You're doing well," she told her. "Keep at it, and you may just surprise yourself."

As Amanda packed up her materials, Allison smiled. Maybe, just maybe, she could handle this.

Chapter Ten

"Good morning, Miss Allison," Jeeves' calm, crisp voice announced. "Today is Tuesday, October 14, and the time is 7 a.m. The weather in Manhattan is currently 42 degrees, with a forecast high of 61 degrees. You are scheduled to arrive at Vanguard at 8 a.m. Shall I adjust the lighting?"

Allison groaned and shoved her face into the pillow. Before she could respond, the windows shifted from opaque to translucent, gradually allowing a warm, golden light to fill the room. She blinked against the brightness, reluctantly sitting up.

"Breakfast will be served in twelve minutes," Jeeves continued. "Today's breakfast options include pancakes, a goat cheese and spinach omelet, or Greek yogurt with assorted fresh fruit. Shall I inform Maria of your selection?"

"Pancakes," she mumbled, dragging herself out of bed.

"Very good, Miss Allison. As a reminder, Miss Trevelyan will arrive at precisely 4:30 this afternoon."

Allison rolled her eyes and shuffled to the bathroom. The cool water jolted her awake, but not enough to shake off the exhaustion. She missed mornings without schedules, without someone announcing her exact departure time like she was on a military mission. She missed her dad's house in Hamburg.

She missed home.

An hour later, the pod glided smoothly along the elevated roadway, the city skyline shifting past tinted windows. Allison slouched in her seat, her backpack tucked by her feet, fingers idly tracing patterns along the soft leather armrest.

Outside, Midtown Manhattan glittered in the morning light, its towering glass buildings reflecting sharp angles of gold and silver. As they passed one of the larger office complexes, a massive video screen flickered to life on the side of the building.

She barely glanced up. Ads were everywhere, but the familiar imagery caught her eye. A woman, glowing in golden light, cradled a baby in her arms. She gazed up at the clouds, serene. Behind her, a man rested his hand on her shoulder, his expression firm but kind. A sunburst halo radiated behind them, the words shimmering across the screen: *A Call to New Jerusalem: Restoring Family, Faith, and Freedom.*

The pod's interior lights dimmed slightly as a voice filled the cabin, low and authoritative. "Motherhood," the voice intoned, "is the most important vocation a woman can embrace. In a world lost to chaos and confusion, the family is our last bastion of hope."

Allison blinked. What the . . . ? She hadn't touched anything. Why was this ad playing inside the pod?

Her fingers scrambled along the panel beside her seat. There had to be a way to turn it off. Had she accidentally triggered something?

The voice softened but kept going, slipping into the practiced warmth of a pastor's cadence. "Join us this Tuesday evening for our Women's Bible Study. An evening of reflection, tea, coffee, and sweet treats, as we reclaim the timeless wisdom of Scripture."

Allison jabbed at the touchscreen. Options flickered to life, but none of them included a mute button.

"How the heck do I turn this thing off?" she muttered under her breath, tapping at the controls almost at random.

"A Call to New Jerusalem: Restore what has been lost. Reclaim your purpose. Together, we can restore our nation. One family, one purpose, one faith . . . "

Restore what has been lost. What did that even mean?

Her great-uncles had used the same kind of words when they talked about Aunt Chloe. About how the family needed to get back to its roots, which apparently didn't include women running companies.

And one family, one purpose, one faith? Yes, marriage and family were important. Pastor Black had said that plenty of times. But he'd also talked about grace, faith, and individual purpose. He never made it sound like women only mattered if they had children. He never said that being a mother was their highest calling.

She grimaced. This wasn't just some random ad. Messages like this were everywhere, on buildings, at school, even in the new Bible study guide from church. She wasn't sure what bothered her more: that she was starting to notice how often she heard it or that part of her was starting to believe it.

Enough. "Omega, a little help here?"

A chime echoed through the cabin, followed by, "External advertisement audio disabled."

The pod fell silent, but the ringing in her ears lingered.

Omega turned her seat slightly, looking at her. "My apologies, Miss Maxwell," she said. "I didn't realize that external advertisements hadn't been disabled. This was the next vehicle in rotation. I'll make sure to double-check this in the future."

"Thanks, Omega," she said, leaning back against the seat.

She glanced out the window again. The ad had looped back to the beginning, golden light bathing the building as the smiling family reappeared.

Allison shifted in her seat, tucking her hair behind her ears. The ad had stopped playing, but the words refused to fade. She crossed her arms, watching the water below lap against the buildings. It didn't sound like the faith she'd grown up with.

The pod slowed as they neared her school. Allison sat up, smoothing her skirt with careful precision.

Was this God's way of telling her she'd lost her way?

Allison barely heard the murmur around her. The dining room bustled as always, with utensils clinking against plates, chairs sliding across the floor, and quiet conversations weaving through the space. But it all felt distant, like she was hearing it from underwater.

Her morning classes had blurred together. It wasn't that the material was hard; most of it was familiar. But none of it felt real.

Language Arts was another round of analyzing texts for moral lessons, always from the approved list. Social Studies focused on historical diplomacy, but it was framed as proof of the need for strong, unquestioned leadership. Life Science had shifted into yet another lecture on how a woman's role in society was essential and sacred. It was a phrase she kept hearing lately, and each time it landed a little heavier.

Even Patrick's voice wouldn't leave her alone. You're not even family.

She'd proven him wrong. The wedding album was real. Her parents had been married. But why had he said it?

The ad played again in her mind, repeating words about motherhood, duty, and reclaiming what was lost. It almost sounded like they were talking about faith.

She'd been taught that faith wasn't about proving herself or following a strict set of rules. It was about grace. About trust. Salvation was a gift, not something you earned by doing everything right.

But here, faith felt different. It wasn't just about believing. It was about following the right order, about knowing your place. And the way they talked about women . . .

She glanced around the room, taking in the quiet, controlled conversations of the girls at their tables and the easy confidence of the boys. She'd always known men and women had different roles. Her dad led their family, but her mom was more than just someone's wife. She built businesses, managed investments, and made things happen. She led, just not in the way her dad did.

But that wasn't what they said here. Here, they talked about God's order and how a woman's job was to be quiet, to nurture, and to follow. Not because they wanted to, but because that was how it was supposed to be.

"Allison?"

She looked up. Across from her, Michelle was watching her. "Are you gonna tell me what's going on, or are you just gonna sit there and play with your food?"

Allison realized she'd been dragging spirals into her mashed potatoes without eating. She dropped her fork with a clink.

Michelle leaned in. "How was your weekend?"

She hesitated, her fingers tightening around the napkin on her lap. "It was fine."

Michelle gave her a look, obviously not believing her.

Allison sighed. "It's my cousin."

Michelle arched an eyebrow. "Okay . . . what about your cousin?"

Allison hesitated. "Patrick," she said finally. "He's my oldest cousin, and he's just . . . awful."

Michelle frowned. "Like, how awful? Steals-your-stuff awful? Or, like, lies-to-get-you-in-trouble awful?"

"Both," Allison admitted. "He's the meanest person I know. He's always taking things from his younger brother and our other cousins, then blaming them when he gets caught."

Michelle made a face, tossing a piece of bread onto her plate. "Okay, so what'd he do this time?"

Allison wanted to brush it off and pretend it didn't matter, but Patrick's smug voice wouldn't go away. Finally, she set her fork down. "He said that my mom got disowned because of me."

Michelle's mouth opened, then closed, her expression shifting from shock to something darker. "What is his problem? Why would he even say something like that?"

Allison swallowed hard, her eyes flicking to the back of the room. Tomas was watching her again, like he knew something. His smirk was infuriating.

She looked back at Michelle. "He just likes to ruin things for me," she told her. "My birthday. Holidays. Everything."

"What a jerk," Michelle said. She frowned. "He probably made it all up."

"What if he didn't?" The words came out so quietly Allison almost didn't hear them herself. She felt the tears burn in the corners of her eyes, but she blinked hard. She wasn't going to cry in the middle of the dining room. Not here.

Michelle hesitated. "Okay, let's say he's not lying," she said carefully. "You're not just gonna take his word for it, right? I mean, this is your family. You could ask your mom."

"I tried," Allison whispered. "She told me Patrick repeats everything he hears and uses it like a weapon to hurt other people."

Michelle blinked. "So, your mom agreed that she was kicked out of the family?"

Allison shook her head. "Not exactly," she admitted. "We mostly talked about Patrick and my Aunt Chloe."

"Do you want to just let this go?" Michelle asked.

"No," she replied, looking down at her plate. "I just don't know how to find out the truth without upsetting my mom."

Michelle glanced around, lowering her voice. "What about looking through her home office? She's got stuff in there, right? Papers? Files on the family share drive, maybe?"

Allison frowned. "You'd really go through your mom's stuff?"

Michelle didn't even hesitate. "Yeah." She shrugged. "If it were me, I'd find out for myself."

It felt wrong to snoop through her mom's files. It bordered on stealing. But what other choice did she have? Ask her mom again? She'd tried and all she'd gotten was some pat answer about Patrick learning to use words to hurt other people.

She glanced out of the dining room's windows. The city skyline loomed outside, bright and sharp in the midday sun. Restore what was lost. One family. One purpose. One faith.

Hadn't she always believed that God loved everyone? That He cared about her? That faith was about trusting in the Lord and not about proving yourself?

Lately, the way people talked about faith made it seem like a test. Like some people were better at being faithful than others. Like men were meant to lead and women were meant to follow, and if you didn't fit the right mold, you weren't part of His plan.

Maybe Patrick was wrong about her parents not being married. But what if he was right about everything else? What if she wasn't really family?

She pushed her plate away, feeling sick. "I'll think about it," she said, her voice quiet.

Civics class. Last class of the day.

Allison barely registered the murmur of students settling into their seats. The chairs were arranged in a wide semi-circle around the front of the room, where Mr. Reynard stood waiting for the last of them to take a seat. The side desk swiveled up silently when she touched it. She placed her tablet in front of her and automatically crossed her ankles so that her skirt covered them.

At the front of the room, Mr. Reynard stood in his crisp suit, hands clasped neatly behind his back. "Good afternoon, ladies," he greeted them, the American flag pin on his lapel catching the light.

Tomas stood off to the side, watching.

Civics was only taught by male instructors. Something about ensuring proper guidance. It also meant an upperclassman was always assigned as an assistant. Today, that was Tomas.

The smart wall flared to life behind Mr. Reynard. The Tenets of Graceful Citizenship appeared in bold, white letters.

"Today," he said, "we'll be exploring societal roles. This week's assignments include a short essay and a flowchart on how structure creates harmony within a nation. But for now, a video to set the stage."

Civics always walked the line between education and indoctrination, dressed up in clean graphics and careful wording.

Allison's stomach sank as he swiped a quick hand over his tablet, and a video began to play on the screen. She already knew what was coming.

The screen lit up with scenes of a perfect neighborhood: a dad playing football with their son in the backyard, girls Allison's age helping their mom prepare dinner, and a younger girl carefully setting silverware next to simple china on a dining room table. "Motherhood is the most important vocation a woman can embrace," the narrator intoned. "In a world lost to chaos and confusion, the family is our last bastion of hope."

Allison bit her lip, glancing sideways. Michelle was blank-faced, and perfectly still. Playing along.

The final scene of the video showed children standing in neat rows, hands pressed over their hearts as they recited the Pledge of Allegiance in unison.

The screen faded to black and Mr. Reynard stepped forward.

"Ladies," he said, his words carefully measured. "Stability allows individuals to thrive, families to prosper, and communities to flourish. Interdependence is the foundation of a strong nation. Think of society as a tapestry. Each role is a thread, and together, they form something strong and beautiful. But if one thread is pulled away, the entire structure can unravel."

He paused, letting the words settle over the room. Allison noticed how the other girls sat up straighter, their attention fixed on him.

"Consider the role you play," Mr. Reynard continued. "Leaders set the vision and guide others. Supporters ensure that the vision becomes reality, providing strength and structure. Contributors bring unity and creativity. Each role is vital, and understanding this balance is key to graceful citizenship."

His gaze swept the room, briefly looking at each student. "As you begin your essays, reflect not only on these roles but also on where you see yourself. What role do you think you're best suited for? Where can you contribute most effectively? These questions aren't just academic. They're the first steps to discovering your place in society.

"Your tablet should have downloaded today's lecture on defining societal roles and the value of interdependence in society," he said. "You'll have twenty minutes to review the text.

The rest of the time may be used to begin your essay about how interdependence supports societal stability."

Allison tapped the corner of her tablet, and the text popped up: Interdependence ensures harmony within society, enabling leaders to guide, supporters to strengthen, and contributors to unify.

She stared at the words. They felt flat and heavy at the same time, like they were trying to push her into a box she didn't belong in. Leaders, supporters, contributors. What about the people who didn't fit neatly into those roles? What about people who asked questions? Where did they belong?

Allison stared at her tablet. The rest of the lecture blurred. What about her?

You're not even family.

Even though the wedding photos showed her parents together, she couldn't shake the feeling that Patrick had meant something else.

"Miss Maxwell."

Allison didn't look up right away. Instead, she took a steady breath before looking up. Tomas was watching her.

His expression was polite, his tone smooth. But she knew better. Everything about him was calculated.

"I'm curious about your thoughts," he said softly, almost as if he didn't want to interrupt. "Surely, your time in Europe has given you an interesting perspective."

Allison kept her face neutral. "Maybe."

"Come now," Tomas said lightly. He leaned on the edge of her desk, close enough to make her want to shrink away. "What do you think about the value of interdependence?"

Her fingers tightened around her stylus. "It depends," she said, tapping her screen with deliberate slowness. "Sometimes it helps people. Sometimes it's just a way to control them."

His smile didn't waver, but it felt colder now. "Control? Without order, society falls apart."

"Order and control aren't the same thing," she said, her voice steady despite the way her heart was beating faster.

Tomas tilted his head, his eyes narrowing slightly. "Nǐ bù yìng gāi tiǎozhàn zhìxù," he told her. You shouldn't challenge the order.

Allison felt her stomach drop. Not a casual challenge. A warning.

She knew what he was doing. Reminding her that he had power and she had none. For a single second, she considered not answering.

Then, carefully, she responded. "Wǒ zhǐshì xiǎng xúnzhǎo zhēnxiàng." I'm just looking for the truth.

For the briefest second, his smile flickered. Then, just as quickly, it was back. "A worthy pursuit." Tomas straightened, tucking his hands behind his back. "I look forward to reading your essay." And just like that, he moved on to the next desk.

Allison let out a breath she hadn't realized she was holding, her shoulders sagging as she reclaimed the space around her. Her fingers tapped absently against her desk as she looked out the window. Everything here was shiny and perfect, built to look good on the surface. But that wasn't how the world worked.

Back home, things had been messy and complicated, but honest. Her dad would have argued with her over breakfast, debating every point, and making her back up her arguments. But he would have let her ask the questions.

Here? Questions were dangerous. She swiped to the next page of text. She didn't have to believe any of this. She just had to play along.

For now. But she wondered to you play if no one has shared the rulebook?

Chapter Eleven

Allison dropped onto the floor in front of her couch, legs crossed as the smart wall flickered to life. A swirl of colors blurred before settling into the familiar faces of Clara, Lena, Greta, and Mila. They were piled onto Clara's couch. A curved mid-century modern arc lamp cast a warm glow over the girls, highlighting their faces as they lounged under blankets.

It felt like home.

"Allie! Wie geht's?" Mila grinned, practically bouncing, as she waved. Allie! How are you? Behind her, Allison could just see the moon peeking in through Clara's living room window.

Allison exhaled. Ah-lee. Soft and familiar, the way it was meant to sound. Not Al-ee with that sharp, cutting punch.

"Mir geht's gut," Allison said, her German slipping out like a sigh of relief. "Ich vermisse euch so sehr." I'm good. I miss you so much.

"We miss you too!" Clara said, tugging a pillow under her chin. "Sleepovers aren't the same without you."

Greta held up a plate of lumpy, uneven brownies. "We even tried to make those microwave brownies you love."

Allison couldn't help laughing. "Did you use chocolate milk and chips instead of cocoa powder again?" she asked.

"Of course we did!" Mila made a face. "Chunks of chocolate make everything better."

"It's wrong," Allison told her. "You need cocoa powder, not chocolate milk!"

"Then come back and fix it!" Mila demanded with a dramatic pout.

Allison's throat closed up. *I wish I could.*

She glanced at Michelle, who was sitting on the edge of the couch, hands clasped in her lap like she wasn't sure if she should be there. Right. She hadn't introduced her yet. "Oh, um, this is Michelle. She's a friend from school."

Michelle smiled a little awkwardly and gave a small wave. "Hi. I don't speak German, but it's nice to meet you."

Clara squinted. "It's early for a sleepover. What class are you studying for?" she asked in English.

"Nothing," Michelle quickly answered. "We're just hanging out."

That seemed to satisfy them, and the conversation quickly shifted back to more important things, with Clara rolling her eyes as Greta defended her failed attempt at microwave brownies.

"You should've let me do it," Mila said between bites. "You over-mixed the batter."

"I did not," Greta shot back. "You're just mad because I wouldn't let you dump all of the chocolate into the mix."

"That's what makes them good!" Mila threw up her hands. "Even Allie says so."

"Yeah, but you can't just dump a whole bag in there and hope for the best," Allison automatically added.

The teasing continued, bouncing between who burned what, whose brother was the most annoying, and the usual back-and-forth about their teachers. The familiar rhythm of it should have been comforting, but Allison found herself struggling to keep up.

The glow from the wall cast long shadows across her lap. Voices drifted through the room, the conversation shifting around her, but it all felt distant, like she was watching from behind glass.

That morning's ad was still looping in her mind. And then there was Patrick. What was she missing?

She barely noticed when the conversation shifted to weekend plans. Mila was heading to the lake, Greta was stuck visiting grandparents, and Clara and Lena complained about having a mountain of homework to get through. She nodded when someone asked her a question, but had no idea what she was agreeing to.

Finally, after another round of swapping stories and half-hearted teasing, Clara let out a yawn and stretched. "We should go to bed," she said. "Big day tomorrow."

"Yeah, yeah," Mila muttered, already burrowing under her blanket.

Allison forced a small smile. "I miss you guys."

"We miss you, too," Greta said. "It'll be summer before you know it."

"Hopefully," Allison replied.

The screen faded to black. Allison let out a breath she hadn't realized she'd been holding.

Michelle nudged her. "You okay?"

"Yeah," Allison lied.

Michelle picked up the wedding album from off the floor, flipping through it lazily. "You've got a whole other world back there. It's cool."

"I guess," Allison mumbled, pulling her knees to her chest.

"Is this your parent's wedding album?" she asked.

Allison nodded as she got up to grab a Spezi and Fizz out of her mini fridge.

"Who's this?" Michelle asked, pointing at the group photo.

Allison glanced over as she sat down. "That's my cousin Patrick," she said, passing Michelle her Fizz.

Michelle nodded. She squinted at the toddler in the picture. "Why is your cousin Patrick wearing a dress?"

Allison blinked. "What? He's not—" She stopped, staring at the photo. The toddler's dress was off-white with lace around the hem. "Oh."

Michelle shook her head. "That can't be Patrick. That kid looks like a baby. Not even walking yet. Patrick is older than you, right?"

"Yeah, he's almost two years older," Allison said slowly, a weird feeling in her stomach. "But then who—"

Michelle pushed the album closer to Allison, her face suddenly serious. "Allison, this kid has auburn hair. None of your mom's side of the family have red hair, do they?"

Allison stared at the photo, her heart pounding. "No. They don't."

Michelle met her eyes with concern. "That's you," she said.

The realization hit like a punch. "No, it can't be," Allison whispered, shaking her head.

"There's only one way to find out," Michelle told her.

Allison turned toward her. "I am not asking my mom if I was at her wedding!" she snarled.

"Fine." Michelle dropped the album onto her lap and held her hands up in surrender. "There has to be another way to find out. Did your mom keep a baby book for you?"

Allison hesitated. "She journals everything. I'm sure she has one. I just don't know where."

"Your library?" Michelle suggested. "That's where you found this, right?"

Allison nodded, mentally combing the bookshelves in her mind. Then she jumped up, grabbing Michelle's hand. "Let's go."

Michelle groaned. "Now? Can't it wait until later?"

"No," Allison hissed. "I need to know."

The hallway was dim, but the late afternoon sun from the first floor cast long golden streaks across the polished wood, breaking up the shadows. Voices drifted up from the family room.

"The reconstruction's hit a delay," her dad was saying. "More supply chain issues."

Her mother's voice was too quiet to make out.

Slipping inside the library, Allison shut the door behind them. She scanned the bookcase nearest her mom's desk. It was filled with random hardcover books, ancient weekly planners, spiral-bound project planners, and old albums. She crouched near the bottom shelf, pulling out a thick album labeled Allison's First Year. Her fingers brushed against another one called My Journey. It had a watercolor of a pregnant woman cradling her pregnant belly on the cover.

"Got 'em," she whispered. "Let's go."

Back in her room, they settled onto the floor and opened the first album. At first, the baby album looked normal. There were pictures of her parents cuddling her, too many shots of her napping in her crib, piles of pastel blankets, and lots of 'baby's first time' stories. But after the six-month mark, something shifted.

"Where's your mom?" Michelle asked, flipping through the photos. "She's barely in these."

"She moved to Massachusetts for school," Allison said, swiping her hand flat across the page so that Jeeves would throw the images onto the smart wall. "I stayed with my dad while he finished his degree in Wisconsin."

Most of the pictures were with her dad. He was holding her in front of Haggerty Hall on Marquette University's campus, feeding her at a holiday dinner, and even had her dressed as a lobster for Halloween. Her mom was either in the background or not there at all.

Michelle pointed to a video still. "What about this?"

Allison frowned. It looked like a screenshot from a video call. "No idea."

Michelle paced toward the smart wall. "When were your parents married?"

"May," Allison said automatically. "I was born in April. So if they got married after I was born, I'd have only been a month old." She swallowed hard. "But that baby is older. This doesn't make any sense."

"And Patrick is almost two years older than you," Michelle mused. She pulled the photo album onto her lap. "I don't know a whole lot about babies, but that baby doesn't look like a toddler."

They kept looking. Most of the pictures were candid. Her dad holding her in a blanket on some college campus. A chubby hand reaching for a stuffed animal. Allison giggling in a high chair with mashed sweet potatoes smeared across her face.

Then they turned the page.

A professionally taken portrait. Baby Allison sat on a pillow in front of a soft cream-colored backdrop, her auburn hair combed neatly, the fine strands held back by tiny barrettes. Her dress was pale yellow, with lace trimming along the sleeves. She was grinning, her baby teeth just starting to show.

The caption below the image read: Baby's First Birthday – April 8, 2030

Michelle sucked in a breath. "Okay . . ."

Allison didn't answer. Her fingers slowly traced the edge of the image. Then, she reached over and scooped up the wedding album from the floor. Her pulse pounded as she flipped to the family photo taken at the altar.

She brought the two albums together side by side, her heart hammering as she compared the photos. The baby in the wedding picture, small and dressed in lace, cradled in her aunt's arms, looked exactly like the one in the professional portrait.

Allison's chest tightened. She leaned in closer. Very light skin, auburn hair pulled back with tiny barrettes. She couldn't quite make out the baby's eye color in the wedding photo, but she would recognize that goofy smile anywhere.

It was her dad's.

"That's you, isn't it?" Michelle asked hesitantly.

Allison swallowed hard. "It's me," she whispered.

Michelle's voice was quiet but firm. "Did your parents tell you if they got married before or after you were born?"

Allison didn't answer. She just stared at the picture, tears burning in her eyes. So, her mom must have been disowned because she wasn't married before Allison was born. What else hadn't her parents told her?

Michelle wasn't supposed to stay the night. But last night, everything had shifted. It felt like someone had rewired her drone. The frame was the same, but the circuits were different, and nothing was working the way it should. She'd shut down.

And Michelle, being Michelle, hadn't even asked if she wanted company. She'd just stayed.

Now, the dining room felt too still for a Saturday morning. The clouds outside kept shifting, like they couldn't decide if they wanted to block the sun or not. Light spilled across the table in patches, making the silverware and glassware glow strangely.

Maria had gone all out with strawberry crêpes, fresh Brötchen, and thick-cut bacon. It smelled good, but everything smelled wrong when your stomach was tied in knots.

Allison stabbed at her crêpes with her fork. Her mom had been disowned because of her.

Patrick's voice kept looping in her head, smug and sharp. She had spent so much energy proving him wrong, and yet, he hadn't been lying.

Her fork scraped against the plate.

"Are you gonna eat that or just destroy it?" Michelle asked, already dressed in a black sweater and slouchy pants, casual as always. She looked normal, like nothing had happened. Meanwhile, Allison was still in pajamas, her hair a mess, stomach churning.

She shrugged.

Michelle studied her, head tilted. "Still thinking about yesterday?"

"No," Allison muttered.

Michelle sighed. "Look, I get it. It's a lot. But stabbing your breakfast isn't going to help."

Allison clenched her jaw. "I didn't ask for your advice."

"Yeah, well, you got it anyway." Michelle nudged her plate away, as if moving the poor crêpes would make her stop. "Come on. Let's do something. Shopping, smoothies, anything but sitting here thinking about it."

Allison frowned at her plate, eyes unfocused. "I don't feel like it."

Michelle groaned. "It's Saturday. You wanna just sit here all day?"

Before Allison could snap back, her mom stepped into the dining room with a coffee in hand, flawless as always in a teal silk blouse and skirt, with perfect hair and makeup. Clearly, she hadn't spent the night spiraling like her daughter.

Her eyes flicked between them. "What's wrong?"

"Nothing," Michelle said smoothly. "We were talking about getting out for a bit. Maybe shopping, maybe get some smoothies."

Her mom set her mug down. "That's a great idea," she said. "Allison, sweetheart, you've been inside all week. A little fresh air and time with your friends might help."

Allison didn't look up. "I don't want to."

Her mom pulled out a chair and sat. "Sometimes getting out of the house helps, even when you don't feel like it," she said, her tone softening. "You don't have to buy anything, but spending time with your friends might help."

"It'll be fun," Michelle chimed in. "We can grab Harper, Cecelia, and Marjani. Maybe hit the mall downstairs or even a few of the shops on Madison Avenue. Whatever works!"

Allison stayed quiet, staring at her plate. The thought of leaving the penthouse felt exhausting. But maybe if she went out, she wouldn't have to think about the photo or her mom. Finally, she sighed. "Fine. But I'm not buying anything gray. If anyone tries to make me wear that color, I'm leaving."

Gray was the color of those miserable Vanguard uniforms. Allison promised herself she'd never wear that color again after she left Manhattan.

Michelle smirked like she'd just won a prize. "Deal."

Mom took another sip of her coffee and stood. "Good," she said, smoothing her blouse. "I'll be at the Women's Club for lunch. Make sure you're back before dinner. I'll order pizza."

"Got it," Michelle said, practically bouncing out of her chair. "Come on, Allison. Go get dressed, and I'll send out the all-call!" She reached up, slid her AR band down over her eyes, and flicked her fingers as she scrolled through the unseen message app. "Who's up for an awesome day of shopping?" she asked. "Meet at Allison's in ten minutes!"

After a moment, she flipped up her AR band. "Harper's in. Cecelia, too. Marjani's a maybe," she told Allison.

Allison pushed her chair back slowly and headed toward her room, her feet dragging against the polished floor. Behind her, she could hear the faint sound of Maria humming in the kitchen.

Whatever.

The escalator hummed under Allison's flats, and she tapped the toes of one foot against the edge, watching the golden panels slide by. Omega was right behind her, standing tall like she always did, her sharp eyes scanning everything. The other two guards flanked the group at a comfortable distance, their movements quiet but deliberate.

Michelle let out a dramatic sigh. "Seriously, why do we need this much security? It's not like we're looking for trouble."

"We either take security with us or my mom," Allison muttered. "Which would you prefer?"

Michelle groaned. "Security, I guess."

Allison shoved her hands into the pockets of her coat. Soft music floated through the air, blending with the murmur of the sparse crowd below. The floors reflected the bright digital ads flickering across storefronts, showcasing sleek clothing, designer bags, and futuristic gadgets Allison had never seen before.

Harper wrinkled her nose as they stepped off the escalator. "This place is dead. Does anyone actually shop here?"

Cecelia huffed. "It's for old people with no taste."

"And lots of money," Michelle added under her breath.

"My mom calls this mall a 'curated lifestyle hub'," Harper said.

Marjani veered toward a café with frosted glass walls. "Come on, let's grab something to drink."

Inside the small shop, the air smelled like vanilla and spice. The robotic arm behind the counter whirred to life as Marjani selected a mango smoothie from the touchscreen.

Allison ordered strawberry, watching as the machine precisely measured and blended the ingredients before snapping the lid onto the travel cup with a clean click. She took the drink from the robotic arm.

"This never gets old," Marjani said, sipping her smoothie. "It's like magic, but with robotics."

Allison forced a smile and took a sip, letting the cool sweetness distract her. The others laughed and chatted as they left the café, the hum of the mall fading into the background.

They didn't stay long. The storefronts all looked the same, filled with things none of them actually wanted.

"Time to move on?" Michelle asked, a wicked grin on her face. "Or should we stay and take in a movie?"

After a solid round of boos, Allison turned to Omega. "I guess that means we're moving on to Madison Avenue." Omega nodded and they headed out.

Allison ducked into the curbside pod Omega gestured to, waving a hand for her friends to follow. The pod was large enough for all of them to sit in the back, including Omega. The two other security agents sat up front.

As the pod pulled away, Allison leaned against the cold window, her breath fogging the glass. Outside, the towering designer stores flowed past, gleaming with excess. Then, the pod turned a corner, and the city shifted.

These shops were smaller, their signs mismatched, their windows a little dusty. Christmas lights blinked haphazardly above a row of doors. A faded wreath hung on one of them, slightly lopsided. It reminded her of home in Hamburg, where she and her dad had spent hours wandering little side streets, hunting for Christmas gifts.

"Omega," she said, pointing. "Can we stop here? Some of the shops look interesting."

Michelle leaned over her to get a better look. "Ooh, yeah! This is cute."

Marjani grinned. "Maybe we won't get yelled at for touching stuff," she added.

Omega glanced out the window, scanning the street. "Looks low risk to me," she said. "Pull over, Rho. The girls are going for a walk."

The pod slowed to a stop, and the door slid open with a quiet hiss. A blast of crisp air hit Allison's face as she stepped onto the sidewalk. It smelled like cold metal and street food, familiar and foreign at the same time. She tugged her coat tighter around her.

Harper headed toward a shop with a tiny tree in the window. "This looks interesting!" she said.

Inside, the shop was warm and packed with soft sweaters, scarves, and jackets along the walls. Omega and the other security agent waited at the entrance as the girls stepped inside. Behind the counter, a salesperson glanced up from her tablet and gave them a quick, polite nod before looking back down.

Michelle pulled a dark blue scarf from one of the racks and held it up. "Allison, this would look amazing on you."

Allison shrugged. "Maybe."

"You didn't even look at it!" Michelle said, draping the scarf over her shoulders. "See? It's totally your color." She paused and then added, "And it's not even black or gray!"

Allison caught her reflection in a mirror near the counter. The scarf was nice—soft, simple, and not too flashy. "You know what? I'll get it for my mom," she said, pulling it off.

By the time they stopped for lunch, Allison was feeling better. The little café they found had a warm, cozy atmosphere, with the smell of fresh bread and sizzling meat filling the air.

They grabbed seats at the counter by the window, trays piled with burgers and fries.

Allison took a bite, the taste of the spiced meat and pretzel bun hitting her like a memory. Her dad grilling in their tiny backyard garden. Chasing fireflies with the neighbor's kids. Home.

"This is amazing," she mumbled, still chewing.

Michelle grinned and stole a fry off her plate. "Told you."

Cecelia gestured dramatically toward the street outside. "This is what the 'other half' eats. Can you imagine?"

Harper snorted. "You say that like we're at an outreach hub. These burgers are way better than that."

The group laughed, their voices overlapping. Then, Michelle's elbow jabbed into her ribs. Hard.

"Look," she whispered, her voice tight.

Allison turned just as a man in a dark hoodie briskly weaved through the crowd outside. A black mask covered most of his face, leaving only his eyes visible. Something about him felt off. His shoulders were tense, and his movements were too precise.

"Do you see him?" Michelle whispered.

Allison put her burger down. The man stopped near a woman by the curb. A split-second hesitation. Then his hand moved.

Metal flashed in the winter light. A weapon.

Allison gasped.

The woman dropped her bag, her eyes wide with panic. She stumbled back, and the man scooped it up, bolting down the street. He disappeared between the moving pods and stunned pedestrians.

For a second, no one moved.

Then, a bystander shouted. The woman turned and ran, disappearing into the crowd.

One of the security guards was already in motion, chasing after the man. The other positioned himself outside of the café entrance, scanning for more threats.

Allison sat frozen, her breath stuck in her throat.

Omega's voice cut through the shock. "Did you see his face? Any identifying details?"

Allison tried to replay it in her mind, but all she saw was the hoodie. The mask. The way he moved. Her fingers clenched the edge of the table. "No," she whispered.

The others shook their heads.

More security arrived, wearing armor. The entire street suddenly felt tense, like something could still happen. Pedestrians were pushed back against the far side of the street.

Omega stood abruptly. "Grab your bags," she said, her voice clipped. "We're leaving. Now."

Michelle stood first, her jaw set as she slung her bag over her shoulder. "That guy—he could still be around, right?" Her voice was steady, though her hands were shaking.

"No worries, miss," Omega said, her tone firm but reassuring. "You're safe, and we'll get you home shortly."

Allison grabbed her shopping bag, the handle digging into her palm as she followed the group. The restaurant door swung open, letting in a gust of cold air. It smelled like snow. She shivered as they stepped outside, the street now feeling louder, more menacing.

The group hurried outside, clustering together as two black security pods pulled up. The doors popped open.

"Michelle, Harper, and Cecilia, into this pod," Omega directed, her sharp gaze scanning the surrounding street even as she spoke. "These guards will be taking you straight home. No stops."

Michelle turned to Allison. "You okay?" Her voice was low.

"Yeah." Allison nodded, even though it wasn't true. "Go ahead. I'll see you Monday."

One hand still on the door, Michelle hesitated. "Call me, okay?"

"I will." Allison swallowed hard, her throat tight.

The other security guards took their places in the front seat. It looked like the one on the left had flipped the pod from self-driving to manual mode.

As the first pod drove away, Omega turned to Marjani and Allison. "You're with me. Let's get moving."

The second pod waited, its door already opened. Omega gestured for them to get in. She waited until they were settled in the back, then took a seat up front. She flipped on the full protection mode: All four doors locked automatically and protective panels covered the windows.

Marjani twisted the strap of her bag. "Why do you think he did that?" she asked nervously.

Omega met her eyes in the rearview mirror. "Because some people don't care who they hurt," she said, her voice quiet but sure. "What matters now is you're safe. Your parents have been notified."

Omega stepped out first, scanning the street and building entrance before opening the car door. "Let's get you inside."

A uniformed security guard stood just outside, speaking quietly into a comm. He straightened as they approached. One hand held a scanner, already sweeping the air in front of them to confirm their identity.

He looked over at Omega. "Any issues?" he asked in a low voice.

Omega shook her head once. "All clients are secure. Sector's sealed."

He glanced at the girls, then back at Omega. "Protocol Six is in effect."

The doorman gave them a polite nod. Omega held the door open for the girls, her eyes still sweeping the street, sharp and restless.

Inside, the lobby was quiet, the marble floors gleaming under warm lights. Nothing looked out of place, but Allison noticed the doorman didn't return to his desk after they passed. And the concierge, usually chatty, didn't even look up from her terminal.

The elevator doors opened without anyone pressing a button. Omega guided them inside and tapped a discreet panel with her wristband. There were no lights, no sound, just a faint buzz as the system registered her clearance.

When they reached Marjani's door, Omega waited until she was safely inside, keyed in the lock override, and double-checked it herself. Then, without a word, she led Allison to a second elevator, unmarked and hidden behind a mirrored wall at the end of the hall. Allison hadn't even known it existed.

This elevator was narrower, with no floor buttons, only a single biometric scanner built into the panel. Omega scanned her wristband, then placed her palm flat against the sensor. The doors closed silently behind them.

Allison's heart thudded in her chest. Omega was acting as if something bad was about to happen. Protocol Six? Unmarked elevators?

The elevator rose smoothly, not a whisper of movement. Just a soft chime as the doors opened into a private vestibule she'd never seen before.

Omega stepped out first, did a quick visual sweep, and then nodded. Allison followed her into the vestibule, watching as Omega keyed a command into a wall panel, locking down the entry behind them.

Omega gestured, and Allison walked into the living room. She found herself standing next to the glass windows that led to the patio garden. As she dropped her bag onto a nearby chair, the panel closed behind her. It was as if it had never existed.

Omega followed her into the living room. "You're safe," she said. Her voice was softer now. "Your mom's expecting you to check in." She paused and looked at Allison. "I'll stay until your mom tells me otherwise. I promise."

"Thanks, Omega," Allison said, her voice sounding strange even to herself, flat and hollow. She could hear Maria singing in the kitchen.

She headed to her room, her legs heavy with each step. The walls of the hallway felt too big, too cold. By the time she reached her couch, she was trembling. The attack kept replaying in her mind: the flash of metal, the way the woman had dropped everything and run away, the heavy sound of the bag hitting the ground.

"Jeeves," she said, her voice dry. "Call my mom's private number."

Her mother's image flickered to life on the smart wall, her face pale with worry. "Oh, thank God! Are you okay?"

"I'm fine," Allison murmured, her voice barely a whisper.

"I'll be home in less than five minutes," her mom told her. Allison could hear the anxiety in her voice. "Just stay in your room, okay?"

Allison ended the call and lay down on the couch. The memory of what she'd seen stayed sharp, refusing to blur.

She closed her eyes, pulling a throw pillow close to cuddle under her chin. Mom would be home soon. Omega was downstairs. It was going to be okay.

Chapter Twelve

The school's mirrored facade gleamed in the winter sun, reflecting the sharp blue sky and the steady stream of students pouring down the front steps. Transport pods lined the curb in a neat row, their muted colors shifting like liquid metal under the afternoon light.

Allison trailed a hand along the cold metal railing, the sensation grounding her in the moment. Normally, she loved this time of day. The sunlight made everything look brighter, like the city was holding its breath just before nightfall, which always felt comforting.

But today, everything felt off. Too bright, too sharp, too normal after what had happened Saturday.

Michelle sighed. "I'm serious. If I never had to take another class about how to be a 'well-rounded young woman,' I'd be thrilled."

"You'd get bored with regular classes," Sophie teased, nudging her playfully. "Admit it."

Michelle scoffed. "Maybe, but at least I wouldn't have to sit through Life Science pretending I care about what fork to use for dessert."

They giggled, but Allison barely heard them. Her mind kept drifting back to Saturday. Omega's eyes sweeping the apartment like even the walls couldn't be trusted. Her mother's tense hug when she finally walked through the door. The way she'd stared at the ceiling for hours that night, the mugging replaying on a loop in her head.

"Don't forget the concert on Saturday," Michelle added, her tone dry as she adjusted her bag. "My mom's already planning for which senators she'll 'accidentally' bump into at the event."

"My dad said it's about making connections," Sophie said, shifting her bag on her shoulder. "It's not who you know. It's who knows you!"

Allison sighed, scanning the line of waiting pods. Sometimes, Omega got a late start and was further back in the line.

And then she saw him. A figure standing by the curb, his auburn hair catching the afternoon sun.

Her dad.

Not on a screen. Not in some faraway country. Here.

"Dad!"

Her school bag slipped from her shoulder, thudding onto the pavement, but she barely noticed. She ran, lifting her skirt to keep from tripping, feet barely touching the ground as she closed the distance.

He caught her like he always did, his arms strong and steady, spinning her around before setting her down.

"I missed you!" she said, holding on to him, afraid to let go.

"I missed you too, sweetheart." His hands rested on her shoulders for a moment, like he was afraid she might disappear. Omega stepped forward, and with a practiced motion, she scooped up Allison's bag from the pavement, brushing at the scuffs before nodding at her dad.

Allison pulled back slightly, looking up at him, her pulse hammering. "You're here," she breathed. "Does this mean—?"

"We'll talk about it when we get back to your mom's," he said, his tone warm but firm. He guided her toward the pod waiting at the curb. The door slid open with a quiet hiss, and a wave of warm air spilled out.

She climbed in first, sliding onto the leather seat, feeling the warm cushions through her uniform skirt. Her dad followed, taking a seat beside her.

Omega passed over her backpack before climbing into the front seat and sealing the door behind them. The pod eased into motion, its electric hum blending with the faint sounds of the city outside.

Allison slowly exhaled and snuggled up against her dad. *He's taking me back to Germany,* she thought. *A cease-fire must have been announced.*

She looked up at him. He looked back, his face calm but unreadable. Outside, the city shifted again as the bright afternoon light faded into shadow.

She whispered a silent prayer. *Please, Lord. Let this mean we're going home.*

Allison perched on the armrest of her dad's favorite chair, swinging her legs as he hung up his coat in the front hall closet. A fire crackled in the fireplace, throwing flickering shadows across the room, but the warmth didn't make her feel any less jittery.

Her mom walked in from the dining room, dressed in a navy silk dress and dark pearls. It was one of her dad's favorites. He'd once said that it made her mom look like someone out of an old movie.

She carried two glasses of white wine. The crystal stems caught the light as she handed one to him. "Welcome home, Sam," her mother said with a warm smile.

Her dad took the glass with a nod but set it on the coffee table. Instead, he pulled her in for a slow kiss. Allison groaned, slapping her hands over her eyes. "Do you have to do that right in front of me?"

Her parents chuckled. "You'll understand someday," her dad teased, ruffling her hair before sinking into the couch. Her mom sat beside him, crossed her legs smoothly, and cradled her glass.

"Why don't you have a seat, kiddo?" he asked. "We need to talk."

Something was wrong. Dad never called a family meeting unless something bad was going to happen.

Allison nodded and slipped off the armrest. She sat down and cuddled the throw pillow as she tucked her legs beneath her.

Her dad loosened his tie, rolling his shoulders before leaning forward. "I wish I could've gotten here sooner. Are you okay?"

Allison blinked. "We weren't the ones who got mugged," she told him. "We were inside, honest. And, we had security with us the whole time!"

Dad glanced at her mom. "Even so, I thought that security kept crime under control here."

Her mom took a sip of wine before responding. "They do. But the girls decided to venture outside the designated safe zone."

Designated safe zone? "We weren't doing anything wrong," Allison protested. "No one told us not to go there!"

Her dad sighed. "It's not about rules, Allison," he told her. "It's about risk. Some people out there are desperate, and desperate people don't care about laws." He leaned forward and rested his elbows on his knees. "You're safer here in this part of Manhattan than you'd be elsewhere, but I need to know you're being careful."

Allison hesitated, then took a deep breath. "D-does that mean that I'm not going back to Germany?"

Dad sat back. "I wish that I could tell you that you were, but things aren't looking good," he told her. "Russian forces are claiming southwestern Latvia, and refugees are pouring into Poland. The EU Defense Force is to avoid an all-out war, but . . . " he trailed off, running a hand through his hair. "It's just not safe right now."

She hesitated. "So . . . are you moving out of Hamburg?"

Her dad rubbed the back of his neck. "Not yet," he told her. "But I don't know how much longer I'll be there. If the situation gets worse, I'll have to relocate operations to a different country."

Her mom set down her wineglass. "What about the last lock?" her mom asked.

"It's in Germany," he told her. "And we're facing significant supply chain issues. It's a real mess." He ran a hand through his hair, reworking the mess so that his hair leaned more to the left. "I have to go back." He looked down at her mom. "But I'll be back as often as I can. Even if I have to rent a private plane."

Her mom arched a brow. "From the company we're buying?"

"Convenient, isn't it?" Dad said with a smirk. "Moving on." He leaned forward to grab his wineglass and took a sip. "The important thing is that we've started looking at what part of the U.S. would be best for you to go to high school."

Allison nodded, swallowing hard. She hated Manhattan. It felt like the folks who lived here were isolated from the real world. Maybe they could go back to Wisconsin, where Dad's family lived?

Before she could say anything, Maria appeared at the entrance. "Dinner will be ready in five minutes."

Her mom gave a tight nod. "Thank you, Maria. We'll be in shortly."

Maria hesitated, her gaze flicking toward Allison, as if sensing the tension. Then, she disappeared down the hall.

Her mom stood, smoothing down the fabric of her dress. "We should move to the dining room."

Her dad stretched and got to his feet. "Come on, kiddo. Let's eat." Allison reluctantly followed. She wasn't hungry.

The oval dining table was set like something out of a holiday gathering. Flickering candles reflected off the silverware. Mom's china rested in the antique chargers she'd received as a birthday gift years ago, the deep blue pattern standing out against the crisp white linen tablecloth. A floral centerpiece, arranged in a Waterford crystal bowl, sat in the middle of the table, filling the air with a faint, fresh scent.

Allison swallowed. This wasn't just dinner. It was a statement. The kind of effort her mom made when she wanted to remind people of something. Maybe that this was still her home, still part of the life she'd built, even if Dad spent most of his time across the ocean.

Her dad pulled out her mom's chair before taking his own, glancing at the spread with an appreciative nod. "Maria, this looks amazing," he said as she set down the last dish.

Maria smiled, smoothing her apron. "It's good to have you home, Mr. Maxwell."

Allison sat down slowly, her fingers brushing the rim of her charger.

Before they could begin, her dad reached for their hands. "Let's pray," he said, his voice steady.

Allison bowed her head.

"Come, Lord Jesus, be our guest, and let these gifts to us be blessed," her dad said, the familiar ritual helping her relax. The rest of the prayer rolled off her tongue, almost as naturally as breathing. "Amen."

Her mom lifted her glass of wine with a soft smile. "To your dad's safe return," she said.

"To Dad," Allison echoed, lifting her water glass as her dad clinked his wineglass against hers.

She had a sip of water before putting the glass down, quietly watching her dad as he placed a few slices of roast beef on his plate. He passed the serving dish to her mom, then picked up the bowl of mashed potatoes. "There's something else that we need to talk about, Allison," he said. "You're going to start taking a self-defense class."

Allison looked up from spooning some green beans on her plate. "What?"

Her mom looked down at the bowl in her hand, obviously not agreeing.

"It's important," Dad said, his voice calm but firm. "You'll learn Krav Maga at your mom's social club. They've agreed to let us use one of the smaller yoga rooms."

Krav Maga. Allison's stomach twisted. "Isn't that what soldiers learn?"

Dad nodded. "You're going to focus on situational awareness and protecting yourself if security can't get to you immediately. And you won't be the only one. There will be other girls there, too."

Allison looked at her mom, expecting her to argue. Instead, she said, "We'll need to meet with the instructor ahead of time. The board is selective about who leads classes on their premises."

Dad exhaled with a nod. "Fair enough."

"Sounds like a lot," she said with a frown. "But I can try, right?"

Her dad smiled, the tension in his shoulders easing slightly. "That's my girl." He handed her the roast beef. "I have a meeting with Vanguard's headmaster tomorrow to discuss what can be done about your academics," he told her. "I don't like you being overloaded with two competing sets of schoolwork. Time to dump what's not working and move on."

Her mom nodded. "Amanda will arrive early for Allison's tutoring session tomorrow so that we can talk things through," she said, her tone brisk. "Would you like to go out for dinner after they're done for the afternoon?"

Allison barely touched her food. Her parents kept talking, about her coursework, about meeting with her tutor, but she just sat there, staring at her plate.

Everything was piling up. The mugging. Europe. The fact that her mom had been disowned because of her.

She glanced up at her parents, still deep in conversation. They didn't even notice how quiet she was.

Slowly, she set down her fork. "May I be excused?"

Mom looked at her, concerned, but Dad nodded. "Go ahead, Allie."

She pushed back from the table, her chair scraping softly against the floor. The carpet muffled her steps as she walked toward her room.

The moment the door shut behind her, she exhaled sharply, pressing her forehead against the wood. She had no idea what to do next.

She made herself walk across the room and flopped onto her bed, staring at the ceiling. School, a tutor, double the homework, the chess club, and now self-defense classes. It was just too much.

Even worse? She couldn't wrap her head around the idea that her mom had been disowned, let alone that it was because of her. Should she talk to her dad, maybe? Look for more clues to confirm that they were married after she was born? Pretend like Patrick had never told her and just ignore it?

She pulled a pillow over her head. "One thing at a time," she mumbled. "Just take one thing at a time."

The next afternoon, Allison stepped out of the elevator, her flats squeaking against the marble as she hurried inside. Outside, the rooftop garden was covered in a thick layer of snow, untouched except for a few bird tracks. Normally, she'd have stopped to look, but not today.

She shrugged off her coat and quickly hung it up. Then, she grabbed her backpack and headed for the living room. From the entrance hall, she could see weather updates and boring headlines about global supply chains on the smart wall. The voices coming from the living room were louder now, and she practically race-walked her way into the living room.

She slowed as she reached the doorway. Her parents were on the couch, her dad scrolling through his tablet, his eyebrows pinched together like they always were when he wasn't thrilled about something. Mom sat next to him, nodding like she already knew whatever he was about to say. Across from them, her tutor sat perfectly straight, a tablet resting on her lap.

Her mom glanced up. "Allison. Perfect timing!" She smiled. "Why don't you have a seat?" she asked. "We're just about finished with the update to your educational plan."

Allison had a seat next to Amanda, barely able to contain her excitement. Were they going to completely pull her out of school, maybe?

Her dad set the tablet aside. "Starting tomorrow, you'll be meeting with Amanda for some of your classes at school."

Allison's eyes widened. "Really? That's amazing!"

"Don't get too excited," her dad warned with a wry smile. "You'll have a dedicated study space on the Sanctuary floor from 8:45 until noon every day." He shrugged. "The headmaster was rather vague about this floor, but I'm told that it has several private study rooms to 'help young women focus'."

Her mom frowned and shook her head.

"The dean of women will be monitoring your progress weekly to ensure everything meets Vanguard's oh-so-rigorous standards," he told her. "The headmaster made it sound like he's doing us a massive favor."

Her mom nodded. "We need to finalize things now that we've got the go-ahead, but I'm sure it will be fine," she said, glancing at Amanda. "Are you comfortable with the schedule adjustment?"

Amanda smiled warmly. "Absolutely. I'm happy to take on a more structured schedule. This will give us a chance to work more closely on the subjects that matter most to you."

"What classes will we cover?" Allison asked excitedly.

"Mandarin, Social Studies, Life Sciences, and Algebra," her dad replied.

Her mom leaned forward. "It's a good opportunity, Allison, but it's also a huge responsibility," she said. "Don't forget that."

"I won't," she promised quickly.

Her dad checked his watch. "Why don't you two head upstairs to get started on tonight's homework? We're leaving for dinner at 6."

Allison turned to Amanda with a grin. "Ready?"

"Of course," the tutor replied, gathering her tablet.

Upstairs, they gathered around the small table. Snow drifted past the windows, soft and silent. They'd only just started reviewing her Algebra homework when Allison paused, her stylus hovering above her tablet.

"Amanda?" she asked tentatively.

"Yes, Allison?" Amanda asked.

"Can I ask you about something personal?"

Amanda sat back in her seat. "Of course. What's on your mind?"

"It's something my cousin told me," Allison began, the words tumbling out quickly. "At first, I thought he was lying, but now, I'm not so sure. It's . . . it's a family thing, and I can't go to my parents about it. Not yet. But now I don't know."

Amanda's face didn't change, but she tilted her head, thoughtful. "Do you think knowing the truth will help?"

Allison thought about it. "I don't know," she admitted. "But I think I have to find out."

Amanda nodded. "Then it's worth exploring," she told her. "Just make sure you're careful. The truth matters, but so does how you go about finding it."

Allison let out a slow breath. "That helps."

"Good," she said with a smile. "Now let's tackle this next equation."

Allison nodded, feeling better. The truth matters. Simple but true. She took a breath and turned back to her tablet, trying to focus.

The restaurant was quiet. Only a few tables were taken, and the two waiters moved between them like they had all the time in the world. Allison glanced around, noticing how the chandeliers sent golden light bouncing off the dark green walls and polished wood.

The plates the waiters carried were small and perfect, each dish arranged like a tiny work of art. The whole place smelled rich and buttery, with something sharp and herby in the background.

She looked around. She was used to busy, buzzing restaurants, but here, the quiet made everything feel a little too important.

A waiter arrived at their table with the first course, placing a delicate porcelain bowl in front of her. The dish was instantly familiar: *Hummersuppe*, a lobster bisque with a swirl of fresh cream and a sprig of fresh dill. The presentation was fancier than she was used to, with tiny edible flowers placed around the edge of the bowl, but the rich, briny smell brought her right back to Germany.

Her dad picked up his spoon first, giving the soup a little stir before taking a sip. "Just like Hamburg," he said, his hazel eyes warm as he looked at her. "They've outdone themselves."

Allison dipped her spoon into the velvety liquid. The first taste was perfect. Smooth, buttery, with just the right hint of sweetness from the lobster. It tasted like home. For a moment, she forgot everything else and just ate.

"Good?" her dad asked, his voice light.

Allison nodded, swallowing quickly. "Really good."

Her mom smiled as she reached for her glass of sparkling water. "This was a great idea," she said, dabbing her mouth with a napkin. "I'm glad you suggested it, Sam."

"It's all about balance," her dad replied, taking another spoonful of soup. He winked at Allison.

As the soup disappeared from her bowl, Allison looked up, unable to keep her excitement bottled up. "I can't wait for tomorrow," she blurted out.

Her dad set his spoon down, amusement flickering across his face. "Really?"

Allison nodded eagerly. "Yes!" she told him. "It's going to be so much better than my regular classes. Amanda, I mean, Miss Trevelyan, is going actually to teach me stuff I need for high school."

Her mom gave her a knowing look. "I know this semester hasn't been easy," she said, "but this should help you get back on track."

The waiter returned to clear the bowls, and her dad took a sip of water. "I'm glad we finalized everything with Vanguard," he said.

A moment later, the next course arrived: *Wiener Schnitzel*, served with potato salad, cucumber slices, and a small dish of lingonberry sauce. The schnitzel was golden and crisp, the buttery aroma mixing with the tang of vinegar and mustard from the potato salad.

"This," her dad said, cutting into the schnitzel, "is exactly what I need after all of that airplane food." He dipped a small piece into the lingonberry sauce before taking a bite. "Crispy, buttery, with just enough lemon. And the sauce is perfect."

Her mom laughed softly, slicing into her portion with careful precision. "I'm impressed they managed to make it this authentic," she said. "I expected something a little more ... modernized, given that Le Privé has a Michelin star." She glanced at Allison, who was already digging in. "What do you think?"

Allison chewed, savoring the contrast between the warm crunch of the schnitzel and the creamy potato salad. She gave a quick nod. "It's really good."

Her mom smiled. "I'll have to let the chef know. He said he wanted to keep it traditional, just for you."

The mention of the chef made Allison pause mid-bite. "Why?" she asked, looking up.

Her dad chuckled. "Because I told him you've been missing Germany. He wanted to make sure you felt a little more at home tonight."

She blinked. For a second, she wasn't sure if that made her happy or if it just made everything worse. She took another bite, forcing herself to focus on the food, on how familiar it all was. If she closed her eyes, she could almost imagine she was back in Hamburg, sitting in one of the little restaurants her dad loved.

They finished the main course in relative silence. By the time the plates were cleared and the waiters brought out key lime pie for dessert, Allison wasn't sure she had room for dessert. But when the pale green slice was set in front of her, she gave in.

She took a bite, the bright citrus cutting through the heaviness of dinner. For a moment, everything felt normal. Just a fancy dinner with her parents, good food, and soft music.

Then, her dad set his fork down, the untouched pie still in front of him. His expression had shifted, and Allison's stomach tightened.

"Now might be a good time to talk," he said.

She froze mid-bite, her fork hovering over her plate. Slowly, she set it down. "Talk about what?"

Her dad took a sip of water before answering. "About what comes next," he said carefully. "Your mom and I have been discussing what's best for our family, going forward. But we want to make sure you're okay with everything."

A strange unease settled over her. "Like what?"

"I'll only be in Manhattan until Wednesday morning," he said, reaching out to cover her mom's hand. "I'm meeting with potential clients—one in Vancouver, the other in Veracruz."

"Veracruz?" Allison repeated, her voice smaller than she wanted it to be. Not Europe?

He nodded. "It's a major port city with some very complex issues to solve. The kind of project I love. But..." He hesitated. "With the supply chain issues I'm dealing with, the Elbe project may not wrap up for another six months. After that, I'd rather take a job closer to you and your mom."

She pushed her fork against the remains of her pie, her appetite gone. "So, you're not going back to Germany?" she asked, barely above a whisper.

"I am," he said firmly. "For now. But once Hamburg is done, I want to make sure I'm closer to you."

Her mom leaned forward, her voice calm but certain. "Your dad and I have talked about this. If he takes the job in Vancouver, he'd be within driving distance of Seattle. I haven't had time to investigate high schools out that way yet, but I have a list for us to look through over the next few weeks."

"Veracruz would be harder," her dad added. "Your mom would need to relocate to someplace nearby, like San Antonio. It's a bit closer and a lot more stable. We'll talk through the options."

Allison nodded, but she barely heard them anymore. No matter what her parents said, it felt like they'd already made the decision.

And the worst part? She wasn't sure if she belonged anywhere anymore.

Chapter Thirteen

Allison rolled over, sighing. "Jeeves," she mumbled. "Start my day."

"Good morning, Miss Allison," the AI responded. The windows lightened to allow some early morning sunlight to enter. "Today is Monday, December 6 and the current time is 6:55 a.m. The weather in Manhattan is currently 32 degrees. Flurries are expected this afternoon."

She grunted and threw off the blanket. Saturday evening had been straight out of one of her mom's old movies, glamorous and over-the-top. The courtyard at Vanguard had shimmered with lights, tables set so perfectly they didn't seem real. The orchestra had been incredible.

As always, her mom owned the night, slipping between conversations like it was choreographed. People leaned in, laughing too easily, nodding like everything she said was brilliant. It looked effortless.

Allison wished she could be like that. Instead, she'd stuck with her friends, sipping mocktails that were too tart and pretending her vintage necklace didn't feel weird against her skin. It was beautiful, gold links and tiny pearls, but it belonged to someone else. Someone who didn't constantly worry about saying the wrong thing.

Sunday had been better. Quieter. Church as a family. It had been strange, watching people who usually fussed over her mom turn their attention to her dad. The men clapped him on the back, shaking his hand like they'd always known him. The women smiled with that perfected, polite smile she'd seen everywhere.

Afterward, they stayed for brunch. Her mom chatted with the pastor's wife while her dad joked and ate waffles like everything was normal. But, it wasn't.

You're not even family. The words crept in between the musical notes played by the orchestra, bites of food during brunch, and every pause in conversation.

Patrick just liked to stir up trouble. That's what her mom said. But if it wasn't true, why did some pieces of it make sense? Like finding out that she had attended her own parent's wedding. But how could her grandparents have been there if her mom had been disowned?

There were holidays, visits, family outings. But sometimes, there were side glances, offhand comments, a feeling like everyone was keeping score. Her mom always seemed so careful around them, her words perfectly chosen.

She wanted to ask her dad. What if he shrugged it off, too? Or worse—he confirmed it? What if she really was the reason her mom wasn't part of the trust and was the reason she worked so hard to prove herself to everyone?

Allison yanked on her uniform, grabbed her backpack, and hurried downstairs.

In the dining room, the morning sunlight spilled across the table. Maria placed a blueberry muffin and orange juice in front of her.

"Good morning, Allie." Her dad sat at the head of the table, nursing some coffee. He smiled, faint and wistful.

Her mom glanced up from her emails. "Ready to start your new schedule?"

Allison slouched, her backpack slumping against the chair leg like it didn't want to go either. "I guess." She tore off a piece of muffin, rolling it between her fingers until it crumbled.

Her dad set his mug down. "I know you're sad that I have to leave," he said gently. "It's going to be okay."

Allison's fingers froze mid-pick. She stared at the crumb, then let it drop onto her plate. "It doesn't feel okay," she mumbled. "I don't want you to go." She bit her lip.

Her mom gave her a sad smile.

Allison looked between them, then looked down at her ruined muffin. "Sorry," she muttered.

Her dad reached across the table, his hand warm over hers. "You don't have to apologize for how you feel, Allie." His voice was quiet but firm. "Feelings aren't right or wrong. They just are."

She nodded, throat tight.

Maria quietly cleared the plates, her head down, so she didn't interrupt.

Her dad pushed his chair back. He stood, stretched, and ran a hand through his hair. "Come on," he said, like he was trying to convince them both that everything would be fine. "Let's not keep Omega waiting."

Allison grabbed her backpack. Her mom followed them to the entrance hall.

Her dad pulled on his coat and kissed her mom. "I'll call when I land," he told her.

Allison looked away, shrugging into her own coat.

The elevator chimed. She stepped inside with her dad, adjusting her bag as he fixed his jacket. He caught her staring and gave her a reassuring smile. The kind that didn't fix anything, but made her feel a little steadier.

"You know, change is always hard," he said as the elevator descended. "But you're tougher than you think. You've got your mom's drive and my stubbornness. That's a pretty unstoppable combination."

Allison gave him a half-smile. She wanted to believe him. But her chest still felt tight with unspoken questions.

The elevator doors slid open. Footsteps echoed, voices murmured, and the scent of coffee seemed to linger in the air. Security stood at their posts. The concierge desk was busy.

Outside, their pod idled at the curb. Omega stepped out and opened the door. Her dad gestured for her to go first. She slid onto the leather seat, warm against her uniform, and stared out the window. The city glinted in the morning light.

Her dad climbed in beside her. Omega took a seat in the front and the door shut with a slight hiss.

"It's not forever, you know," he said as the pod pulled away. "Someday, all of this will make sense."

Allison tilted her head against the window. "I guess," she murmured.

But she wasn't sure how long someday would take. Or if she'd ever really find the answers she was looking for.

Allison stepped out of the elevator as the doors whispered shut behind her. Today had been a good day, maybe even a great one.

Her new schedule worked. The headmaster had agreed that mornings should be structured. She still attended the morning assembly, but then she was released for the rest of the morning for her real lessons.

The best part? With only one subject per day, there was no endless pile of homework. Fridays were for review, with Amanda making sure she fully understood the material and that her work met Vanguard's 'high' standards. Her afternoons were predictable: Lunch, Civics, Language Arts. And on Mondays, Chess Club.

Chess Club had been fun today, too. She'd nearly won her last match, but lost at the end. Still, it was progress.

She tugged off her winter coat and set her boots on the drying rack in the closet. The apartment was warm, the scent of something rich and savory filling the air. Her stomach rumbled.

Maria appeared from the kitchen, her apron dusted with flour. "I'm glad you're home, Miss Allison," she said, handing her a small plate. "I made *Flammkuchen*." The thin, crispy flatbread was topped with caramelized onions, crisp bacon, and creamy cheese.

Allison grinned. "Thanks, Maria. It smells amazing."

"Your mom will be home in a few hours," Maria said, brushing flour off her hands. "This should hold you over until dinner."

Allison nodded and headed upstairs to her room. The familiar space wrapped around her like a soft blanket. She set the plate on her worktable, tossed her bag onto the couch, and pulled out her tablet.

She hesitated. No more after-school tutoring. No one watching over her. If she didn't do this now, she might lose her nerve.

"Jeeves," she said, her voice unsteady. "Activate incognito mode."

"Incognito mode activated."

She sat on the couch and took a deep breath. "Jeeves, find a copy of my birth certificate and my parents' marriage license."

The smart wall flickered to life. Two documents appeared side by side.

On the left was her birth certificate: April 8, 2029, with her name, Allison Isabelle Williams Maxwell, neatly typed on the document. Her parents' marriage license, dated May 18, 2030, was on the left. Both had official State of Wisconsin seals.

Her heart sank. The documents confirmed that her parents weren't married when she was born. She sank onto the couch, the *Flammkuchen* completely forgotten.

She pressed her back into the couch, her arms wrapping around her knees. The redheaded baby in the family photo was her. She'd never thought to ask about their anniversary before. They celebrated quietly. No big parties. No public acknowledgment.

Now she understood why.

Her fingers trembled as she rubbed her face. What if Patrick was right about everything else? She wanted to just erase the wall and exit incognito mode. To pretend she hadn't looked. But the unanswered question made her feel sick.

"Jeeves," she whispered, "is there any way to confirm if someone's been disowned?"

A pause. "Disownment does not typically involve legal documentation," Jeeves replied. "However, if it resulted in removal from a family trust, court records or amendments may exist."

Allison's heart pounded so hard it felt like it wanted out now!

She could stop this. Turn off the smart wall and force herself to eat the *Flammkuchen* that Maria had made specially for her.

Instead, she took another breath and forced the words out. "Search for any legal documentation regarding Rylee Williams Maxwell. Specifically, anything about being disowned or removed from a family trust."

"Searching."

The silence was almost suffocating. Allison found herself pacing her room, her hands gripping the edges of her blazer.

This was stupid. A waste of time. Jeeves was going to come back with nothing, and she'd feel ridiculous.

"I have located electronic copies of the Williams Family Trust from 2019 to 2029," Jeeves finally told her. "Displaying now."

The smart wall filled with overlapping documents. She walked closer, her eyes blurring as she tried to understand the legal jargon.

"Jeeves," she whispered, "is there anything that mentions my mom being removed from the Williams Family Trust?"

A pause. Then a single document opened in the middle of the wall.

This document, dated February 23, 2029, serves as an amendment to the Williams Family Trust, approved by the board of trustees and executed on November 11, 2001, by Albert Williams, hereinafter referred to as the Settlor.

Allison barely breathed. It was right there in front of her.

"WHEREAS, the Settlor desires to make specific provisions regarding the beneficiaries of the Williams Family Trust;

"NOW, THEREFORE, in consideration of the premises and for other good and valuable consideration, the receipt and sufficiency of which are hereby acknowledged, the Settlor hereby amends the Williams Family Trust;

1. For all purposes hereunder, I am specifically not making any provision for my granddaughter Rylee Annabelle Williams or her issue or for Samuel Maxwell or his issue (if any).

2. Rylee Annabelle Williams is removed from any and all benefits, distributions, and entitlements from the Williams Family Trust. This disinheritance includes, but is not limited to, any share of the trust principal, income, or other assets.

The words hit her like a punch to the gut.

Removed from everything. Her issue. No provision.

It was too much.

Her vision blurred. A tear slipped down her cheek before she even realized she was crying. She clenched her fists, nails digging into her palms.

"Save it," she managed to choke out. "Save a copy to my personal drive under a private encryption key."

"File saved."

Allison stumbled to her bed and collapsed into the pillows. The tears kept coming, soaking into the pillows. She could feel a wail building in the pit of her stomach and she rolled onto her back, stuffing a pillow into her mouth to muffle it.

Patrick hadn't lied. Her mom had been disowned, cut out from the family trust. Because of her.

Chapter Fourteen

The pod came to a quiet stop and the doors sliding open with a soft hiss. Allison didn't move right away. She stared at the building in front of her. It wasn't like the towering glass skyscrapers around it. It was shorter, maybe twenty stories, with sleek stone steps and wide glass doors that reflected the dull gray sky. It looked more like a luxury apartment complex than a women's club.

A man stood at the top of the stairs, watching them. His long coat moved slightly in the wind, but he didn't shift his weight or fidget. He wasn't dressed like a regular doorman. His coat was sharp and expensive-looking, but there was something in the way he stood, scanning the street as if waiting for something to go wrong.

Security.

He quickly moved down the stairs. Then, he offered her mom his hand. "Mrs. Maxwell," he said smoothly, as if he'd done this a thousand times.

Her mom smiled, one of her perfect, camera-ready smiles, and took his hand, letting him help her out like she was a movie star at a premiere.

Allison sighed and slid out after her, shoving her hands deep into her jacket pockets. The cold wind stung her cheeks, and she hunched her shoulders against it.

She followed them up the stairs. The man opened the door, giving her mom a small nod as she stepped inside without looking back.

The warmth hit immediately, wrapping around her like a heavy blanket. The floor gleamed gold under the soft lighting, some kind of marble polished so perfectly she could see her reflection. A massive chandelier hung above them, its crystal arms sprawling like a frozen explosion. Instead of being beautiful, it just made her feel small.

Her mom walked straight to the front desk, heels clicking against the marble floor as if she owned the place.

The receptionist, a woman with sleek black hair and a name tag that simply read Ava, looked up with a bright, practiced smile. "Mrs. Maxwell! How lovely to see you this brisk December afternoon. The Young Women's Group is meeting in the yoga studio on the third floor."

"And my meeting?" her mom asked lightly.

"The response has been higher than expected," Ava replied. "It's been moved to the Presentation Room on the fifteenth floor. It starts at 4 p.m."

"Thank you." Her mom flashed another dazzling smile before turning to Allison. "Let's get you upstairs."

Allison didn't argue, but she didn't hurry either. She dragged her feet behind her mom, her school bag slumping against her back. She didn't want to be here. Not in this building, not in Manhattan, not even in this country.

Rylee Annabelle Williams and her issue... removed from any and all benefits...

Her stomach burned. She sucked in a breath, staring at her shoes as they rode the elevator up.

It was her fault. All of it. If she hadn't been born, her mom wouldn't have been disowned. She wouldn't have been cut out of the trust. She wouldn't have had to continually try to claw her way back into her family's good graces.

"Allison."

Her mom's voice snapped her back. The elevator doors were open, and she was standing there, waiting.

Allison forced herself to move, stepping out onto the plush carpet of the hallway. They walked in silence, the soft lighting making the corridor feel almost too calm. A few turns later, they stopped outside a door labeled Yoga Studio. Her mom turned to her, expression unreadable. Was she annoyed? Concerned?

"Are you okay?" she asked.

Allison forced a nod. "I'm fine, Mom," she mumbled. "I just don't see why I have to do this."

"Your dad and I feel that learning some basic self-defense might help," her mom said. "Try it for a few weeks. Please."

Allison hesitated, then pushed open the door.

Inside, the floor was lined with thick blue mats. A punching bag hung in the corner like a weird, deflated balloon. She ducked into the dressing room. The room smelled like fresh linen and eucalyptus, a subtle nod to the spa-like surroundings.

Each girl had a private dressing room, sectioned off by floor-to-ceiling panels with smooth, light woodgrain finishes. A touch panel at the entrance of each stall controlled the lighting and climate settings. With a quick tap of her security bracelet,

Allison activated hers, and the space adjusted to her preferences. The temperature cooled slightly, and the lighting shifted to a warm glow.

She pulled back the drape at the entrance and stepped inside. Her sports bag landed on the bench with a gentle thud. She unzipped it, pulling out her training gear and setting aside her street clothes. She pulled on the stiff uniform her mom had bought for her. The tight white shirt clung uncomfortably to her arms, and the padded pants felt like they belonged to someone else. She tugged at the hem of her shirt, scowling at her reflection.

She looked ridiculous. Like she was trying too hard to be something she wasn't.

By the time she came back out, a few other girls had arrived. Most were younger than her and whispered nervously to each other. One girl stood apart from the rest. She was taller, with a blonde ponytail that swung every time she moved. She didn't look nervous. She looked like she already knew what to do.

Allison's stomach tightened.

At the front of the room, a woman stood with her arms crossed. Mrs. Ashcroft. Her white uniform was crisp, her hair pulled back so tightly it looked painful. She had the kind of eyes that made you feel guilty, even if you hadn't done anything wrong.

"This is Krav Maga," she said, her voice cutting through the murmurs. "It's not a sport. It's not a game. It's about survival."

Allison shifted on her feet. The room went silent.

"Krav Maga is about quick thinking, controlled aggression, and using everything at your disposal to protect yourself," Mrs.

Ashcroft continued. "Rule number one: Decide not to become a victim."

Allison frowned. Decide not to become a victim? How was that a choice?

The door opened behind Mrs. Ashcroft, and a man stepped inside. He was tall, with gray hair and ordinary clothes that looked completely out of place in the yoga studio. Allison hesitated. Wasn't this supposed to be a women-only social club?

And then, without warning, he lunged.

Allison barely had time to react before Mrs. Ashcroft moved.

It happened so fast: an elbow strike to his chest, a sharp twist, then a flip that sent him crashing onto the mat with a solid thud.

Allison staggered back, her breath caught in her throat. Around her, a few girls gasped, one clutching her friend's arm.

The man laid still for a second. Then, he grinned. "Still got it."

Mrs. Ashcroft didn't return the smile. She reached down, pulled him up with one strong grip, and turned back to the class. "Thank you, Mr. Carrington," she said, her tone sharp. She turned back to the group, her green eyes sweeping over them like she was counting heads. "This is why we train."

Allison swallowed hard. Her eyes followed Mr. Carrington as he left.

"This is not about looking for a fight," Mrs. Ashcroft said. "It's about making sure you can survive one."

"All right," Mrs. Ashcroft said, clapping her hands once. "Line up. We start with the basics."

The girls shuffled into a line across the mats, their movements hesitant and awkward. Allison ended up near the middle, glancing nervously at the others. Most of them were fidgeting, looking everywhere but at Mrs. Ashcroft. The tall blonde girl stood at the end of the line, her stance steady, like she wasn't worried at all.

Mrs. Ashcroft stepped forward, holding up her fists. "First, you learn how to make a proper fist. Thumb outside. Fingers curled tightly. If your wrist isn't straight, you'll hurt yourself more than your attacker."

She demonstrated, showing how her knuckles lined up. "Straight punch." Her fist darted out. "Jab." Another snap. "Cross." Her torso twisted, adding power. "These are your basic strikes. Everything builds from here."

"Begin," Ms. Ashcroft said, pacing in front of them. The room filled with the soft sound of fists hitting the air as the girls tried to follow her lead.

Allison copied her movements, but her punches felt awkward.

"Your wrist is too loose," Mrs. Ashcroft said, stopping in front of her. "Straighten it. Again."

Allison reset her stance, clenching her fist tighter as she tried to ignore the flush creeping up her neck. She threw another punch, focusing on keeping her wrist straight.

"Better," Mrs. Ashcroft said with a small nod. "Keep going."

The drills went on forever. Straight punch, jab, cross. Change arms. Straight punch, jab, cross. Allison's arms started to ache, and sweat dripped down her forehead.

Finally, Mrs. Ashcroft clapped her hands. "One by one," she said. "Punch me. I'll call out corrections."

Allison's stomach dropped. Punch Mrs. Ashcroft?

"Maxwell."

Her name cut through the room.

She hated how shaky her legs felt, but she wasn't about to freeze up now. She stepped forward. Mrs. Ashcroft raised the padded mitts, her expression unreadable. "Straight punch. Jab. Cross," she said. "Go."

Allison threw the punches. The first hit felt weak. It barely made a sound.

She adjusted her stance and tried again, her knuckles landing harder this time. The soft thud sent a strange wave of satisfaction through her. She wasn't sure why, but it felt good.

"Good," Mrs. Ashcroft said. "Again. Faster."

Straight punch. Jab. Cross.

Her arms burned, but she kept going until finally Mrs. Ashcroft gave her a nod. "Not bad."

By the time class ended, sweat dripped down her back. Every muscle ached. But under all that exhaustion, something flickered.

Pride.

She grabbed her water bottle and towel. Decide not to become a victim.

As she walked to the changing room, she imagined Patrick standing in front of her.

Straight punch. Jab. Cross.

She imagined him going down on the floor, mouth gaping as she stepped back.

She grinned. Nope. She wasn't anyone's victim. And she was going to find out what else her mom was hiding.

Dinner had been quiet, but for the first time in a long time, Allison didn't feel weighed down by it.

She still had that energy buzz under her skin from class. Her arms ached, and her knuckles were sore, but that didn't bother her. She wasn't a victim. She was going to take control of her life, starting now.

She was curled up on the couch, her blanket draped over her. Outside, the city lights twinkled like frozen stars and the waxing moon nestled in the lower corner of her window.

Her tablet sat beside her, screen dimmed, displaying her half-finished visual summary of the U.S. government. She glared at it.

Checks and balances between the legislative, executive, and judicial branches. What a joke. It wasn't like it worked, anyway!

The government was supposed to protect people. But she'd already learned firsthand that courts could control lives, dictate choices, and decide futures. She shoved the tablet aside. It didn't matter. What mattered was getting answers.

She walked over to the smart wall and tapped the side panel. The control menu flickered on, and with a few quick selections, soft instrumental music filled the room. It wasn't really for her. She just didn't want anyone downstairs to hear what she was about to do.

"Jeeves," she said in a low voice. "Incognito mode."

"Incognito mode activated."

She slowly walked back to the couch. "What happens if a kid's parents aren't married before they're born?" she asked.

"In many jurisdictions, custody is determined based on legal agreements or court orders," Jeeves replied. "If the parents are unable or unwilling to take responsibility, the child may be placed with a relative or, in some cases, enter state care as a ward."

She hesitated, lowering herself onto the couch. "A ward?" she asked. "How does that work?"

"A minor can become a ward of the court when the state determines that their parents or guardians cannot provide adequate care," Jeeves explained. "This can result from legal disputes, neglect, or other risks to the child's well-being. A court-appointed guardian is assigned to manage the child's care until they reach adulthood."

Allison frowned. "Does that include unborn children?" she asked.

A pause and then a definition appeared on the smart wall. "Unborn children may be made wards of the state when a court determines that intervention is necessary to protect their health and well-being," Jeeves replied. "This typically involves the appointment of a guardian ad litem to represent the interests of the fetus until the child reaches legal adulthood."

Allison sat down on the couch, slouching down to get comfortable. "What about Wisconsin?" she asked. "Are the laws different there?"

"Accessing Wisconsin statutes."

A longer pause. A pair of documents appeared on the smart wall.

"Wisconsin law under statutes § 54.42 and § 54.25 outlines the rights and responsibilities of wards and their guardians," Jeeves told her. "For minors under state protection, custody arrangements require court approval. Guardians are obligated to act in the child's best interests, but oversight from the court ensured compliance."

"What kind of oversight?" she asked, her voice sharper now.

"Records indicate that custody agreements could involve measures such as mandated court oversight, restrictions on travel, and requirements for guardians to reside within court-approved boundaries," Jeeves explained. "In some cases, GPS tracking devices have been used to monitor compliance with court orders."

Allison stood up and gave her head a quick shake. Restrictions on travel. Court oversight.

It was just too much. The more questions she asked, the deeper she seemed to sink.

Focus, Allison, she told herself. "What's a guardian ad litem?" she asked.

"A guardian ad litem, or GAL, is a court-appointed advocate responsible for representing the best interests of a minor or unborn child in legal matters," Jeeves explained. "This includes providing recommendations to the court regarding custody, care, and welfare decisions."

Allison sat up, her motion so fast that she almost rolled onto the floor.

She'd heard that before, somewhere, a long time ago. "Am I a ward of the State of Wisconsin?" she whispered.

A pause. "Accessing public and family drive data," Jeeves responded.

Allison's heart pounded in her chest and she grabbed the blanket, twisting the fabric with shaking hands.

Then a document appeared on the smart wall.

"Allison Isabelle Williams Maxwell, born April 8, 2029, is a ward of the State of Wisconsin," Jeeves said. "Her guardian ad litem is attorney-of-record James Mueller, appointed August 25, 2028."

She froze.

The words stared back at her. A ward of the State of Wisconsin.

James Mueller. She knew that name.

She saw him every year when her parents met with him. He was always polite. Professional. Just another boring lawyer in a long line of lawyers that her parents employed.

But he wasn't just a lawyer. He was the one in charge of her life.

She slowly covered her stomach with both hands, her breathing shallow as she slouched back on the couch. "Oh," she whispered. "Okay, then."

She pushed herself up, legs a little shaky, and walked over to the small fridge built into her bookcase. She grabbed a Spezi, cracked it open, and took a long drink.

The fizziness burned her throat, but it didn't help with the acid in her stomach. "So, someone was making decisions about my life before I was even born?" she muttered.

"That is correct, Miss Allison."

She squeezed the bottle tighter.

"Court records indicate that the guardian ad litem was also present for all subsequent custody hearings and major decisions involving you."

Her head shook. "Why?"

"Records indicate that on August 24, 2028, your mother voluntarily visited Faith and Prayers Pregnancy Crisis Center for a routine pregnancy check," Jeeves told her. "Based on information provided during that visit, authorities took her into custody under an emergency order. She remained in detention until August 28, 2028, when further court proceedings were held."

"They detained her?!"

"Emergency court orders were issued based on allegations that her actions or circumstances posed a potential risk to the fetus," Jeeves told her.

Her stomach churned, and she had to set the Spezi down on the worktable. "Why?!"

"As part of these proceedings, your mother was temporarily detained for evaluation. Your father was served the following day, and both were required to appear in court."

She stared at the smart wall, not even blinking. "What happened?" she asked.

"Rylee Williams, age 18, was remanded to her parents' custody," Jeeves said. "Samuel Maxwell and Rylee Williams were required to participate in the Wisconsin Individual Family Educational Program. The court also ordered them to cohabitate from Rylee's third stage of pregnancy through their offspring's six-month birthday."

She felt lightheaded. "What about after I was six months old?"

Another pause. "Court records show your parents finalized a custody agreement," Jeeves told her. "You were to live with your mother during elementary school, live with your father during middle school, and return to your mother's custody for high school. The agreement also included a holiday schedule designed to give you equal access to both sides of your extended family. International travel for all three family members was prohibited without prior authorization."

The words landed like a punch. She'd always thought the back-and-forth between her parents was just how they worked things out.

It wasn't their choice. A judge had to decide.

Allison stared at the documents on the wall, her heart pounding. Detention? Court hearings? The whispering at family gatherings, the way her mom's family seemed to treat her like an outsider, the annual meetings with that attorney. It was all starting to make sense now.

She swallowed hard. "Jeeves, save a copy of all legal records and a copy of those Wisconsin State statutes to my personal drive. Encrypt it under my private key."

"Understood. Files have been saved and encrypted," Jeeves replied.

"End incognito mode and turn off the music," she told the AI.

There was a chirp followed by silence. Allison leaned up against a chair from her worktable, staring out at the moonlit skyline. Her mom's faint voice drifted up from downstairs, casually chatting with Aunt Mackenzie on a video call.

Her hands tightened on the back of the chair. She was going to figure out how to take that control back. Period.

Chapter Fifteen

Allison floated on her back, ears just below the warm water. The quiet around her felt safe, like a shield between her and the mess in her head. Sunlight filtered through the glass ceiling, making the water shimmer. She closed her eyes, trying to push the thoughts away, but they were impossible to ignore.

Michelle floated nearby, balanced against a bright orange pool noodle. Her arms draped loosely over the sides, her neck resting perfectly on its curve, keeping her effortlessly afloat. She flicked a splash of water at Allison.

Michelle frowned. "Are you gonna tell me what's going on, or do I have to guess?" Her voice was soft but insistent, her Italian accent lingering lightly on each word.

Allison licked her lips, staring at the rippling water. "It's everything," she said, her throat tight. "My whole life. Everything I thought I knew. It's all a lie. My parents, my family, even our so-called attorney, Mr. Mueller. They've all been lying to me."

Michelle tilted her head. "Okay, you're gonna have to spell that out because I have no idea what you're talking about."

Allison pressed her palms on the edge of the pool, her knuckles white. "I'm a ward of the state, Michelle. Wisconsin owns me. I didn't know until last night that someone else has been making decisions about my life since before I was born."

Michelle struggled to untangle herself from the noodle before treading water. "Woahwoahwoah," Michelle said. "What?"

Allison swallowed hard. "The State of Wisconsin literally appointed someone—not my parents—to make decisions for me. He's been doing it my whole life." She shivered, despite the warmth of the pool.

Michelle's face softened. She slid closer, lowering her voice. "That's messed up."

Allison's chest tightened, and suddenly the tears came. She couldn't hold them back. Michelle pulled her into a hug, and Allison didn't fight it.

When she finally pulled back, wiping her face with her hands. "Mr. Mueller isn't just some lawyer my parents hired. He was appointed by the Court. He's been my Guardian Ad Litem my whole life."

Michelle blinked. "Wait. Why?"

Allison's fingers curled around the towel in her lap. "Because my mom got detained before I was born," she said quietly. "Something about 'protecting the fetus'. The state didn't trust her to make decisions for herself, so the court stepped in. And they've been stepping in ever since."

Michelle let out a low whistle. "No wonder you're freaking out."

"Freaking out doesn't even cover it," Allison snapped, her voice cracking. "My whole life has been a lie. Like I've been living in a glass bubble, and everyone knew except me."

Michelle hesitated, then nudged her shoulder. "Come on. Let's get you wrapped up and into the sauna."

They waded toward the shallow end. The pool's edge blended seamlessly into the smooth tile. No steps, no border—just a gentle slope that led them out onto the patio. Michelle handed her a fresh towel that she had scooped up from a nearby recliner.

Inside the sauna, heat wrapped around them like a heavy blanket. Allison leaned back against the wooden wall, letting the heat seep into her skin.

"Start from the beginning?" Michelle asked gently.

Allison exhaled. "Patrick told me about my mom. That she was disowned."

Michelle frowned. "Still doesn't explain why Wisconsin—of all places would—" She paused, realization flickering across her face. "Wait. Was it because your mom got detained?"

Allison nodded, sniffling. She could feel the tears threatening to stream down her face.

Michelle stayed quiet for a moment. "So, what are you gonna do?"

"I don't know," Allison admitted. "I just—" She broke off, her voice catching. "I can't stay here. I want to live with my Uncle Josh and Aunt Elena. At least they're normal."

Michelle chewed her lip. "But how do you make that happen?" she asked. "Isn't your guardian, the Mueller guy, in charge of stuff like that?"

Allison hesitated, then nodded. "Yeah. But how do I even talk to him about it? What am I supposed to say? 'Hey, I'd like to move out of state because I hate my life'? That's not exactly gonna win me any points."

Michelle leaned back against the wooden seat. "Well, if he's supposed to look out for you, maybe just tell him," she told her. "Tell him you're not happy and see what he says." Michelle squeezed Allison's shoulder before standing. "Come on. Let's cool off and grab some fresh towels."

Allison slowly got up. "I could probably use some water," she told Michelle as she opened the sauna door.

"Agreed."

She followed Michelle out of the sauna, the rush of cooler air making her shiver. They grabbed fresh towels and water bottles from the cabana shelves, swapping out the damp ones, before heading to the recliners.

Michelle wrapped a smaller towel around her hair and sat down, stretching out. "So . . . are you going to call him?"

Allison shook her head. "I don't know," she replied. "He's been part of this whole mess from the beginning and never explained who he is and why we have to visit him every year. How am I supposed to trust him?"

Michelle sighed. "I don't know. But you're not gonna figure it out by just sitting here."

Allison shot her a glare. "I'm not just sitting here."

Michelle glanced at her lounger, then at her face, then back at the lounger. "Looks like it from here," she said, trying to hide a smile.

Allison let out a reluctant laugh, pulling her feet up onto the recliner. "Better?"

"Much better," Michelle said with a smirk.

Allison relaxed back into the recliner. Michelle was right. Maybe it was time to talk to Mr. Mueller.

Allison sat on the couch in her bedroom, rubbing her hands over her jeans. The familiar fabric, soft and worn, was the only thing that felt normal. She had hoped the shower would help, but she still felt like her skin didn't fit right.

She exhaled sharply. Enough waiting.

"Jeeves," she said, barely above a whisper. "Incognito mode."

"Incognito mode activated," the AI responded.

The room felt different now, quieter. She hesitated, then took a deep breath as she turned to look at the smart wall. Do it, she told herself.

"Jeeves, call Mr. Mueller's office." Her pulse jumped as the call connected. What if this was a mistake? What if he told her to talk to her parents instead? She stood up, ready to cut the call—

The screen flickered, and Mr. Mueller's face appeared.

Allison froze. She hadn't expected him to actually answer.

His sharp blue eyes dropped to his screen, then looked up at her. He was wearing the same dark blue suit, white shirt, and black tie he always wore. His brown hair was still combed perfectly, but there was more gray at the sides than she remembered. He squinted a little, like he wasn't sure why she was calling.

"Allison," he said, polite but cautious. "I wasn't expecting to hear from you." He glanced off-screen. "We're not scheduled to meet for a few months. Let me check . . . Yes, not until April."

Her stomach twisted. *He's already looking for a reason to end the call*, she thought.

Allison clenched the hem of her sleeve in her hand. "I know," she said, her voice too quiet. She cleared her throat. "I just—" *Say it!* "I needed to talk to you. Privately."

His expression didn't change, but she saw the slight shift in his posture. He was listening now. "Alright," he said. "What's wrong?"

She hesitated, her fingers nervously twisting the fabric of her sleeve. This is it, she told herself. No turning back.

"I want to live with my Uncle Josh and Aunt Elena in Wisconsin," she told him, surprised that she had been able to get that out without stuttering.

A brief pause. Not long enough to be surprised, but long enough that she knew he was weighing the request. "That's a big ask," he said evenly. "Can I ask why?"

Her stomach twisted with anxiety. Just tell him, she told herself. And don't let him talk you out of it!

"It's . . . everything," she said, forcing the words out. "I wasn't supposed to be back in the U.S. yet. I was supposed to stay with my dad in Hamburg until high school. But now, because of the war, I'm here, and nothing feels right."

Mr. Mueller just nodded. She hated that. Like he already knew the answer, but wanted to see if she did.

"In Hamburg, school was about learning real stuff. Like science, history, languages," she said, the words tumbling out. "Here, it's like all they care about is how we look and act. They keep talking about the 'role' we're supposed to fit into. Like we don't get a choice."

She swallowed, her jaw tightening. "And the classes? They're not normal. They mix in religion everywhere. They tell us women are supposed to be 'helpmates' and 'submissive'. That we should focus on being good wives and mothers instead of anything else."

She forced herself to keep going. "That's not what I believe. That's not what my family believes."

Mr. Mueller watched her. He seemed too calm. Shouldn't he be upset for her?

"What do you believe?" he finally asked.

Allison blinked. What kind of question was that?

She stood up straighter. "That men and women are equal," she said, firmer this time. "Women aren't supposed to just sit there and let men tell them what to do."

Another pause. "Have you talked to your parents about this?" he asked.

"They know," she said, gripping her sleeve again. "That's why they hired a tutor. They wanted me to keep up with what I'd be learning in Hamburg. And I am, kind of. But it's not enough. I don't belong here." She exhaled sharply. "I need to get out of Manhattan."

Mr. Mueller didn't nod this time. He leaned back slightly, considering. "And you believe your aunt and uncle would provide a better environment?" he asked.

"Yes."

"Why?"

Allison's pulse jumped. "Because they're normal," she said quickly. "They don't live in a locked-down city. They don't send their kids to a school that pushes a completely different religion on them. They care about what's happening in the world."

"Your parents also care about your education," he told her. "They picked out a top school in the area and brought in a tutor when it wasn't enough to keep you academically challenged."

Allison's nails dug into her palm. "My mom only cares about how that school looks. My dad won't come back here even though he could be killed in that stupid war."

Silence stretched between them.

"Allison," Mr. Mueller finally said, his tone coolly neutral. "Something like this needs court approval. There has to be a documented reason to change custody, something concrete."

Her stomach sank. "So, it's not enough to just say I'm unhappy?" she asked.

He exhaled. "The court looks at stability, maintaining strong relationships with both parents, making sure there's a measurable reason for change."

She turned away, backing up until she was able to sit on the couch. "So, what I want doesn't matter," she muttered.

Mr. Mueller's lips pressed together slightly. "I can understand why it feels that way."

She closed her eyes. She didn't want his understanding. She wanted an answer that wasn't no.

Her head dipped in a slow nod, but she was already moving ahead. If her feelings weren't enough, she'd find something else. Something that would prove she didn't belong here. Something they couldn't ignore.

"Okay," she said softly.

"We can circle back around this at our April meeting," Mr. Mueller said. "Take care, Allison."

The call disconnected, and the screen went dark. Allison found herself staring at the blank wall.

One thing was clear. This wasn't over.

Allison sat curled up in the big chair in the corner of the living room. The city lights made the sky too bright to see any stars. Snow was falling, but it melted as soon as it touched the stone path outside.

She held her mug of hot chocolate close to her face. It smelled like cinnamon. Her mom always added some. The marshmallows were almost gone, just blobs of sugar floating on top. She set it down on the side table. Her stomach was too upset.

Her dad sat on the couch, scrolling through his tablet. He'd flown in for Christmas, but he was already talking about leaving early because certain pieces of a critical component had unexpectedly come through. Her mom sat across from him, legs crossed, a book in her lap.

The room felt too still. She took a deep breath. "Dad?" she asked, her voice soft.

He looked up immediately. "What's up, kiddo?" He set the tablet aside and patted the cushion next to him. "Come sit."

Allison didn't move. She glanced at her mom, who lowered her book slightly to look at her.

"Why is everything changing?" she asked.

Her mom frowned. "What do you mean, sweetie?"

"At school. At church. Everywhere!" Allison told them. "It's like all the rules are different here, somehow. The boys are in charge, and no one questions it. They tell us we're supposed to be 'compliant' and 'submissive', like we're stupid or something. And if we say anything, they just—" She clenched her jaw. "They laugh. Like we don't even matter."

Her mom sighed. "I'm sure they don't mean it that way—"

"They do mean it," Allison interrupted. "They say it. To our faces. 'There they go again, opening their mouths again.'" The words came out fast, sharp. "And at church, it's even worse. They changed the guides for Women's Bible Studies. I know because I downloaded the originals." She looked up, meeting her parents' eyes. "They're completely different."

Her dad frowned. He glanced at her mom, who let out a slow breath and set her book aside.

"I'll look into it," he said after a moment.

Allison looked down at her hands. "You always say that," she muttered. "But nothing ever changes."

Her mom came to sit on the arm of Allison's chair. "It's okay to feel upset, Allison," she said. "I know it's hard. But you need to talk to us about these things."

Talk? That's what she was doing!

Her mom rested a hand on the back of the chair. "What you've been noticing isn't isolated. It's real. And it didn't start at your school or church."

She paused for a moment, choosing her words. "Men in this country have been angry for a very long time," she said. "Especially white men. They've been told they're at the top of the food chain. But every time someone else, someone not like them, gets an opportunity, they feel like they're losing something. Like their power is slipping away."

Allison looked up at her mom. "That's dumb," she said.

"Maybe," Mom said, her voice soft but steady. "But that's how they see it. And they're scared. The world is changing, sweetheart. Most of the opportunities aren't even in this country anymore. They're in places like Argentina, China, and

Kenya. And the men here? They see that, and they hold on tighter to whatever they have."

Allison blinked. "Is that why mixed marriages are illegal?" she asked.

Mom nodded. "It's all about control. About keeping things the way they've always been."

For a moment, Allison didn't say anything. The snow outside had slowed, blowing across the garden in small bursts of flurries.

She swallowed. "It's not just school or church," she said. "It's Patrick, too. He told me I'm not a part of the family. That Mom was disowned because of me."

Her dad sat up straighter. "Patrick said that?" he asked with a frown.

She nodded. "He hates me."

Mom exhaled, shaking her head. "Patrick doesn't hate you," she said, her voice calm. "But he is angry. At a lot of things."

She stared up at her mom, waiting for her to keep going. The firelight flickered across her face, and for the first time, Allison saw tiny stress lines around her eyes.

"Patrick's life is complicated," she said. "Your Aunt Chloe wanted a lot out of life. She thought she could balance everything. But our society doesn't let women 'have it all'. Not without consequences."

Allison frowned. "What kind of consequences?"

Her mom hesitated. "We talked about how your Aunt Chloe was removed as CEO by the family board of directors," she said. "There's more to the story."

Allison nodded.

"Well . . . " Mom glanced at Dad. He gestured for her to continue.

"Your great-grandfather told your aunt that she'd married down," Mom said, moving back to the couch. "Uncle Alexander didn't come from money. And he has spent years trying to prove he was good enough for The Firm."

She glanced at Dad. "Unlike your father, who doesn't care what anyone thinks. He built a global company from scratch and never looked back."

Her dad snorted.

"Patrick grew up hearing that his mom cared more about the business than about being his mom." Mom paused, looking up at the ceiling like she was trying to find the right words. "Aunt Chloe wanted to prove she could run the company. Your uncle turned it into a competition. Every time she succeeded, he acted like she'd beaten him, no matter how much money he'd made."

"So, Patrick got stuck in the middle?" Allison asked, confused.

Mom nodded. "Your aunt and uncle are legally separated. Not divorced, because that's nearly impossible. But they might as well be."

Dad leaned forward, his voice quieter now. "Look . . . whatever Patrick said to you, whatever he thinks, that doesn't make it true."

Allison blinked. "He said I don't belong. That Mom was disowned. That I'm not really family."

Her dad's jaw tightened. "You are. You've always been. Patrick's wrong. You are part of this family. And no one gets to take that away from you."

She didn't say anything for a second. "It doesn't feel like I matter," she whispered.

Her dad reached out, pulling her off her chair and into a hug. "You do matter," Dad said. Her mom came to sit next to him and rested a hand on Allison's back.

"I'll have a conversation with your aunt Chloe," her mom said. "I promise."

Allison leaned her chin on her dad's shoulder. They thought a hug and a promise would be enough. That she'd wait for them to handle it.

But she wasn't a little kid anymore.

She pulled away and went back to her chair. Decide to not become a victim.

Her mom was right. The world was changing, and she'd figure it out on her own.

Chapter Sixteen

The chess club was quiet except for the tapping of chess pieces on the boards. More of the seats were full today. Their etiquette teacher had mentioned that men appreciated women who understood the basics of the game. Not enough to win, just enough to be 'interesting'.

Allison adjusted the stiff collar of her blazer and stared at the chessboard, barely seeing the pieces. Across from her, Michelle tapped a captured rook against the table. "Well?" she asked in a low voice. "What happened over break?"

Allison exhaled through her nose. "Nothing useful."

"Puh-leez!" Michelle replied. "Your dad was home, right? So, give me the details!"

Allison rubbed at the side of her skirt. "I told my parents everything. About school, about church, about how none of it makes sense anymore. My dad actually made some calls and even talked to our pastor. But I don't think anyone took him seriously because he was talking about 'my concerns'."

Michelle frowned. "And your mom?"

Allison shook her head. "She said she's looking at high schools for me, but how does that fix anything now?"

Michelle sighed. "So, they're stalling." She looked down at the board. "It's your move," Michelle said, her voice soft but firm.

Allison reached for her knight. "They think things will just magically get better if we wait long enough." She moved the knight across the board and sat back. "I'm not even sure that working with a tutor is keeping me at grade level. Pastor is completely oblivious to the changes to Bible studies. And home? It's like I don't exist again. My mom's too busy trying to close some big deal."

Michelle leaned forward. "You talked to your attorney, right? What did he say?"

"Not much." Allison crossed her arms. "There's a family meeting in April. I can't wait that long. I need to move now."

Michelle made a face. "I'm sorry."

"More talking is not going to solve anything," Allison told her. "They all know what the problems are. No one is willing to step up and fix them." She closed her eyes.

Michelle picked up her stylus, twirling it between her fingers. "Your lawyer needs more, then."

Allison frowned. "More?"

"More to work with," Michelle told her. "Something solid."

Allison hesitated. "Like what? My parents aren't breaking any laws. I have a 'stable environment'." She made air quotes with her fingers. "On paper, I have everything."

Michelle tilted her head. "It's not about laws. It's about proving how this is affecting you. If there's anything—at school, at church, even at home—that shows how bad things are, you should start keeping track of it." She set her stylus down. "Write it down. Take videos. Whatever you can to prove that you need to leave here."

Allison tapped a finger against the table. "That feels . . . sneaky," she said with a small smile.

Michelle shrugged, a slight smirk on her face. "It's not sneaky if it's the truth. You deserve to be heard, Allison. If your parents won't listen, maybe this attorney guy will."

Allison didn't answer right away. Document it. She'd already started doing that, right? She had her birth certificate, her parents' marriage license, the family trust amendment.

"What do you think would count as proof?" she asked.

Michelle's frowned, thinking about it. "Anything that shows the pressure you're under," she finally said. "Vanguard school assignments, recorded lessons, notes of conversations. If the school's teaching something that doesn't match the school's written policy, that's a problem."

Allison nodded slowly. "I could check the school's handbook. Grab the comparison between Vanguard and Kaiserhof."

"Exactly." Michelle leaned in. "And if the Bible study guides are significantly different, it's time to download and compare them."

"I already downloaded the old guides," Allison said. "I just need to go through them."

Michelle smiled, looking down to study the board. "See? You're already ahead. Now, keep going." She tapped her stylus against the chess board. "Move your queen. I'm about to win, and I don't want to hear any complaints later."

Allison rolled her eyes and shifted her queen to safety. "Fine. But this game doesn't count."

Michelle grinned. "They never do."

Allison stepped into the changing area, listening to the murmur of voices as the group got ready for their next Krav Maga class. She let herself into a private dressing room and tapped her security bracelet to activate it. Then, she pulled the drape across the entrance and got into her training gear.

She unrolled her wrist wraps, sliding her thumb through the loop before winding the fabric around her wrist. Tight, but not too tight. Support, not restriction.

She pulled the second wrap tight; the material pressing into her skin. A chime signaled that class was starting. Outside, she heard Lexi teasing Rowan about taking too long.

Allison exhaled, shoved her bracelet and regular clothes into the storage drawer, and stepped out.

Lexi was already bouncing on the balls of her feet. "Ready?"

Not even close. But Allison nodded anyway. No more waiting.

The other girls followed her into the yoga room. The studio was cool, the rubber mats freshly scrubbed. Shelves along one wall were stocked with focus mitts, padded vests, and forearm guards.

Mrs. Ashcroft stood at the front, arms crossed. "All right, everyone, line up."

Allison took her place between Lexi and Rowan. Feet planted. Hands relaxed. Breathe.

They started with the warm-ups. Deep stretches. Controlled movements. The usual burn in her legs.

She ran through the motions but couldn't seem to focus. Instead, she found herself running down the list of things she needed to do. Find the prenup, if it existed. Have Jeeves do a systematic comparison of the differences between Vanguard, Kaiserhof, and the high school by her Uncle Josh's house. Save everything and keep digging.

Mrs. Ashcroft's voice cut through her thoughts. "Break up into pairs."

Allison barely registered the command before Lexi was standing in front of her, hands raised.

Lexi moved first with a jab. Not full force, just a drill. But Allison reacted a second too slow. She blocked, but her form was off. The impact rattled her arm.

Lexi didn't comment as she stepped back. Jab. Cross. Feint. Allison's right hand shot up to block a punch that never came.

Lexi dipped left instead. Allison tried to compensate and almost went down as Lexi's glove brushed her chin.

Dammit. She should have seen that coming.

"Maxwell." Mrs. Ashcroft's voice rang out. "Pay attention."

Everyone paused to look over at them. "Any distraction can be deadly," Mrs. Ashcroft said, slowly pacing along the side of the mat. "Situational awareness is key." She stopped in front of Allison. "You deal with this." She tapped the side of her head. "So you can deal with everything else."

She nodded at Lexi to step aside, then turned to face Allison directly. Allison barely had time to reset before Mrs. Ashcroft slid a focus mitt onto her hand and raised it.

"Punch me."

Allison clenched her jaw and struck. Her knuckles connected with the center of the mitt, the *thwap* of impact sharp in the silent room.

"Again."

The slap of leather against flesh echoed as Allison's punch landed harder.

"Again."

The next strike hit dead-center, sending a dull vibration through her arm.

"Harder."

Allison widened her stance, exhaled sharply, and drove her fist into the mitt. A satisfying crack filled the air.

"Faster."

Her heartbeat pounded in sync with the strikes. Each strike felt sharper. More controlled.

Mrs. Ashcroft's eyes stayed locked on her. And then—a blur of motion.

A sharp pop landed against Allison's shoulder, redirecting her punch. She wobbled. She hit the mat before she could recover.

Mrs. Ashcroft didn't move. "Good," she finally said, extending a hand to help her up. "Now, it's time you learned an offensive technique."

Allison stared up at her for a beat, heart pounding. Krav Maga was about control.

She gripped Mrs. Ashcroft's hand and let herself be pulled to her feet.

This time, she steadied herself before nodding. She clenched her fists, standing taller. "Show me."

Allison sat at the worktable in the middle of her room, her fingers tapping a restless rhythm against the smooth surface. The overhead lights were dimmed, casting long shadows along the edges of the room. The smart wall's glow was the only real illumination, its cool white screen waiting for her command.

"Jeeves," she said quietly. "Incognito mode."

The AI responded immediately. "Incognito mode activated."

Good. She straightened in her chair, choosing her words carefully. "I need to understand the legal process for modifying my court-ordered placement," she told Jeeves. "Specifically, what options exist for a ward of the state to request a change in residence that does not involve living with either biological parent?"

There was a pause. "Under current Wisconsin law, modifications to such an arrangement typically require evidence of extenuating circumstances," Jeeves told her. "Would you like an overview of the conditions under which a ward may request a reassignment to extended family?"

"Yes," she replied. "And filter for cases where the decision was based on stability, well-being, or emotional health."

"Understood." There was a pause, and then Jeeves responded. "Miss Allison, I have reviewed relevant legal precedents regarding the reassignment of wards of the state to extended family. Would you like a summary of my findings?"

"Absolutely," she said, straightening in her chair.

The smart wall lit up, displaying a streamlined report as Jeeves spoke. "Under Wisconsin law, a ward of the state may be reassigned to an extended family under specific conditions," the AI told her. "The courts prioritize keeping children with their biological parents whenever possible. However, reassignment may be considered if substantial evidence demonstrates that the current placement is unstable or detrimental to the child's well-being."

Allison leaned forward. This sounded different from what Mr. Mueller had told her. "What qualifies as 'substantial evidence'?"

"Cases that result in reassignment typically include a documented history of emotional distress, verified by school counselors, therapists, or guardian ad litem reports," the AI responded. "Courts also considered evidence of instability in the current placement, such as frequent moves, major disruptions, or a lack of parental engagement. Additionally, the child's preference could be weighed, but it is rarely the deciding factor. A strong pre-existing relationship with the extended family members petitioning for reassignment was also crucial, as was their demonstrated ability to provide long-term care."

Her stomach tightened. "So, I'd have to prove that my current situation is bad for me."

"Correct, Miss Allison," Jeeves replied. "Each case is unique. The court will evaluate a variety of factors to determine the most suitable living arrangement."

She pushed a hand through her hair, exhaling sharply. The system wasn't built for her. It was built to keep her where she was.

"What about the cases you found?" she demanded. "Do any of them match my situation?"

"There are no exact matches. However, in the cases where wards were reassigned to extended family, several common factors emerged," Jeeves told her. Several documents moved to the left side of the wall. "The most significant was ongoing emotional or physical distress in the current home, documented through multiple reports over time. Stability played a key role as well. If the current guardians could not provide a consistent, structured environment, the court was more likely to consider alternative placements. Another critical element was the child's relationship with the extended family members seeking custody. The courts favored situations where the child already had a strong bond with them and where those family members had demonstrated they were capable of providing a stable and supportive home."

Allison tapped the table, restless. "Jeeves, flag this research as ongoing," she ordered. "Update it with any new findings. And set periodic reminders to document anything that could support my case."

"Understood, Miss Allison," Jeeves replied. "Research flagged for continuous monitoring, and I have set periodic reminders for review."

She got up and paced. That wasn't going to help. Both of her parents provided stable homes and were supportive in their own way. What else?

She stopped, considering. What was on the family drive?

"Jeeves, access the family drive," she ordered. "Pull any documentation about the original placement plans or any documents that describe or impact my placement."

Jeeves paused for a fraction of a second. "There are a number of records, including the original custody agreements, archived guardian ad litem reports, state placement orders, caseworker notes, private school enrollment contracts as well as school performance records. Would you like me to retrieve the most recent files?"

"Yes. And highlight anything that mentions my emotional well-being." She hesitated, then added, "Especially anything about how custody was affecting me."

"Retrieving now."

Allison got up and paced in front of the smart wall again. Maybe she'd find something useful, something that would prove Manhattan was bad for her. Maybe there was an old report where she'd told a counselor she hated moving away from family.

"Compilation complete. Displaying relevant findings now."

Allison walked back to the worktable, watching as documents started to fill up the wall. Too many of them.

"Jeeves, provide key summaries for each document, one at a time," she told the AI.

"Understood," Jeeves replied. A line of documents appeared at the bottom of the wall. The farthest document on the left moved up and text appeared next to it:

Guardian Ad Litem Report, Age 6 (NYC - Living with Rylee Maxwell)

Miss Maxwell has successfully transitioned to living full-time with her mother after spending her early childhood with her father. While she has adjusted to her new routine, she occasionally expresses frustration with structured expectations and limited autonomy. She has indicated a strong attachment to her father and finds the infrequent visits with him difficult.

Allison's jaw tightened. "Save a copy to my personal drive under my private encryption key," Allison told Jeeves. "Next document." The document moved off-screen and was replaced with the next.

Guardian Ad Litem Report, Age 9 (NYC - Before Moving to Europe with Samual Maxwell)

Miss Maxwell has expressed a preference for spending more time with her father. While her mother provides a structured environment with extensive educational support, Allison appears more relaxed and engaged when discussing time spent with her father. Transitioning between parents may pose challenges due to differences in lifestyle and expectations.

She nodded, pursing her lips. So even back then, Mueller had noticed. "Save a copy to my personal drive under a private encryption key. Next document." Again, the current document moved off-screen, and another document took its place.

School Report, Age 10 (Europe - Living with Samuel Maxwell)

Miss Maxwell demonstrates strong academic progress and social adaptation. Teachers report that she is highly independent and well-adjusted. No behavioral concerns have been noted. She has briefly expressed concern about potential relocation, but there is no observed impact on academic performance.

She sat down at the table, her pulse speeding up. This was exactly what she needed, proof that she'd been struggling with this arrangement for years.

"Jeeves," she whispered, "save all of these to a secure folder with my encryption key. Cross-reference them with the legal cases you found. I need to know if there's a pattern."

"Saving now. Would you like me to draft a summary of the findings for your guardian ad litem?"

She blinked. That was a really good idea. "Yeah," she said, her voice steadier now. "Make it sound professional, like something a lawyer would put together."

"Compiling a draft now."

Time to move on. "Pull the official curricula for Kaiserhof, Vanguard, and Weston Prep," she told the AI. "Then, compare the coursework for my current grade level. Organize the data into a table highlighting key subject areas in STEM, humanities, religious studies, and leadership training. I need to see whether each subject is fully available, limited, or restricted, and flag any ideological or educational biases."

She started with Weston Prep. The Wisconsin school was one of the most prestigious private schools in the Midwest. It offered a full, high-level curriculum in STEM, humanities, and social sciences. It was the kind of education designed to produce CEOs, policymakers, scientists, and innovators. Exactly what she wanted. Plus, it was close to her Uncle Josh.

Next, Kaiserhof. She already knew the academic structure was relentless, designed to push students to their limits in STEM, humanities, international relations, and business. It was a school where excellence was demanded, not requested.

Finally, Vanguard. She forced herself to focus on the academics, skipping over the school's reputation as a breeding ground for America's elite. Full AP and Honors Tracks, with limited enrollment for girls. A dual-track system where male students were trained for leadership, power, and decision-making, while female students were gently guided toward a curated curriculum designed to prepare them for supporting roles as wives and mothers.

"Jeeves, what's the source for the information on Vanguard?" she asked.

"This data comes from Vanguard's website," Jeeves responded. "However, it is from an archived page that is no longer publicly available."

That was strange. "So, it's hidden?" she asked.

"It is no longer linked on their main site, but it still exists in their internal database archives," Jeeves told her. "It may also be accessible through direct searches using specific keywords."

She closed her eyes, shaking her head in disbelief. Wow. Hidden in plain sight.

"Jeeves," she whispered, gripping the edge of the table, "save all of these to a secure folder and end incognito mode." She walked over to the couch and sank into the cushions, staring at the documents on the smart wall. She hoped it was enough evidence to convince Mr. Mueller to help her.

Michelle flopped onto the couch in Allison's room, tugging her sleeves over her hands. "Okay," she said, "let's see what we're working with."

It had taken almost a week for her to work with Jeeves to find the documents, flagged messages, and historical documentation on her parents. She walked to her bedroom door and locked it, then had a seat next to Michelle.

"Okay, Jeeves," Allison said. "Time to go into Incognito mode."

"Incognito mode activated," Jeeves responded.

"Jeeves, open the summary that you created for the Milwaukee Family Court, please," she instructed the AI. The text appeared on the smart wall with key points highlighted.

"Summary of findings," Jeeves told them. "Court documents indicate that in cases where a minor petitions for a custody adjustment, the Guardian Ad Litem's recommendation carries significant weight. Historical precedent suggests success rates depend on the strength of justification. In addition, I have compiled a comprehensive analysis of the impact that the academic curriculum of Kaiser, Vanguard, and Weston Prep Academy would have on Ms. Allison's future grades and career choices."

"That's good," Michelle said.

"Estimated probability of approval based on current documentation: Thirty-eight percent," Jeeves replied.

Michelle groaned, pressing a pillow over her face. "Not great odds," she said.

Allison sat cross-legged on the couch, staring at the screen. "I basically have two choices: I can either send this to Mr. Mueller and hope that we can talk it through, or wait until our annual family meeting." She sighed.

"But you said that the family meeting isn't until April, right?" Michelle pointed out.

"Exactly," Allison replied. "Which means that I might be here for another school year if my mom feels that we need to stay in Manhattan because of her business."

Michelle sat up. "Then we need to do something drastic."

Allison arched a brow. "Like what?"

"Like, we book a flight to Milwaukee," Michelle said, her voice dropping a little. "Quick round trip. You need to meet with Mr. Mueller in person, talk to him face-to-face, and fly back before anyone even notices."

Allison shook her head. "Too much security. Even private flights get flagged in advance."

Michelle groaned. "Then what? Walk?"

Allison's mind raced. Something fast. Something discreet. Something outside her mother's reach.

She flicked her fingers again, closing the legal documents on the smart wall. "Jeeves, check if there's a high-speed train from Manhattan to Milwaukee."

"One moment," Jeeves replied. Then, text scrolled across the screen. "Hudson HyperRail. Daily departure: 10 a.m. Arrival in Milwaukee: 1:35 p.m. Return options to Manhattan proper: 3 p.m. and 5:15 p.m."

Michelle sat up fast. "That's perfect. We could be gone and back before dinner."

"Jeeves, does Mr. Mueller have an opening after 2 p.m. next week?" Allison asked.

"Accessing," Jeeves responded. "Wednesday, February 18, 1:50 p.m. is available."

Allison looked at Michelle and grinned. Allison could already see how it would work. No flight logs, and no security clearances. Just two kids on a train. If they timed it right, her mom would think she was at Michelle's, and Michelle's parents would think she was at hers.

"Book it!" she ordered Jeeves.

"A twenty-minute meeting with attorney James Mueller has been scheduled for February 18 at 1:50 p.m.," the AI responded.

"All we need to do is get the tickets," Michelle said, stretching out on the couch.

Allison smiled. "Leave that to me."

Chapter Seventeen

Today was the day. Vanguard had the week off for something called a 'Mid-Winter' break. Spring break wasn't until April, but this was a perfect time to get things moving.

Allison was sure they had everything covered. They'd told their parents they were going to a 'safe' shopping mall, maybe hanging out with a few friends, and taking some time to relax. Michelle's parents thought she'd be spending the night at Allison's. Allison's mom thought she was spending the night at Michelle's. It was the perfect cover.

They just had to make it to the 10 a.m. train to Milwaukee, meet with Mr. Mueller, and get back before anyone noticed. If they had to take the later train? Well . . . they'd figure it out.

Allison glanced at her security bracelet. The charge was low—just like she'd planned. If it died, it wouldn't ping her location. She slipped it onto her wrist, the weight of her backpack settling against her shoulder. Tucked inside was the data drive. It had everything: court documents, school reports, emails from her school counselors, and notes from the annual meetings with Mr. Mueller.

It had to be enough. It just had to be.

The lobby of the high-rise buzzed with its usual morning energy. Residents strolled through, chatting and sipping coffee while they waited for their pods to arrive.

Their security agent ushered them outside. He was older and part of Michelle's security detail. His black-and-white hair made him look like a low-level office worker, even with his conservative jacket and pants. But it was his shoes that gave him away. They were the standard boots of a security agent.

"Pod's waiting," he said, his voice neutral but firm.

Allison and Michelle exchanged a quick glance before stepping outside. The pod was parked at the curb. The doors slid open with a quiet hiss. The agent motioned them inside first before taking a seat in the front.

The Infinity Galleria wasn't far, but it was far enough that their parents wouldn't let them walk. It was one of the few shopping centers left where ultra-high-end brands coexisted with independent boutiques.

The pod ride was silent except for the occasional thrum as it adjusted speed. Michelle drummed her fingers against the seat, glancing at the agent, who kept his gaze trained on the passing cityscape.

As the Infinity Galleria's glass facade came into view, Allison's heart started pounding. Sunlight bounced off the arching rooftops, blending natural elements with a futuristic design. This was it. No turning back.

The pod doors slid open, and they stepped onto the walkway leading inside. Their agent followed, ignoring the pod as the mall's remote controls moved it to the parking structure.

The mall stretched before them, an indoor-outdoor maze of high-end stores and cafés. The scent of coffee and fresh pastries filled the air. Shoppers weaved their way through the crowd, voices low and shopping bags swinging. It was a busy morning.

Almost immediately, Allison noticed a security agent near the elevators. She seemed to be tracking them with casual disinterest. They had their own security, so they weren't a threat. Two more were positioned farther down, one outside a jewelry store, the other lingering in the courtyard. They all looked bored.

The goal was to slip away without drawing attention. Allison was happy that Omega wasn't with them. She was much more observant than Michelle's guy.

"We need a little space, okay?" Allison called back to their agent, keeping her voice steady. "It's girl talk."

The agent nodded, stepping back just enough to give them some distance. Close enough to watch and far enough away to give them breathing room.

Michelle leaned in, speaking just loud enough for him to hear. "So, did you hear? That boy from Civics class? Beatrice was all over him in the library. I heard they got called to the headmaster's office!"

Allison faked a gasp, barely suppressing a nervous laugh. "No way!"

The agent smirked at their 'girl talk' and backed off a bit more, giving them a few extra feet of space as they walked deeper into the mall. Good, she thought. Now for the hard part.

They walked arm-in-arm, chatting about nonsense, glancing at storefronts, trying to look like they belonged. They wandered past dozens of stores, trying to look like they were interested. Every time they tried to pull ahead, the security agent matched them, step for step.

Michelle tilted her head just slightly, catching the time on a display near the escalators. "It's 9:20," she muttered. "Any ideas?"

Allison scanned the stores. They couldn't just run. They needed a distraction.

Then, she saw it. A boutique nestled between a café and a jewelry store. Stylish but not flashy. Nearly empty. The woman behind the counter was already watching them with a concerned frown.

"Follow me," Allison whispered.

They stepped inside; the door chiming. The woman behind the counter flicked her gaze outside, eyes locking onto their agent standing by the window.

"Hi, welcome to Beyond," the woman said, not quite making eye contact as she continued to keep an eye on the man. "I'm Cassie. What style can we help you create today?" She gestured to the jewelry and clothing racks on either side of the boutique.

Their security agent entered, hovering near the entrance.

Allison stepped closer to the counter, lowering her voice. "That man—he's been following us. We're scared."

Cassie's eyes darkened. "Jasmine," she called, brushing a small pin on her sweater. It was shaped like two hands clasped together. She tapped it twice. "Can you and Esta take another look at the display, please? I believe that dress might no longer be in stock."

Jasmine, who had been folding clothes nearby, froze for only a second. She straightened, smoothing her hands over her dress. "Of course," she said, moving toward the display.

Allison wasn't sure what the pin meant. It had to be important because Jasmine and another associate immediately began to pull everything out of the display case, starting with the mannequins. They stepped between him and the entrance, shifting mannequins, effectively blocking the agent's line of sight.

Cassie turned back to Allison and Michelle. "Hurry!" she whispered.

She led them toward the back. "Beth, bring out the new inventory," she called over her shoulder.

Another woman hurried past them, arms full of clothes. "I can't believe that you forgot to change things up," she said loudly. "This should have been done weeks ago!"

Cassie guided the girls through a door marked Employees Only and into a narrow stockroom. Cassie followed, her voice low as she tapped her pin. "If you need help again, look for someone wearing this symbol."

"Thank you," Allison whispered.

"That's what we're here for," Cassie told her. "Now, go. Out back, there's an alley. Take a right. Now, run!"

Cold air slapped Allison's face as they bolted. The alley was narrow, lined with dumpsters and graffiti-covered brick walls. They raced past a few delivery drones that were parked on both sides of the alley, their status lights blinking in standby mode.

They burst out of the alley and onto a quiet side street. Allison's heart pounded as they frantically looked in every direction. Cassie had told them to make a right. The SkyRail station had to be close. She could see the tracks above the street.

She glanced back. The alley was empty, but that didn't mean that security wasn't looking for them already.

They started jogging. The walkway was slippery, and their shoes slapped against the wet pavement. Up ahead, the transit hub rose above the street, a web of platforms and walkways suspended over the road. The entrance was up on an overpass, with ramps and escalators twisting up toward the main part of the station.

Michelle grabbed her arm. "Come on! Let's get there before he figures it out!" They took off running.

Inside was chaos. People everywhere. Arrival times flashed overhead, changing so fast Allison couldn't keep up. Walkways made of glass stretched across the open space above them. People brushed past her from all sides. Elbows, bags, shoulders, like she wasn't even there. Some rushed toward the platforms, others stopped at kiosks, holding up the lines as they tapped their wristbands or argued with the machines. Even their voices blurred together, mixed with echoing announcements and the rumble of trains overhead.

Michelle pulled her to a nearby kiosk and tapped it. "Which line takes us to Grand Central Terminal?"

"Track 1973," the AI responded in a crisp, automated voice. "Departure is every five minutes." A map flickered to life, a blue arrow pointing them toward the far right side of the concourse.

Michelle grabbed Allison's hand as they weaved through the crowd. The entrance to Track 1973 was lined with translucent security barriers, scanning commuters as they stepped inside. No turning back now.

The doors slid open, revealing a sleek monorail cabin. Unlike the compact four-seater pods, these were larger transit cars with glass walls, designed for longer trips. Each car had eight seats. The seats were padded but firm, with slim digital panels embedded into the armrests.

They slipped inside just as the doors sealed shut. They barely had time to grab an open seat before a gentle vibration ran through the floor. The cabin disengaged from the platform and began to accelerate along the track.

Allison exhaled, heart racing. The city outside rushed past in a blur of towering buildings and illuminated transit lanes. The ground below looked impossibly distant, an endless sprawl of buildings and glowing highways, the lower city nearly swallowed in darkness.

Allison hesitated, rolling her security bracelet between her fingers. It was warm from her skin and the was charge completely drained. If it was dead, did she really need to get rid of it?

She glanced at Michelle. They couldn't be sure there wasn't an emergency tracker inside. Better safe than caught. She shoved it under the cushion, pressing it deep into the fabric, then sat back. Michelle did the same.

She glanced at Michelle. "We actually did it," she whispered, almost not believing it.

Michelle grinned. "You were right. This worked." She leaned back, shaking her head. "When we get home, we'll just say we accidentally left them in a boutique. We have no idea how they got on the SkyRail."

As the capsule glided toward Grand Central, Allison ran through the plan again. Stage one: Ditch security. Done.

Stage two: Get on the train without drawing attention. Two unaccompanied kids were suspicious. Luckily, Jeeves had been able to help with that.

The doors slid open, and they stepped onto Grand Central Station. A rush of people moved around them, fast and unpredictable. Rolling suitcases bumped along the floor, voices echoed overhead, and the sharp chime of a departure bell rang through the station.

Allison stole one last glance at the seats where they'd hidden the trackers. Her hands were shaking. Was it fear? No ... excitement. Yeah. That had to be it.

The terminal was huge. The ceiling stretched high above them, painted with constellations in faded blues and golds. She'd read once that the stars were painted backward, a mistake no one had ever fixed. It made the whole place feel upside down, like she was standing under a sky that wasn't really there.

Announcements crackled over the speakers, calling out train departures. People hurried past, some scanning their bracelets at kiosks, others heading straight for the platforms.

Michelle leaned in close, practically buzzing. "This is it. Next stop, Milwaukee. We're gonna make this work."

Allison nodded. Now, they just needed to find their train!

They wandered through the crowd, following the signs for regional departures. It took a few wrong turns and one escalator ride too far before they finally found the right level. The train to Milwaukee was tucked away on a sublevel. It was much quieter than the upper platforms, with fewer people and lower ceilings. Everything down here looked older, like it had been part of the station forever. When the train slid into view, sleek and silent, Allison took a deep breath. This was it.

Allison stepped onto the train, her flats barely making a sound on the smooth, frictionless floor. The doors closed behind them. The maglev superconductors buzzed underfoot, a quiet reminder that they had started moving.

Michelle stuck close behind, gripping her backpack straps. She leaned in. "Where do we go?"

Allison scanned the car, her stomach tightening. The rows of gray seats stretched forward in identical sections, passengers already settling in. No signs or arrows pointed them toward the staterooms, just an overhead display with random letters and numbers.

"I don't know," she admitted. Her only experience with public transport was airport shuttles and short-range pods. Trains weren't part of her world.

Michelle sighed. "Great."

Allison pulled out her travel tablet and tapped through the booking details. "State Room E," she read aloud, glancing at the numbers along the overhead displays.

Michelle squinted at the signs. "Okay, so would that be SR E. So, that way?" They started walking, dodging rolling suitcases and stepping aside for passengers to settle into their seats.

They'd changed at Grand Central, swapping out their usual clothes for hoodies and jeans. Just comfortable, ordinary clothes. Allison hid a smile. They needed to be forgettable and blend in. Just two kids on a train.

Sunlight streamed through the panoramic windows, flashing across the aisle as the train shot past glass towers and smaller buildings. Allison adjusted her backpack, pretending she wasn't scanning for security cameras or suspicious glances. If they acted like they belonged, no one would question them.

"Keep walking," Michelle whispered, nudging her shoulder.

They hadn't made it far before a voice cut through the quiet. "Excuse me."

Allison's stomach flipped. She slowly turned around.

A man in a black-and-white uniform stood a few feet away. His badge caught the light. Chadd. He looked them over, lingering on their hoodies and backpacks. Not a good sign.

"Tickets?" His tone was polite, but something in the way he said it made her feel like they'd already been caught.

Allison forced herself to breathe and pulled her tablet from her pocket. The screen blinked awake as she tapped the screen. "Here," she said, keeping her voice even. "Stateroom E."

Chadd studied the screen. His frown softened when he saw the reservation details. Staterooms weren't cheap. But then he scrolled lower, and his expression changed. "Unaccompanied minors?"

Allison forced herself to nod. "Yes, sir. This trip was a gift from my grandma. My mom dropped us off, and my uncle's picking us up in Milwaukee." She shrugged like it was no big deal. "It's his birthday."

She swiped to the next screen, showing the approval note. "See? The NYC terminal cleared it." Thanks to Jeeves sending an alert through to cover us, she thought.

Chadd hesitated, then smiled. "Let me show you to your stateroom," he said. "It's at the very end of this car. This way, please."

She exhaled slowly and tried not to look nervous. Just act normal, she told herself. She looked back at Michelle, who gave her a quick thumbs-up, barely moving her hand.

They followed Chadd to the back of the train, weaving past rows of gray seats. Business people were busy with smart displays, parents tried to wrangle bored kids, and a bunch of students sat with their AR bands on, totally zoned out.

No one even looked at them. Good. When they reached their stateroom, Chadd slid open the door and stepped aside.

"Meals, drinks, and snacks are included," he said, pointing to a slim touch panel on the wall. "Here's the menu and the button if you need any assistance."

"Thank you," they said in unison. The door clicked shut behind him.

For a second, neither of them moved. Then, Michelle dropped onto one of the couches, her arms and legs sprawled like she owned the place. "Grandma, huh?" Michelle drawled with a grin. "Lemme guess. You had Jeeves hack the transit system."

Allison set her backpack on the seat next to her. "No," she said with a small smile. "Even Jeeves isn't that good."

Michelle raised an eyebrow. "So, where'd you get the money?"

Allison adjusted the strap on her bag. "The money's mine," she admitted. "I used my credit card, signed my grandma's name for authorization, and had Jeeves file the unaccompanied minor paperwork."

Michelle blinked, then let out a low whistle. "Okay, you're a legend."

Allison shrugged, trying to play it cool. "Took you long enough to notice."

Michelle rolled her eyes. "I don't know about you, but I'm starving!" Michelle told her. She got up and looked over the menu. "I know what I want. Now, what are you having?"

Allison got up and ordered something at random. She couldn't focus. Her stomach was still upset, but maybe food would help.

Their meals arrived pretty fast. For a moment, it was easy to pretend this was just a normal trip. Michelle's French toast was stacked with berries and powdered sugar. Allison's scrambled eggs and crispy potatoes tasted way better than she expected. The sparkling water fizzed against her tongue, crisp and cold.

By the time the plates were cleared, the city had disappeared. Endless fields stretched out behind them. In the distance, wind turbines dotted the horizon, their giant blades turning slow and steady.

Allison pressed her forehead against the window. The train was too fast to make out anything for long. She glimpsed worn roads, barns, and the occasional highway exit. It felt unreal, like a dream she'd barely remember when she woke up.

"Relax," Michelle said, nudging her knee. "We've got this."

Allison nodded. The truth was, she had worked hard to make this trip seem easy. Like sneaking away to board a maglev train and tricking a corporate AI booking system was just another day for her. But for Allison, this wasn't just an adventure. It was about her future.

"What are you gonna say to him?" Michelle asked, stretching out her legs. "Your lawyer, I mean."

Allison pulled up her notes on the tablet, the screen casting a faint glow on her face. "I'm going to remind him that the Unborn Child Protection Act gives me rights," she said. "That's why I have a Guardian Ad Litem in the first place. He's supposed to be on my side." She scrolled through her notes. "If I can show him that living with my Uncle Josh is better for me, legally, he has to take it to court."

Michelle tilted her head. "And if your parents find out?"

"Hopefully, by the time they even realize what's happening, it'll be too late," Allison told her. "The court will have ruled in my favor and there's nothing they can do about it."

She glanced at the window, watching the fields blur by. "I can't keep living like this, Michelle. It's just too much." She swallowed hard. "Uncle Josh is my best shot at a normal life. I like the Mequon area. I love the church they go to and I miss my cousins. They don't treat me like my mom's family does."

Michelle didn't answer right away. Then, finally, she nodded. "Okay. I'll wait outside while you talk to him. Just . . . don't let him shut you down." She nudged Allison's foot.

A small smile tugged at Allison's lips.

Chadd was waiting for them as the train slid into Milwaukee. When Allison opened the door, he gave a quick nod. "This way, please."

Cold air blasted in the second she stepped onto the platform. It crept through her hoodie, biting at her fingers and ears. Way colder than New York.

She hunched her shoulders and followed Michelle, moving as fast as she could. The platform was half-covered, wind cutting through the open edges. Ahead, a wide walkway led toward the main station, its glass doors sliding open as people streamed inside.

The station was warm but loud. Voices bounced off the high ceiling, a mix of conversations, rolling luggage, and the occasional announcement over the PA. Near the entrance, a woman in a black-and-white uniform stood waiting.

"She'll take you to your car," Chadd told them.

The woman smiled. "Right this way, girls."

Allison tapped her tablet, summoning the auto-drive pod she'd reserved. As it pulled up, she and Michelle waved like someone inside was expecting them.

"Thanks for your help," Allison said smoothly. The woman nodded, satisfied, and went back inside.

As soon as they climbed in, the doors sealed and the pod hummed to life. For a long second, neither of them spoke. Then, Michelle let out a shaky laugh. Before Allison could stop herself, she laughed too.

"We made it," Michelle said with a wide grin. She stretched her legs out, knocking Allison's foot. "Plenty of time to get to your attorney's office."

Allison leaned back against the seat. Almost done, she told herself. *Mr. Mueller has to fix this. It's his job, right?*

The pod slowed to a stop, its doors sliding open with a soft hiss.

Allison stepped onto the sidewalk and slung he backpack over one shoulder. The cold air bit at her cheeks, the sky overhead a dull, overcast gray. The office tower in front of her was nothing like the sleek, polished buildings in Manhattan.

Michelle followed, adjusting her backpack. She looked around, frowning at the quiet, mostly empty street. "So, this is what the rest of the country looks like?" Her accent made it sound more curious than rude.

"It's Milwaukee," she replied, tugging her backpack higher on her shoulder. "They don't rebuild everything every five minutes."

The building was plain, all straight lines and gray stone. No flashy digital signs, no sky bridges—just an old-school metal entry door and a lobby barely big enough for a security desk.

They took the elevator up in silence. It creaked as it rose; the panel lighting up with each floor.

When the doors finally opened, they stepped into a long hallway. Every door looked the same with frosted glass with names printed in blocky black letters. Some of the letters were faded, like no one had updated them in years. Framed posters and papers covered the walls, some in English, some in Spanish. Know Your Rights. What to Expect in Family Court. Legal Aid Hotline. All of them with the same serious, don't-mess-around font.

Between them were old black-and-white photos of Milwaukee. Bridges, factories, people standing around looking important. Someone had tried to make it look historic, like it mattered. It just made the place feel old.

"Come on," Allison said, gesturing for Michelle to follow. At the end of the hall was a frosted glass door with 'James Mueller' etched in black letters. Allison pushed it open and stepped inside.

A woman sat behind the reception desk, using a flat-panel screen with an old-school keyboard. Her gray hair was pulled into a neat bun, and glasses perched low on her nose.

"Hi, I'm Allison Maxwell," Allison said. "I have a meeting with Mr. Mueller."

The receptionist nodded, fingers flying across the keys. "He'll be with you shortly. Please have a seat."

Allison hesitated before sinking into one of the black leather chairs. Her confidence had faded, her fingers gripping her backpack straps. Michelle sat next to her, bouncing her foot.

A few minutes later, the door to the inner office opened, and Mr. Mueller stepped out. He was tall and wiry. His eyes flicked around the room before landing on them.

"Allison," he said with a nod. "Come on back."

She stood and looked at Michelle. "Will you come with me?" Allison asked.

Michelle nodded. They followed him down another short hallway and into his office. It was bigger than the waiting room. A heavy wooden desk sat in the center of the room. Bookcases packed with thick, ancient legal volumes lined the walls.

He gestured for them to sit down as he shut the door. He moved around to the other side of the desk, looking from Allison to Michelle and back.

"I'm sorry, I don't believe we've met before, Miss . . . " He waited for Michelle to answer.

"Michelle Bartoni," Michelle responded. "I'm a friend of Allison's."

Mr. Mueller inclined his head to her. "It's nice to meet you, Michelle." Then he turned to Allison. "Where are your parents?" he asked, his voice firm. "According to my calendar, this was supposed to be a family meeting."

Allison took a deep breath. "I came alone," she admitted. "I need to talk to you about the custody arrangements."

Mr. Mueller's lips pressed into a thin line. If anything, he looked disappointed. "You know I can't meet with you without notifying your parents. We've had this discussion, Allison."

He looked at Michelle. "Would either of you like something to drink?" he asked.

Michelle looked at Allison, a worried frown on her face. She shook her head as she turned back to Mr. Mueller. "No, thank you."

Mr. Mueller nodded and pressed a button on his desk. "Zoe, could you step in for a moment?"

A few seconds later, a young woman with auburn hair entered the room.

He spoke to her quietly. "Please notify Allison Maxwell's parents that she's here in my office, along with her friend, Michelle Bartoni. Michelle, Zoe will need your parents' contact information."

Michelle nodded.

"While Zoe takes care of that, why don't I have a quick conversation with Allison?" Mr. Mueller said as he looked at Allison.

Her stomach sank. She glanced at Michelle, but there was nothing either of them could do now.

She got up and followed him into the conference room next door. Glass walls faced the hallway, making the room feel too open, like anyone could be watching. Across from the door, tall windows showed off the skyline. To the right, a huge bookcase sagged under old legal books, their cracked spines stuffed tightly together. A smart wall glowed with documents and what looked like case files.

Allison paused. The glowing tech felt out of place. The rest of the room looked like some old professor's office.

They sat down at a small oval table in the center of the room. Allison placed her backpack on the floor and dug out the data file.

Mr. Mueller folded his hands on the table. "Allison, I shouldn't be meeting with you without your parents." His voice had that calm, patient tone, like he was explaining something obvious.

Allison swallowed hard. "I had to come. I found things that might change the custody arrangement." She pushed the data file across the table.

Mr. Mueller hesitated, then picked it up and plugged it into the smart wall. Documents spread across the screen. "What am I looking at?" he asked.

Allison took a deep breath. "Reports about how I handled all the moves, school counselor reports, grades." She tapped a finger against the wooden table. "But I added more."

She sat up a little. "There's a report about how the war in Russia is affecting families in Hamburg. My dad's stuck there, and it's not safe, but the supply chain issues keep him from leaving."

She hesitated, then said, "I also included some stuff about the Church of Rising Grace Fellowship. They're everywhere now. In my school. In Bible study. Even in my mom's church."

Her voice wavered. "It's not what my parents taught me. It's not what church used to be. But now it's in school lessons, the homework, the prayers . . . like someone changed everything when nobody was paying attention."

She swallowed hard. "I don't know who to talk to about it anymore. Everyone just acts like it's normal."

Mr. Mueller nodded absently as he scrolled through the files. He stopped on one, moving it to the front. "What's this?" he asked.

"It's an amendment to the Williams Family Trust," she told him, feeling the tears start.

Mr. Mueller sighed. "I shouldn't—"

"Please," Allison blurted out. "They disowned my mom because of me!"

Mr. Mueller turned around, adjusting his glasses as he looked at her. His expression remained unreadable.

"Allison," he said carefully, "I understand why this would be painful for you to read, but this is something that you should have talked over with your parents."

"I did!" Allison told him, almost yelling in frustration. "But my mom brushed it off! Neither of them care about what's happening to me." She clenched her hands into fists. "I can't live in Manhattan anymore. I just can't."

Mr. Mueller leaned back, looking sympathetic and maybe even a bit sad. "I'll review these documents and anything else you find," he said, "but this isn't enough to take to court." He leaned back in his chair. "I will, however, recommend that you receive counseling. Your sudden relocation to the U.S. and the Russian invasion seem to be causing you significant distress."

Counseling?! Before she could respond, there was a sharp knock followed by Zoe peeking her head in, her expression tight.

"Allison's mom is here," she said.

Mr. Mueller glanced at Allison. "That didn't take long," he said. "Bring her back, please."

Chapter Eighteen

The pod hummed as it moved through the streets, the gentle vibrations buzzing against Allison's back. Through the tinted window, Midtown loomed with its gleaming towers and elevated streets, the carefully curated version of Manhattan. The version they wanted you to see.

But beyond the security barriers, past the checkpoints and restricted zones, there was another city. The one slowly being swallowed by the ocean. The one left behind. The one no one talked about.

Allison clenched the hem of her hoodie, her fingers curled tight in her lap.

Her mom sat beside her, silent and stiff. She hadn't looked at Allison once since they left the private terminal in Milwaukee. Hadn't spoken since the plane landed, except for one sentence: "Your father's flight lands in six hours."

That was it. Not 'Why did you do this?' or 'What were you thinking?'

Just silence.

On the plane, her mom hadn't even touched her tablet. No emails, no voice messages, no conference calls. It just sat in her bag, if she'd brought it at all.

That was the worst part.

And when the plane landed, she had turned to Michelle with that same eerie calm. "Your parents should be here to pick you up."

They were. Their limo pod waited on the tarmac. Michelle's mother didn't say a word. She pulled her inside without looking back. Her father followed, scolding in rapid, clipped Italian.

Michelle glanced over her shoulder one last time. A quick wave. A frustrated shake of her head. Then the door closed, and she was gone.

It was Allison's fault. All of it.

Her dad had dropped everything to rush back. He'd abandoned the Elbe Project, the one thing not even a Russian invasion could make him leave. Because of her.

She swallowed hard and pressed her forehead against the cool glass.

They'd known Vanguard was bad. That's why they hired a tutor. She'd told them religion had seeped into her classes, that something felt off. Not loud or obvious, just steady and constant, like a drip. But they hadn't listened.

Now it was clear. They weren't just teaching obedience. They were training her to be a perfect wife. To marry the right man. To uphold a new tradition, so carefully and quietly stitched into American life that no one stopped to ask where it came from.

She once heard a story about boiling a frog. Drop it into hot water and it will jump out. Heat the water slowly, and the frog won't notice until it's too late.

Is that what happened to her mom? Had she even noticed? Or had it all changed so slowly that it felt normal?

Allison shook her head in frustration. If she had never moved to Germany, would she have asked why her classes were getting smaller, why her books were shorter, why everything felt easier? Or would she have just gone along with it?

Just that thought made her stomach churn.

She hadn't meant to scare her parents. But if she didn't leave now, she knew what would happen. One day, she'd stop arguing. She'd stop fighting it because she'd stop being herself.

The pod slowed as it neared the high-rise, its steel-and-glass entrance glowing under the golden lights. Two security guards at the door stood at attention.

Allison inhaled sharply, gripping her seat. Six hours before her dad came back. And she had no idea what to do.

Jeeves' voice cut through the darkness. "Good morning, Miss Allison. Today is Thursday, February 18, and the time is 7 a.m. The weather in Manhattan is currently 15 degrees, with a forecast high of 37 degrees."

She groaned, pulling the blanket over her head. Her body felt heavy, her eyes swollen, like she hadn't slept at all.

"Your parents are waiting for you at the breakfast table."

That jolted her awake. Her dad. He was here.

She sat up too fast, her head spinning. Swallowing hard, she yanked a brush through her tangled hair, wincing at the knots. Jeans, flats, her purple hoodie. Her favorite t-shirt underneath, soft and worn. Something familiar. Something safe.

The apartment was too quiet as she walked toward the dining room. Normally, Maria would be working in the kitchen, music playing. But now, it was just her own footsteps against the carpet.

She hesitated at the doorway. Both of her parents sat at the table, coffee cups in front of them.

Something was wrong with her mom. No makeup. Puffy eyes. Her hair was pulled back like she didn't care how she looked. Had she been crying?

Maybe. But it was her dad who caught her attention.

He looked exhausted. She'd seen him pull all-nighters before, but this was different. His skin looked pale, almost gray, like someone had wrung him out and left nothing behind.

Maria quietly slipped in to refill their coffee. When she returned to set a glass of orange juice in front of Allison, she didn't even make eye contact. That was a bad sign.

"Allison." Her dad's voice was calm. "Are you okay?"

She nodded, swallowing against the lump in her throat. "Yeah. I'm fine."

He sighed, rubbing his forehead. "Your trip to Milwaukee had . . . consequences."

Her mom's arms were crossed, lips pressed tight. She didn't say a word, just held her coffee mug close and let her dad speak.

"When you left Manhattan, it triggered an emergency alert. A full lockdown."

Her stomach dropped. "What?"

"They shut down all of Manhattan." His voice was too steady, too controlled. "There were raids into lower Manhattan and parts of the upper west side. Immigration blocks searched. Suspected crime fronts torn apart. People were detained, Allison."

Her throat tightened. "I—I didn't know."

"People who commute to Midtown have lost security access," he continued. "They had to let security search their homes. If they refused, they were arrested." He paused to look at her. "Going forward, all workers who work in Midtown will only be given daily passes. This means that anyone who works here must have their access reauthorized every single day. No authorization, no access."

Allison looked down at her hands.

"The official story is that you were abducted while shopping," her dad told her. "A team found your security bracelet in a SkyRail capsule. A federal terrorist alert went out."

Her heart started pounding. "Terrorists?" she whispered.

Her dad nodded slowly. "Because of our family's status, they assumed—" He stopped, exhaling sharply. "They assumed you'd been taken as some kind of political statement."

Allison stared at him, acid pouring into her stomach. She had known she was taking a risk, but she hadn't thought—hadn't realized—

"You have no idea what you set in motion," her mother told her in a gentle voice. "Businesses have been closed down. Security has been increased because you exposed a loophole in Manhattan's security coverage."

Her dad closed his eyes for a moment before looking at her. "I'm not angry," he said quietly. "I just need you to understand."

Allison gripped her orange juice, her fingers pressing into the cold glass. She had wanted to convince Mr. Mueller to let her move in with her aunt and uncle. Instead, she had set fire to an entire city.

"Michelle's parents have asked that you no longer socialize with their daughter outside of school," her mother said. "Since you will be leaving Vanguard at the end of the year, they did not request you be pulled out early."

The world shrank around her. Michelle was gone. Just like that.

"As far as your security bracelet goes, it will have to be reprogrammed," her father added. "You'll be allowed access to our home, your school, and your mother's women's club. That's it. If you try to go anywhere else, your mother will have to authorize it in advance." He paused, sighing. "I've also been advised that they need your original building pass card."

Allison looked from one parent to the other, horrified. So, not only was she grounded, but she couldn't visit any other part of the building without authorization? What was this, a prison?

"Starting today, Jeeves will monitor all of your communications. That includes calls, messages, and anything that isn't school-related. Even to family," her dad continued. "Your tablet will only be able to connect to the local network. No AstrisLink Global access."

Her fingers curled into a fist in her lap.

"And every night, your tablet, AR band, and bracelet will be docked in the living room," her dad finished. "We'll have to review your activity." He turned to her mom. "I'm missing something, aren't I?"

Her mom smiled weakly. "Yes," she replied, looking at Allison. "A meeting with Mr. Mueller is still scheduled for the afternoon of April 13th. The agenda includes our next steps for high school." A lump settled in Allison's throat. Two months.

Her mother's voice softened. "We've also been advised that you need counseling. The Russian invasion forced you to leave Germany. I'm sorry that we didn't realize how much that affected you. That was a mistake. I've scheduled an appointment with Pastor Black later today."

Allison flinched. Oh, my God! she thought. Mr. Mueller told her parents that she was doubting her faith.

"Ah, I just remembered one last thing," her father said. "You'll have to meet with the head of the enclave's security. They need you to walk them through exactly how you and Michelle evaded security."

Her breath caught. "But they should have video footage," she managed to say.

"There are gaps," her dad told her. "They need to confirm the route you took out of the store and anyone you spoke to."

A chill ran down Allison's spine. Cassie, the sales associate. The pin.

It meant something, and she couldn't tell them about that. She wouldn't.

She looked down at the table. She didn't want to give up, but how could she convince anyone to let her leave Manhattan now?

Allison sat in the reception area outside Pastor Black's office, her hands in her lap, fingers pressed together so tightly they ached. The smooth wooden floor beneath her feet gleamed under the fluorescent lights. She stared at the nameplate that hadn't changed since she was five.

Rev. David Black, Senior Pastor. Familiar and foreign all at once.

Her mother sat next to her, scrolling through her tablet with sharp, deliberate movements. She had barely spoken since they arrived, her expression unreadable.

Janice, the parish secretary, had been here for as long as Allison could remember. Her desktop smart board hummed as she worked. She barely looked up as she focused on whatever task she was handling. The scent of polished wood clung to the space, triggering memories of Sunday school lessons, Advent by

Candlelight, and church lunches. But those memories felt so distant now.

Back then, everything had been so . . . normal. That was before the Russian invasion. Before her parents made her leave Germany and come back to the States. Before she realized just how much had changed while she was gone.

Allison swallowed hard, her fingers tightening in her lap. No one here really talked about it. About how the EU Defense Force was pushing back. About the evacuations. About the people left behind. About her friends.

Her dad said that Germany was still safe. He looked so tired of dealing with all the issues the war had caused. And now, he was stuck here, in Manhattan, because of her.

Janice finally looked up. "You can go in now."

Allison felt her mother glance at her, but she didn't move. After a moment, Allison stood and crossed the room, her steps slow, deliberate.

The office door handle was cool under her fingers as she stepped inside. The room was exactly as she remembered. The bookshelves packed with thick theological texts behind a sturdy mahogany desk, and a cross hanging on the wall. A place of learning. A place of comfort.

Or at least, it had been.

Pastor Black stood up from his chair, his smile warm but measured. "Allison," he said, his deep voice steady. He gestured to the chair across from him. "It's been a while."

She hesitated in the doorway. Every part of her wanted to turn around and walk out, but what was the point? She couldn't get out of this conversation. With a small sigh, she dropped into the chair, crossing her arms tightly over her chest.

"Your mother mentioned you've been struggling since moving back home." He sat down in the chair next to her, his eyes sharp with concern.

She rolled her eyes toward the ceiling. "Struggling," she repeated. "Sure."

Pastor Black frowned slightly. "How would you describe it?"

Her jaw tightened, fingers digging into her sleeves. "Like I can't breathe. Like everyone wants me to be something I'm not."

He nodded slowly, considering her words. "Something like what?" he gently prompted.

She hesitated. Saying it out loud felt dangerous, like it would make everything worse. She let out a sharp breath.

"My parents told me that I was going to one of the best schools in Manhattan," she told him, trying to keep her voice even. "But Vanguard isn't even teaching us real stuff. Not like Kaiserhof did. Everything's watered down or twisted, like the only thing that matters is what kind of family I end up in someday."

Pastor Black leaned forward, resting his elbows on his knees. "That's a serious concern, Allison."

She let out a bitter laugh. "You're the first person who thinks so."

He studied her for a moment. "You've always picked up on things most kids didn't," he said quietly. "Even back in Children's Bible Study. You were the one asking questions no one else thought to ask." He paused. "That kind of awareness isn't always easy to live with."

She swallowed hard. "Then why does no one listen to me? Why is everyone just letting this happen?"

Her voice cracked, and a tear slipped down her cheek. "The way people talk about God now, it's so different. Like He's a weapon instead of . . . " She broke off, pressing her lips together. "Instead of who He's supposed to be."

"Why do you say that?" he asked gently.

Allison wiped her face with the sleeve of her sweater. "Did you approve the new Women's Bible Study stuff?"

"No," Pastor Black said quietly. "That came from the Synod. The Education Committee just passed it along."

She looked up at him, feeling the tears starting. "So, they really think that's all we're good for? Submitting. Serving. Making perfect little homes?"

A shadow passed over his face. He stood, walked to his desk, and tapped on the smart screen. His expression darkened as he read.

"Seven Mountains Mandate?" he muttered. His voice was low, almost to himself. "Men are called to rule, and women are called to support them in dominion . . . "

His lips pressed into a thin line. He pulled open another document and turned the screen toward her.

"Allison," he said, his voice more serious now, "this is what the Synod sent for Women's Bible Study."

She leaned in, scanning the title: **The Role of Women in God's Plan.**

Key Scripture: Proverbs 31:10-31.

She skimmed the verses. "*A wife of noble character who can find? She is worth far more than rubies. Her husband has full confidence in her and lacks nothing of value. She brings him good, not harm, all the days of her life . . .*"

She nodded slowly. It was one of her favorites.

She looked up at him. "I don't understand. That's not what we were given."

Pastor Black's expression didn't change. "I don't understand, either," he admitted. "The study guide uploaded to our site is . . . inappropriate and not faithful to what we believe."

"I'm sorry," Allison whispered.

He met her eyes. "Don't be," he told her. "I understand why you're upset. What you're seeing doesn't match what you've been taught, does it?"

She nodded, another tear rolled down her cheek.

He sighed, rubbing his chin. "Your father spoke to me a month ago. He said you had questions about a Bible study guide. I told him I'd look into it, but . . . " He shook his head. "Maybe I didn't look hard enough."

Allison swallowed. "Did my parents tell you about everything else?"

He hesitated. "They said you were struggling with how much religion has seeped into everyday life," he said gently. "And they thought maybe the war . . . the move, being separated from your dad and your friends has been hard on you." He looked at her carefully. "Is that true?"

Allison hesitated, then gave a small nod.

"I don't know if it's just the move," she said, voice small. "I think . . . I think I just don't trust people anymore. Not like I used to."

Pastor Black's expression softened. "Because of the war?"

She swallowed hard. "Because I don't know who's telling the truth." Her voice wavered, but she kept going. "When I left Germany, it happened so fast," she told him. "My dad wouldn't come with me. He said he couldn't leave his work. But now he's here. Because of me. Because I messed up."

She wiped at her face, frustrated. "And the war didn't stop just because he left. It's still happening. People are dying."

She shook her head. "And here? Everyone acts like none of it matters. They talk about weddings, fundraisers, and the right kind of marriage, like nothing outside Manhattan even exists." Her voice broke. "Like my friends don't exist."

Pastor Black exhaled slowly. "We're called to be faithful, not fashionable," he softly said. "But maybe some people have forgotten that."

Allison looked at him carefully, watching for any sign that he was just trying to make her feel better. But he looked serious.

She wiped her eyes again. "Thank you, Pastor."

"Would you like me to speak with your parents?" he asked. "I could explain the changes we found in the Women's Bible Studies guide and the other changes you've noticed."

Allison let out a long breath. "That might help."

Pastor Black nodded, then straightened. "Would you like to pray before you go?"

She almost said no. Almost brushed it off. But something inside her, some deep, tangled knot, started to unravel. She nodded. "Please."

They bowed their heads. Pastor Black's voice was steady and calm.

"Heavenly Father, we come before You today, seeking Your wisdom and guidance. We know that the world is shifting, and sometimes, the path ahead seems unclear. But we trust in You, Lord. We trust that You see all, that You know our fears and our burdens.

"Please grant Your child, Allison, peace in her heart and clarity in her mind. Help her find strength in who she is and the courage to stand firm in her convictions. Remind her that she is not alone, that Your love surrounds her, even in times of doubt.

"And Lord, guide us all to walk in Your truth, unshaken by the voices that seek to twist it. Amen."

"Amen," she breathed, feeling something inside her settle. The weight wasn't gone. But for the first time, it felt like she wasn't carrying it alone.

Monday came too fast.

Allison dragged her fork across her plate, pushing a smear of mashed potato into the roasted chicken. The scent of freshly baked bread and warm butter should have been comforting. It wasn't. Around her, students acted as if nothing had happened.

She was alone. Michelle's usual seat across the table sat empty. No half-smiles. No quiet jokes. They'd been inseparable before, but now Michelle wasn't even allowed to sit with her.

She shifted in her seat. Allison didn't have to look up to know people were watching her. She could almost feel the weight of their eyes pressed against her, sharp and lingering. Someone whispered her name, followed by a muffled laugh.

Some people treated her like a hero and whispered how lucky she was. Others looked at her like she had done something unforgivable. The boys, especially, treated her like she was a villain that had threatened their world.

She shifted in her seat and reached for her glass of water, but her hand hovered over it before pulling away. Everything about this felt wrong.

Her tablet was locked. Her messages screened. Every step she took was monitored and every interaction filtered through the school's security.

She hadn't seen the chaos firsthand, but she could feel it. The city was locked down, sealed off from the rest of the world. All because she had managed to slip through the cracks.

Her parents had let her watch the news reports a few days ago. Now she couldn't unsee it. The footage played in her mind like a scene from someone else's life, looping whether she wanted it to or not.

Sirens screamed through the streets, their wails echoing as they bounced off Midtown's glass and metal towers. Red emergency lights flickering across the helmets of armored security forces moving in tight formations. Streets emptied. Barricades locked into place. Helicopters cut across the skyline. Hundreds and hundreds of people being rounded up for questioning.

All of it because of her.

She could still see the headlines scrolling across the bottom of the screens.

Midtown Heiress Missing.

High-Risk Search in Manhattan: Security Mobilized for Allison Maxwell.

The acid in her stomach burned like it was eating her from the inside. She swallowed hard, trying to push the thoughts down, but they wouldn't go away. They just waited for things to go quiet again.

At least Pastor Black hadn't brushed her off. He'd listened. He'd even said he would investigate who had made changes to the Bible study materials.

Still didn't change anything right now. She was still here. In this dining hall. Alone.

"Allison."

Allison tensed before she even looked up.

"Ah, zhèlǐ shì wǒmen de tiāncái shàonǚ." Tomas's voice cut through the murmur of the dining hall, his tone mocking. *Ah, there's our little prodigy.*

She met his gaze, her expression blank. "Nǐ zhème guānxīn wǒ ma?" *Do you care about me that much?*

Tomas's smirk widened as he pulled out the chair across from her and sat down like he owned the place. His friends hovered behind him, smiling with interest.

"Wǒ tīngdào le zuì fēngkuáng de gùshì," he continued, his voice dripping with amusement. *I've heard the wildest stories.*

A fork clinked against a plate somewhere nearby. A hushed murmur rippled through the surrounding tables, but most of their classmates barely noticed. Most didn't speak Mandarin, or if they did, they didn't speak it well. For now, this was between the two of them.

Tomas glanced at her untouched food, then leaned forward slightly, voice dropping into a conspiratorial whisper. "So, the entire city went on lockdown. Full terror alert. Drones in the sky. All because you went missing."

He smiled, but it didn't reach his eyes. "That's a lot of firepower for one girl." He sat back with a chuckle. "Tīng qǐlái bù tài kěnéng." *Sounds unlikely.*

A slow, hot wave of shame crept up Allison's spine.

He knew something. Not everything. But enough.

She tightened her grip on the fork. The cool metal dug into her palm. "Nǐ wèishéme zhème guānxīn?" *Why do you care?*

Tomas tilted his head, pretending to think about it. Then, in English, he drew out the words like he was savoring them.

"Maybe you ran away and got picked up in a public sweep," he said. "Or maybe your parents had to buy you back from traffickers."

A sharp inhale from somewhere close. The scrape of a chair leg across the floor.

The dining hall went completely silent.

Allison set her fork down carefully. Deliberately. She would not let him get to her. She didn't know why she was on his list, but she'd had enough.

She stood up, moving toward the lobby, but Tomas slid smoothly in front of her. His friends closed in around her, cutting off every way out of the dining room.

Not good. "Ràng kāi." *Move.* She kept her voice steady.

Tomas raised an eyebrow, pretending to think it over. Then, he smirked.

He gestured to the empty space around her. "What's wrong?" He lifted his hands. "No one wants to sit with you. Not even your best friend. And now you're skipping classes and need a tutor?"

He leaned in, his voice almost gentle. "Kànqǐlái nǐ bùgòu cōngmíng, shì ba?" *Guess you're not smart enough for Vanguard.*

She closed her eyes for a second. Don't react. You are not a victim. Her fists clenched at her sides.

"Gǔndàn," she said through gritted teeth. Back off!

Tomas chuckled, amused. "Bùrán ne?" he replied. *Or what?*

The curse slipped out before she could stop it.

"Húnzhàng." *Filthy bastard.*

A WARD OF THE STATE

His face darkened, hands flexing at his sides. For a moment, everything stopped. Then his arm snapped back—

She dropped her weight, right leg kicking back to shift her center. She drove forward under his swing, her left foot moving next to his.

Her fist slammed into his ribs.

Tomas staggered backward. And then he hit the ground. Hard.

Silence.

She took a slow breath, stepping back.

The entire dining hall was frozen. Servers. Students. Everyone watching.

Tomas blinked up at her, stunned.

Allison stood tall. Her heart pounded, but she didn't look away.

She looked down at Tomas, her voice steady. "Bùyào zài hé wǒ shuōhuà." *Don't ever talk to me again.*

She grabbed her backpack from the floor, turned on her heel, and slowly walked toward the elevators. The whispers started up again, but no one tried to stop her. Girls stepped aside as she passed. One of them, wide-eyed and breathless, whispered, "Are you okay?"

Allison gave a small nod but didn't answer. Her mind was already racing.

How long before her parents were called? And more importantly, would she be expelled before or after they showed up?

Chapter Nineteen

The worst thing about the head of security was how unremarkable he looked.

He wasn't tall, wasn't short. Not young, not old. He had the kind of face that wouldn't stick in your mind unless you tried to remember it. He could be a maintenance worker fixing a busted pipe, a tired dad paying for groceries, or a guy scanning IDs at the SkyRail station. Someone who blended in so well that even if he had been watching you all day, you'd never notice.

Dan Mercer sat in one of the sleek, low-backed chairs near the entrance to the outdoor garden, hands resting lightly on the armrests. Relaxed, except for the lines around his eyes.

Allison sat across from him, hands squeezed between her knees, trying not to fidget. She felt like a kid caught sneaking out after curfew. Her mom sat next to her, trying to be supportive.

"You were off-grid for quite a while," he said, his voice as neutral as his face. "That's not easy to do in Manhattan."

Allison swallowed. "We were just trying to get to Milwaukee," she said. She hung her head to avoid looking at him. Her voice felt too small, like she wasn't the one speaking. "I wanted to meet with a family attorney and maybe see my grandpa if we had time." She glanced at her dad, who was sitting stiffly nearby. "He works downtown."

Her fingers curled tighter in her lap. She really didn't want to have this conversation.

So, she stuck to her story. How she'd lied to the woman at the boutique that they were afraid of the man following them. How the woman had pointed them toward the back. How they found an employee exit into the alley and took the SkyRail to Grand Central. From there, it had been an easy hop onto the train.

She'd even admitted they had stashed their security bracelets between the SkyRail capsule cushions.

Mercer just watched her, almost as if he was listening to what she didn't say.

"You got lucky," he finally said. "If either of your bracelets had been fully charged, it could have caused a major security issue."

Allison frowned. "Why?"

Mercer leaned forward, elbows resting on his thighs as he looked at her. "You have higher access than the average citizen. If a criminal had found those bracelets . . . "

She swallowed hard. She hadn't realized that.

Mercer didn't give her time to dwell on it. "We spoke to the women at the boutique," he said, watching her closely. "Their stories didn't match."

He let the silence settle.

"Not unusual on its own," he added. "But, it makes me wonder if they were coached."

"Coached?" she echoed.

He leaned back in his chair. "Something we're still looking into," he said. "It doesn't help that the store's security cameras had been down for over twenty-four hours. The manager didn't report it. The boutique's been fined. The manager's been fired."

He paused for a moment. "We know you and Michelle left through the employee entrance, but we lost visual for several critical minutes," he told her. "We picked you up again just before you boarded the train."

He gestured toward the far wall, and the smart glass flickered to life. The room darkened slightly as a security feed appeared.

The image zoomed in. It showed her and Michelle walking together on a train platform. The timestamp in the corner was from Wednesday morning, not long after they'd fled the boutique. The video quality wasn't great, but the longer she stared, the more she realized that they weren't alone.

A woman walked right behind them. Dark-skinned. Headscarf covering her hair and part of her face. She never looked straight at the camera, her profile angled just enough to stay in the shadows.

But it was the way she moved, always slightly behind but never too close, her hands slightly spread out, that got Allison's attention. The people around them seemed to part, like they were inside some invisible bubble.

"Shepherding," Mercer said. "That's the word our analysts used."

Allison's mouth was dry. She didn't remember seeing that woman.

He gestured at the wall. "Do you recognize her?" he asked. "Did she speak to you?"

Allison leaned in, eyes searching. She realized that she wasn't wearing a pin like the one Cassie said to look for. Or maybe the scarf covered it.

"I don't know who she is," she said quietly. "We didn't talk to her."

Mercer tilted his head slightly. It was the first time he reacted at all.

"Interesting," he said.

Allison swallowed. Was the woman helping them? Watching out for them?

Mercer let the silence hang before standing.

"If you remember anything else," he said, "no matter how small, let me know."

He nodded to her dad, then walked to the elevator. The doors closed, and just like that, he was gone.

Allison exhaled slowly, then turned to her parents. "I'm so sorry," she said, barely above a whisper. "I didn't know."

Her dad sighed, then pulled her into a hug. "I know, Allie," he murmured. "But you're old enough now. You have to start paying attention." He kissed the top of her head, then let her go. "Time for me to pack."

Her stomach clenched. Right. He was leaving again.

She followed him upstairs. Her dad grabbed his work tablet, chargers, and a few other things. He didn't need to pack any clothes. He had what he needed in Hamburg.

The bed was huge, with a sleek black frame and matching nightstands. Soft reading lights curved over each side, casting a warm glow. The far wall was all glass, with floor-to-ceiling windows that showed the city skyline.

But there was nothing else. No dressers. No books. No random things left on the nightstands. Just smooth cabinets along one wall, hiding everything away.

Her dad's house in Hamburg was nothing like this. His bedroom had books stuffed on random shelves, old coffee mugs on the desk, and a leather armchair that was basically falling apart but was 'too comfortable to get rid of.' His house felt lived in.

She sat on the bed, watching him. "Did you decide yet?"

He glanced over at her. "Decide what?"

"Which project you're taking next? Vancouver or Veracruz."

He'd told her that both cities were dealing with climate stuff. Vancouver was fixing seawalls and flood zones. Veracruz needed its whole port system rebuilt.

He sighed, rubbing his neck. "They both have pros and cons."

She folded her arms and leaned against the pillows. "Which one's winning?"

"Vancouver, for now," he admitted with a small smile. "They started prepping earlier, so it won't take as long."

She swallowed hard. That was so far from Hamburg.

"Seattle's right next door," he added. "I can be home every weekend and every holiday."

She frowned. And then what? If the project only lasted a year, would they stay in Seattle? Would her mom make them stay there for her business? Or would she have to get used to another school, another home, only to have to leave again?

"But nothing's final," he said, sitting next to her. "No contracts yet. We can still visit Hamburg in the summer."

She stared at her hands, picking at a loose thread on her sleeve. "It's not the same."

"I know."

His arm wrapped around her shoulders, pulling her close. "All that's left are the final inspections," he murmured. "I should have a final sign-off by early May. We'll have all summer together. We can go back to Hamburg for a while. Okay?"

She wanted to believe him.

"Okay," she mumbled.

He squeezed her, then stood to finish packing.

Allison curled up where she was, arms wrapped around her knees, watching him. Trying not to think about how everything—her home, her school, her friends—hinged on choices she didn't get to make.

Allison stepped into the chess club room, the overhead lights casting a sterile white glow over the wooden black-and-white boards. Students were already at their tables, quietly murmuring as they set up their matches. Some glanced over at her. Most didn't.

Michelle was already at one of the tables in the middle of the room. She'd already set the pieces on the board for the first match. Her blazer hung open over her white blouse, despite the cool air. She tapped her black-painted nails lightly against the edge of the table. And pinned to her lapel was the pin.

Small. Silver. Two hands clasped together.

It was the same pin the woman at the boutique had worn. Allison stared at it, her pulse speeding up. She hesitated. What did that symbol mean?

Michelle met her gaze and jerked her chin toward the empty chair. Allison sat, smoothing her skirt before pulling out her stylus. No one had told them they couldn't play chess together. They just weren't allowed to socialize.

The smart screen built into the table flickered on as Michelle wrote her first message: You okay?

Allison nodded, erased it, and then replied. Yes. Are you?

Michelle exhaled sharply. She wiped the message away with a quick tap and wrote: My parents are so angry. I am grounded until the end of time. You?

Allison moved a pawn forward. The quiet click of wood against the board echoed from other tables. Same.

Michelle moved one of her own pieces. Chess club had always been a safe place, except now they couldn't talk. Not out loud. Not with the judges watching.

Michelle wrote: So, what are you going to do?

Allison moved her knight. I don't know. I just know that I can't stay here.

Michelle hesitated before erasing her words and writing a new message. Same. My parents are taking me back to Italy after the school year. We're Roman Catholic, and everything around us is a reminder that we're not welcome.

Allison frowned, advancing another piece to set up an early defense. I'm sorry. Honestly? I'm not sure anyplace is safe anymore.

Michelle studied the board, then moved her bishop. You're staying in the U.S., right? Not moving back to Hamburg?

Allison hesitated before responding. Still too dangerous in Eastern Europe and I'm not allowed to permanently leave the U.S. until I'm at least 18.

Michelle's stylus hovered over the screen before she wrote: That's just wrong. How were you able to live in Germany for two years?

Allison shifted in her chair and moved her queen, forcing Michelle's knight to retreat. My dad had custody and his job was overseas. Now that my mom has custody, we have to stay in the U.S. I don't know why.

Michelle smirked slightly, countering the move and pressing her advantage. So, what are you going to do?

Allison sighed, making a move to block her. I don't know. I don't seem to have any rights at the moment.

Michelle tilted her head, considering. Then, she wrote: Sure, you do. There's got to be something that lets your aunt and uncle take custody. You just have to find it.

Her stylus hovered over the board before she hesitated and wrote: I'm still amazed I haven't been expelled.

Michelle smiled slightly before she wrote back. Same.

Allison's fingers tightened around the stylus. She'd expected to get called into the headmaster's office. Maybe even have her parents dragged in to discuss her 'lack of respect for authority'. But nothing had happened. The school had pretended like she hadn't hit Tomas. Not even a warning. Very surprising, she wrote.

Michelle studied her for a long moment, then made her next move. Allison didn't even look at the board before moving a random piece. Your pin. Where did you get it?

Michelle's expression didn't change, but her fingers hesitated just a second too long before she erased her message and replied. One of my mom's friends gave it to me. It's an heirloom.

Allison glanced at the tiny silver emblem, tracing its shape with her eyes. Two hands clasped together. A symbol of unity?

From when? she wrote.

Michelle shifted in her chair, making her next move before answering. From when women still had the right to vote.

Allison stared at the words, her fingers frozen over the board. From when women still had the right to vote.

It sounded like a fragment of ancient history, even though her mom had lived through it.

Michelle slid her rook into place. Checkmate.

"I did not see that coming," Allison whispered, her voice barely audible over the murmurs in the room. "Great move."

Michelle leaned back in her chair, arms folded in satisfaction. "And that's why you need to keep going."

The words settled in Allison's mind as she reset the board. Maybe Michelle was right. Maybe there was a way out. She just had to find it.

Allison barely waited for the elevator doors to open before stepping out. She shrugged off her winter jacket and hung it up in the closet before racing for the stairs.

The penthouse was mostly quiet, except for the faint clatter of Maria working in the kitchen. Good. Her mom wouldn't be home for at least an hour.

She took the steps two at a time, gripping the railing to keep from tripping on her long skirt. She could still feel the relief of sitting across from Michelle in the chess club.

She'd missed a few meetings. For all she knew, Michelle's parents had pulled her out, or even worse, Michelle might have decided she wasn't worth the trouble anymore. It wouldn't have been surprising. Allison was the one who had dragged her along to Milwaukee. The one who had gotten them both caught.

She should have gone alone.

But playing chess turned out to be the perfect cover. The smart screens had let them pass notes, a kind of digital whisper instead of spoken words. The judges couldn't see what they were writing, and they'd erased everything.

Allison shut her bedroom door and flipped the lock, her back pressed against the wood. Keep going, Michelle had told her.

She slowly crossed the room and sank onto the couch, pulling a throw pillow onto her lap. "Jeeves," she said, forcing her voice to stay steady. "Incognito mode."

"Incognito mode activated."

If she wiped the logs afterward, would there be any trace? No way to know unless she tested it.

She took a deep breath. "Pull up every document I gave Mr. Mueller," she told Jeeves.

"Acknowledged," the AI replied. A second later, legal filings, school records, and counselor notes filled the wall. Allison tossed the pillow to the floor and walked over to the smart wall. She stared at the documents, arms crossed. It wasn't enough, she thought. Something was missing.

"Run a search through Milwaukee city and county legal records," she told Jeeves. No. Too small. "Actually, search all of Wisconsin municipalities and county records. Hit the state level, too. My name, my mom's name, my dad's. Lifetime records. Download anything we don't already have."

"Processing," Jeeves replied.

Allison exhaled and went to her nightstand. She pulled out the old leather-bound wedding album. She flopped onto her bed and flipped it open. There had to be something missing.

Her parents looked so young. Her mom's head was thrown back, laughing. Her dad twirling her across the dance floor.

Candid shots of them making stupid faces at each other when they thought no one was watching. But something felt off.

She flipped through it again, slower this time. Where were Aunt Chloe, Uncle Alexander, and Patrick?

She frowned at the family photo. They should've been there. Her mom and Aunt Chloe had been close, right? So why were they missing? She shut the album, tapping the cover absently before setting it aside.

Her mom loved to journal. She had even tried getting Allison into it when she was little, but writing about her feelings felt pointless. She preferred sketching them instead.

Maybe, just maybe, her mom had written about the wedding. Something that explained all of this.

Or maybe she was completely wrong, and this was a waste of time. No way to know unless she looked, right?

She slipped out of her room, heart hammering as she padded down the hall. She stopped at the head of the stairs, listening. Silence. Maybe Maria had run out for something quick?

Keep going, she told herself as she quietly moved down the hall to her mom's bedroom and carefully shut the door behind her.

The room had always felt too big. The furniture was beautiful, but the room had no warmth. No dressers, no scattered clothes, no stacks of books or shoes kicked off in a hurry—just the bed and a long row of closets that hid built-in cabinets that swallowed every piece of clothing her parents had in Manhattan.

She moved toward the small couch in the corner. If her mom had kept any old journals, they'd be there.

Allison kneeled and tugged the cabinet door open. Inside, rows of leather-bound books lined the lowest shelf. She ran her fingers along the spines, scanning the dates.

She pulled out one labeled COVID, smirking at the tiny green virus her mom had doodled on the cover before sliding it back into place.

She kept going, moving farther to the right. 2028. 2029. Got 'em!

The 2028 journal cover was covered in watercolor swirls, interspaced with drawings of horses and assorted doodles. 2029's cover was blank, except for a small sketch of a baby crib.

Allison hesitated. Then, she picked them up and tucked them under one arm as she carefully closed the cabinet door. She slipped out and quietly made her way to her room.

Allison curled her legs beneath her on the couch. Jeeves continued to scan for pertinent public documents. The glow from the smart wall flickered, casting shifting shadows across the room as lines of text scrolled by. Documents appeared, text was highlighted, then vanished.

She opened the second journal, flipping through the pages until she found the first entry her mom had written after she was born. The handwriting—familiar and careful—pulled her in, like she was a detective chasing clues in one of her favorite mystery thrillers.

April 10, 2029:

Allison won't sleep unless I'm holding her. The second I put her down, she cries like the world is ending—and maybe it is. My whole body hurts. My milk isn't coming in right, so I'm constantly pumping, hoping it's enough. I don't know if I'm good enough, and Sam refuses to even consider a nanny.

Allison stared at the words. That didn't sound like her. Mom was the one who always took charge. The one who got things done. Always. Just the idea that she had ever doubted herself was strange. She randomly flipped to an earlier entry.

March 26, 2029:

The first of my contractions hit me hard. It's too early. My baby girl isn't ready yet.

Sam was only coming back to the apartment to sleep on the couch before disappearing again.

I tried so hard to deal with it myself. But this wasn't like what we learned in the birthing class, so I called him. He finally picked up. Finally came home.

The triage nurse told us that it was Braxton-Hicks and nothing to worry about. Nothing to worry about?!

At least I got to see my doctor today. Allison is head down and getting ready for her debut! Now, if she'd just stop kicking me under the ribs . . .

Allison giggled. My debut, huh? She imagined a baby being born in a long silk dress and heels, ready to waltz into a debutante ball.

But then, she pressed a finger to the page. Her dad was avoiding her mom. Why? She flipped back through March. Then February.

February 19, 2029:

Sam has been gone for four days. Four. Days.
What if I went into labor early? What if I fell on the stairs?
At church, his mom had the gall to tell me that she knew where he was. Why did he get to go home and I'm stuck here, helpless?

Allison's throat tightened. Her dad had left while her mom was pregnant. And worse—Grandma knew.

Her fingers hovered over the page. Should she be reading this? It felt wrong, spying on her parents' relationship like this.

But she couldn't stop now. She needed to know. There had to be something Mr. Mueller could use. Something that made sense of all this.

January 8, 2029:
I just found out that Sam's family isn't helping out. At. All. No wonder he's stressed about money all the time. I need to go over that budget he's been working on. Find the gaps. Fix this mess!

Now, that sounded like Mom, she thought. But why hadn't her grandparents helped? Her grandfather was one of the most generous people she knew. And Grandma—she was always busy with church, running committees and helping vets get community resources. Why wouldn't they help their own son?

She flipped further back. Some entries were rushed and scribbled. Others were neat, almost casual.

Then, she reached the beginning of 2029. Her mom vented about being forced to move in with her dad. The apartment was too small, had too many stairs, and really old appliances. Not the kind of place she'd ever choose to live in.

Allison rolled her eyes. Spoiled much, Mom?

She picked up the 2028 journal and flipped to the back entries. Advent by Candlelight. Allison's first kick. Doctor visits. Lots of talk about weekly mentoring circles. A few notes about access to money during pregnancy.

The page opened to early September.

September 6, 2028:
Un-fucking-believable. Sam wants me to get an abortion. Wasn't he listening in court? We would be charged with murder. I just can't.

I don't even know how I got pregnant. Doctors told me it was impossible without help—just like Chloe. But here I am. And I refuse to end it.

Allison stood so fast the journal slipped from her hands.

Her dad had wanted her dead. He hadn't wanted her to be born.

A tremor ran through her as she dropped back onto the couch, pressing a pillow to her face, squeezing her eyes shut. A choked sob escaped, and then tears, as her fingers clutched the fabric so tightly her knuckles ached.

He wanted me gone, she thought. If her mom had listened to him, she wouldn't be here.

"Search results updated," Jeeves announced. "Displaying additional legal documentation."

Sniffing, Allison sat up, swiping at her face with the sleeve of her shirt. The smart wall flickered, a new set of documents materializing in crisp lines of text.

She let out a shaky breath, rubbing her damp palms against her jeans. "What did you find?" she whispered, her voice still unsteady.

"Medical notes on 'Labor Simulation', connected to a court case involving Samuel Maxwell," the AI replied, as a document opened. "Arrest records indicating parole violation due to entering an establishment serving alcohol on several occasions. Additional legal documentation submitted by Mr. Maxwell's mentor—"

Allison blinked. "Pause. The mentor's document. What does it say?"

Text expanded across the screen. She tried to read it, but she still couldn't focus. "Just give me a summary," she whispered.

"Mr. Maxwell transferred from Northwestern University in Niles, Illinois to Marquette University in Milwaukee, Wisconsin," Jeeves told her. "His court filing indicates that he requested full custody of Allison Isabelle Williams Maxwell until her fourth birthday and, until that time, he would remain in the Milwaukee area, near family. This would allow Miss Maxwell's mother to receive her undergraduate degree."

Her throat tightened. That didn't make sense. He wanted her gone. So why fight for her?

Another document: It is in the best interest of the child to remain in Milwaukee, allowing both parents the freedom to pursue their academic goals while ensuring strong familial bonds.

Allison let out a shaky breath. "Any other documents to review, Jeeves?"

"None at this time, Miss Allison," it told her.

She wiped at her face again. Time to move on. "Jeeves, how is the expanded search for Rising Grace Fellowship ministry?" she asked.

"Current files include sermons, publicly available financial records, published memos, and references in legal cases," the AI told her. "I've also identified mentions in political lobbying records and Manhattan-based lawsuits. Would you like a summary?"

She swallowed. "No summary. Just flag anything about them controlling personal decisions like schools, family interference, anything tied to my mom or her companies."

She scooped up the journals and placed them into the scanner near the smart wall. "Scan all entries from August 15, 2028 through April 10, 2029," she ordered Jeeves. "Then save everything to my encrypted file. When you're done, erase the last two hours and exit incognito mode."

"Acknowledged."

After the journals popped out of the scanner, she checked the logs. The last two hours were gone.

Relief washed over her, leaving her drained. She stuffed the journals beneath her bed, pushing them deep into the shadows where the vacuum wouldn't find them.

She needed time to think. How was she going to get this to Mr. Mueller? And more importantly, would it even make a difference?

In the end, she found a way. All her activity was monitored at home, but they couldn't tap into the computer system in the school library.

Allison found herself hunched over a computer table, her heart pounding relentlessly. Her trembling fingers hovered over the smart board embedded in the table.

This was it.

She forced herself to glance around. A few students were scattered across the room, heads bent over tablets. One girl traced her fingers over the words of a print book. Across the room, she could hear the sound of muffled laughter and boys shoving each other near the game pit.

No one was watching. No one had any idea what she was about to do.

Her eyes darted back to the screen. This was her shot. Jeeves had pointed her to a secure server for Milwaukee Family Court, one that he could not directly access due to the household restrictions. If she was right, she could upload every file she'd uncovered, bypass the red tape, and get everything directly into Mr. Mueller's hands before the annual family review.

It had to work.

She inserted the file drive into the small slot and typed the command to upload everything. A faint click confirmed the connection. The screen brightened as the library's interface processed the files. She typed out the final command.

A single word blinked on the screen: *Submit*.

Her finger hovered over it. Her mind raced. Was she making the worst mistake of her life? Or was this the only way forward?

She swallowed hard. If she didn't do this, nothing would ever change. Her fingertip pressed the screen.

Loading. And then, *Your documents have been successfully submitted.*

A rush of adrenaline hit her hard, leaving her lightheaded. It was done. No going back.

Breathe, she told herself. She took a slow breath, then another.

She'd done it!

She logged off quickly, her fingers steady despite the churn in her stomach. Then, she carefully wiped the session history, shut the screen down and slid the file drive into her backpack.

Then, methodically, she gathered her things, keeping her movements calm. Normal.

As she stood, she stole one last glance around the library. The world moved on, unaware.

But Allison knew better. Everything had changed. And, ready or not, she had, too.

Chapter Twenty

The days blurred together, each one dragging through the same routine. Wake up. School. Homework. Repeat. And somehow, it was already mid-April. School would be over in a few months, but she still hadn't received an answer from Mr. Mueller.

Now, Allison was back in another custody review meeting, weeks of dread crashing into this single moment.

She knew the documents she'd sent through the secure server had been delivered because she'd triple-checked the confirmation. But as the conversation dragged on, there was no sign that Mr. Mueller had even seen them, let alone read them. Nothing indicated that the effort she'd put into gathering all of that proof had made any difference at all.

Had it all been for nothing?

Mom crossed her legs, adjusting her bracelet. "I'm not saying Manhattan is sustainable," she said. "But moving my entire business to Seattle isn't something I can just do overnight. I need to be sure it's the right decision."

Dad exhaled sharply, rubbing a hand over his jaw. "It is the right decision. I've already signed the contract in Vancouver. We'll be close enough to be a family again, at least on weekends and holidays."

Mom shook her head. "Seattle has its own issues. Puget Sound's been flooding for years. The Duwamish River is unstable. If we move, it has to be long-term. Maybe Redmond. Or Bellevue." She waved a hand. "I don't want to be right in the middle of Seattle."

Dad's jaw tightened. "It's April. Allison starts high school in the fall. We can't keep dragging this out." He turned to her. "You have a list of schools. Why don't we go through them?"

Allison's fingers pressed into the cool leather of the chair's armrests. They'd been having the same conversation for a month. Circling each other but never making a decision.

Just pick a place, she thought. Anywhere but Manhattan. Or let me live with Aunt Elena and Uncle Josh.

She glanced at Mr. Mueller. He was watching, taking notes, letting them talk. But as the conversation spiraled into office locations and school rankings, he finally cleared his throat.

"All right," he said, cutting through their conversation. "You've both given this a lot of thought. Let's table it for now and get me your decision by the end of the week."

"Yes," Dad said immediately.

Mom hesitated, then nodded. "Yes."

"Good." Mr. Mueller leaned forward slightly. "Now, since Allison has turned fourteen, I'd like to meet with her privately."

Both parents turned to him at the same time.

"Privately?" Mom frowned. "Why?"

"We've always been here when you've talked to Allison," Dad added, wary.

Mr. Mueller remained unfazed. "As children grow older, their input matters. Allison must be allowed to express her thoughts freely."

Mom pursed her lips, but Dad was the first to stand. "All right," he said.

Mom sighed and gave Allison a long look before standing up. "We'll be right outside if you need us," she said, smoothing her dress before walking toward the door.

Allison frowned, pushing down that small flicker of hope. He already knew what she wanted. Why couldn't he just do it?

The door clicked shut, sealing the room into silence. Mr. Mueller's chair creaked as he leaned forward. "This is the first time we've had an official private meeting, isn't it?" he asked with a smile.

Allison nodded and looked down. She couldn't look at him. Her eyes traced a deep scratch in the wood, running across the surface of the table. Old. Like something heavy had been dragged across years ago.

Just like her life.

"I know you've mentioned wanting to live with your Uncle Josh," Mr. Mueller said, tapping the screen. "Let's talk about what that would mean legally."

Allison swallowed. "Okay."

"Right now, your parents share custody." He paused. "If we want to request a change, we need to prove that living with your uncle would be in your best interest, emotionally, mentally, or physically. The court will need proof."

She looked up, and her grip tightened on the armrest. "Didn't I give you proof?" The words came out sharper than she meant.

Mr. Mueller didn't react. He just folded his hands on the desk. "The court would need more than your preference. We'd have to show a clear impact on your well-being."

Allison sighed, slumping into the chair. "So, it doesn't matter what I want."

"That's not true." His voice stayed even. "At fourteen, your opinion carries more weight than before. But your parents still have a say."

"And if they say no?"

Mr. Mueller exhaled. "Then it becomes much harder. We'd need extenuating circumstances."

Of course. She already knew the answer.

"I know this isn't what you were hoping for," Mr. Mueller said. "But there is another option we could explore."

She blinked. "Like what?"

"A boarding school."

Allison frowned. "Wait. Like, a real boarding school?"

He tapped the screen again, and a list of schools appeared on the smart wall next to his desk. One in particular caught her eye. A STEM-focused, all-girls academy.

Mr. Mueller nodded. "If your parents agree, we could ask the court to modify the custody arrangement so you could live at a boarding school during the academic year. Your parents would still have custody, so you'd have to live with one of them when school is not in session."

Allison sat up slightly. "And if they don't agree?"

"Then the court will decide." He met her gaze. "And that's where I come in. If this is something you really want, I can help you make a case for it."

Her heart hammered in her chest.

A real school. Away from Manhattan. Away from the expectations and the watchful eyes.

It was a way out. A real way out.

Allison took a slow breath, sitting up just a little taller. "Tell me more about the STEM school," she said.

Allison sat on the couch beside her mom, legs tucked under her, hands pressed against her lap to keep them from trembling. The smart wall flickered, and the screen split down the middle. On the left side, Dad sat in his office in Hamburg, his face lined with exhaustion. Mr. Mueller was on the other side. He was in his Milwaukee office, glasses perched near the tip of his nose as he flicked through files on his desktop smart board.

Mom exhaled slowly, voice measured. "We should consider delaying the move. Six months to a year."

Allison's stomach twisted. No!

Mom kept going. "Allison has a tutor. Amanda Trevelyan has already created a full curriculum for tenth grade and can ensure Allison stays ahead until we relocate. Relocate where? They'd been circling the same argument for months. She was done waiting.

Mr. Mueller's gaze flicked over to Dad. "Mr. Maxwell?"

Dad hesitated. His jaw was clenched, fingers steepled together. Then, reluctantly, he nodded. "It's not ideal," he admitted, "but unless you're willing to let Allison move to Canada with me for a year, it's the best option we have."

Canada. For half a second, Allison let herself imagine it. Wide open spaces. No security. No gated towers or constant reminders that her future was already mapped out for her. And no advertisements telling her that her only choice in life was to be a helpmate.

But she already knew the answer. Mom didn't even acknowledge the suggestion.

Mr. Mueller tapped a few keys on his smart board. With a flick of his fingers, new files spread across the screen below the video feed. "There is a third option," he said.

Allison's heart started pounding. Here we go, she thought.

"A girls-only STEM boarding school in Minnesota. Small campus. All-women faculty. Non-denominational, but with access to a WELS Lutheran church nearby if you approve."

Silence. Allison could almost hear the moment it sank in.

Mom sat forward, back rigid, nostrils flaring. "Boarding school?" The words dripped with disbelief. "She has to live with one of us, James."

Dad's chair creaked as he leaned in, eyes narrowing. "We won't agree to send our daughter away."

We. Suddenly, they were on the same side, even after all the fighting.

Mr. Mueller didn't blink. "As Allison's Guardian Ad Litem, it is my responsibility to ensure her best interests are met. This is my recommendation."

He let the words settle before adding, "A judicial review has already been scheduled for next week."

Allison's fingers dug into the couch cushion. What? Scheduled already?

Mr. Mueller flicked another document into view, the court order glowing in crisp black text. "You both have the option to attend and present your position to the court. The hearing will take place in Judge Harrington's courtroom at the Milwaukee Family Court."

Mom's lips parted slightly, but no sound came out. Dad's mouth pressed into a thin line.

Allison's fingers curled against the fabric of the couch. Every muscle in her body tensed to keep from grinning.

Finally. This was happening.

Not a vague plan. Not another stalled argument. A date. A time. A chance.

No more waiting. No more Vanguard. One way or another, this tug-of-war would be over.

Today was the day, Allison thought as she walked down the marble-lined hallway at Milwaukee Family Court. The marble walls seemed to go on forever, streaked with veins of gray that looked like someone had sketched them in with a pencil. The floors reflected the overhead lights, making everything feel too bright but also weirdly dull, like the glow in a dentist's office.

Every little sound echoed way too much. The click of heels. The murmured conversation. Even someone clearing their throat seemed to bounce off the walls and vanish into the air.

At the end of the hall, the giant wooden doors stood closed, their brass handles dull from so many hands gripping them over the years. Beyond those doors was the courtroom.

And in a few minutes, her entire life could change.

Mr. Mueller stood near the door, waiting for her, his expression calm. He wasn't dressed like the other lawyers she'd seen in the building. No stiff suit or expensive tie, just a simple dark blazer over a neatly pressed shirt. He looked exactly as he always had.

"Mr. and Mrs. Maxwell," he said, nodding politely to her parents.

Her mom acknowledged him with a short, unreadable smile, her fingers stiffly curled around the handle of her purse. Her dad barely nodded, his expression tight. No one spoke, at least not to each other.

Mr. Mueller turned to Allison. "Come with me, Allison," he said. "We can talk while your parents wait for their attorney."

For a moment, she hesitated. She wasn't expecting her mom or dad to stop her, but the fact that they didn't protest made her uneasy. Like they weren't even pretending to fight for her anymore.

She followed Mr. Mueller a short way down the hall to a small meeting room. It was nothing special, just a table and two chairs, a small window letting in the morning light. The moment the door shut behind them, some of the pressure in her chest loosened. No parents. No lawyers. Just the one person who could change her life.

He motioned to a chair. "Why don't you sit down?" Mr. Mueller asked her.

She dropped into the seat, her hands nervously twisting in her lap.

Mr. Mueller set his tablet on the table but didn't turn it on. Instead, he looked at her expectantly. "Are you ready?"

Allison nodded, but the truth was, she didn't know. Could anyone ever be ready for something like this?

He must have seen something in her face because he leaned forward slightly. "Listen, you've done everything right. You know exactly what you want. And I know that, no matter how this plays out, you'll be okay."

She let out a shaky breath. "Are you sure they'll listen to me?"

"They have to," he said simply. "You're not a little kid anymore, Allison." He sounded like he was trying to be reassuring, but what if he was wrong?

Mr. Mueller checked the time. "We should go in."

Allison stood up and wiped her sweaty palms against her skirt. Then, she followed him through the door behind him and into the courtroom.

It wasn't a huge room. There were just four narrow tables arranged in the small, square space. A simple desk sat at the front of the room, bare except for a smart board and a neatly stacked row of documents. That was where the judge sat. Two smaller tables faced it—one for her parents and one for her and Mr. Mueller. The stenographer's desk was tucked in the far corner, her fingers ready to capture every word.

It was smaller than she expected, so that should have made things feel less intimidating. But it didn't.

Allison glanced at the table on the right side of the room. Her mom sat with perfect posture, hands folded neatly on top of her purse, placed carefully on her lap. Dad sat beside her, looking a bit frustrated. It made her feel sad.

Mr. Mueller led Allison to their table and gestured for her to sit. She did, gripping the edge of the table like it might keep her upright. The bailiff walked across the front of the room to stand next to the judge's table.

Take a deep breath, she told herself. This is it.

"All rise," the bailiff's voice rang out, breaking the heavy silence.

Allison stood, her legs unsteady, as Judge Harrington entered the room. She wasn't particularly tall, but she didn't need to be. Her authority filled the room, her sharp gray eyes scanning the space like she already knew exactly how this was going to go.

"You may be seated," she told them. Allison lowered herself into the chair, her pulse hammering against her ribs.

The judge tapped the screen of her smart board. The case details appeared behind her in crisp black text. "We are here today for the judicial review of the custody arrangement for Allison Maxwell," she said. "This court has reviewed documentation from all relevant parties, including the report from Guardian Ad Litem, Mr. Mueller. The question before the court is whether a custody modification is in Allison's best interest." She paused, her sharp eyes scanning the room. "I understand this is a difficult matter for all involved."

Allison's fingers curled together in her lap, her knuckles pressing hard against each other. Please, Heavenly Father, let this happen!

The lawyer representing her parents stood, adjusting the smooth lines of his suit jacket before speaking. His tone was measured and practiced, like he had given this exact speech before in a hundred other cases.

"Your Honor, the current custody arrangement was established to ensure stability in Allison's life," he began. "Both of her parents have prioritized her education, well-being, and safety. A drastic change, such as sending her to a boarding school, could disrupt that stability and negatively impact her emotional and academic development."

Allison barely blinked, keeping her expression still as her mother nodded slightly. Her father sat farther away, and she couldn't see his face without turning. His hands remained clasped in front of him, fingers interlaced like he was praying.

The lawyer's voice remained steady and unwavering. "The mission of this court is to ensure children stay with their families, Your Honor." He paused to look over at Allison. "Given the concerns that my clients have raised, we respectfully request that the current custody arrangement remain in place and that the court deny this petition." Then, he sat down as if the case had already been settled.

Allison's fists clenched beneath the table. They didn't get it. Her entire last year had been nothing but unstable. It was about finally being in control of her future.

Beside her, Mr. Mueller stood, his movements deliberate. When he spoke, his voice was calm, firm, and unwavering. "Your Honor, Allison is at an age where her voice must be considered in decisions that directly affect her," he said. "Over the past few months, she has expressed growing dissatisfaction with the existing custody arrangement and has thoughtfully explored alternatives."

He motioned toward the screen, where information about the boarding school flashed into view. "The boarding school she has selected is academically rigorous, safe, and would provide her with the structure and challenge she requires to meet her long-term academic goals."

Allison inhaled sharply, her breath catching in her throat. Finally. Every word he said just validated what she had been trying to say for months.

Judge Harrington leaned forward slightly, her gaze settling on Allison. "Miss Maxwell," she said, her voice steady and even. "Please stand."

Allison's stomach churned, but she obeyed, rising to her feet. Her knees felt unsteady.

"This is a significant request," the judge continued. "Why do you believe attending boarding school is in your best interest?"

Her throat was dry, but she forced herself to answer. "Your Honor, I love my parents, and I know they want what's best for me," she said, forcing her voice to stay steady. "But changing schools every few years isn't helping me. I need consistency. I need a high school that challenges me academically so that I can get into the college of my choice—like Stanford or MIT."

The words came easier now, falling into place just as she had rehearsed them. "The schools in Manhattan don't meet my academic needs," she told the judge. "Why else would my parents have hired a tutor to help me work through the Kaiserhof curriculum?" She swallowed hard, pushing forward. "I don't need another 'finishing school'. I need an education that gives me a head start to become an engineer." She paused and looked at her parents. "Like my dad.

"On top of that," she continued, her voice quieter now but still firm, "Manhattan hasn't been a good fit for me. I just want to go to school without someone trying to push their beliefs on me all the time." She hesitated, but only for a moment. "Both of my parents' businesses require their full attention. That's not a criticism. It's just reality. The boarding school I want to attend will give me the environment I need."

Her voice steadied as she finished. "That's why I'm asking for this change."

Silence filled the courtroom as Allison sank into her seat.

The judge studied her for a long moment before leaning back slightly in her chair. Then, with slow, deliberate movements, she flipped through the documents on her desk. Allison could barely hear over the pounding in her ears.

Please. Please let this work.

Finally, the judge dismissed the documents on the smart wall. "This is not an easy decision," she said, her tone measured. "However, given the evidence presented, including the recommendation of the Guardian Ad Litem and Allison's own testimony, I find that a modification to the existing custody arrangement is appropriate."

The words hit Allison like a shock wave, and for a moment, she couldn't breathe.

She'd done it. God had listened to her prayers!

Everything else blurred together as the judge outlined the conditions, like holidays with both parents and weekly check-ins, but Allison barely heard them. She'd won.

The hearing adjourned. The bailiff's voice sounded somewhere far away, but all she could focus on was the way her hands shook as she rose to her feet.

Her parents stood, too. No one spoke. They all stood there, looking at each other.

Her mom's face had gone pale, her lips pressed into a thin line. Her dad's jaw was tight, his arms crossed over his chest, his exhaustion even more obvious now. He looked like he wanted to say something, but whatever it was, he held it back.

Allison met her mom's gaze, and for just a moment, there was something unspoken between them. Not quite anger, not quite understanding.

She didn't know what came next. But for the first time in a long time, she felt like she was walking toward something that was truly hers.

Chapter Twenty-One

The evening air carried a faint scent from the vineyard below. It was rich, almost sweet, with something green underneath. Allison sat on the patio, listening to the rustle of leaves and the quiet clatter of silverware inside the house.

The last month had been relatively calm. The Elbe Project passed its final inspections and was credited with saving a coastal town from catastrophic flooding. Her mom had thrown herself into the buyout plan, juggling late-night calls and nonstop meetings. It was the kind of chaos Allison had grown up with. And for once, both of her parents had agreed to give her space to process everything that came with the court's final decision.

Maybe that was why, when school recessed for the summer, they'd chosen a quiet place for holiday. Her mom had picked Deidesheim, a small town in Germany's wine country. They rented a house tucked into the hills. It wasn't fancy, but it was theirs for the week. A place where, just for a little while, they could pretend they were a normal family on vacation.

Allison leaned back in her chair, watching her dad struggle with the grill, muttering under his breath as smoke curled into the air. The sharp scent of burning fish filled the patio, and judging by her mom's expression, dinner was seconds away from disaster.

Her dad sighed dramatically. "I was this close to getting it right." He waved the tongs in the air before setting them down in surrender.

Her mom smiled. "Grilling salmon isn't as easy as it looks," she teased him.

"Fine, fine. We'll eat out," her dad conceded, running a frustrated hand through his hair.

Dinner was simple, but good. They'd let Allison choose the place. The small restaurant had an old-world feel with wooden beams, dim lighting, and the rich aroma of butter-fried schnitzel, caramelized onions, and fresh bread.

By the time they had walked back to the house, the easy laughter and teasing had faded. Tomorrow, they would fly to Hamburg to begin the process of shipping all of Allison's belongings back to the States.

Her dad built a fire in the pit outside, flames crackling softly as the scent of burning wood mixed with the warm night air. As he stacked the logs, her mom disappeared inside and returned with a bag of marshmallows, chocolate, and graham crackers. Mom set them on the small table near her chair.

Her gaze flickered to Allison and then to Dad. Allison recognized that look. Mom was bracing herself for a conversation she didn't want to have.

Her dad handed out the roasting sticks, and they gathered around the fire, their chairs angled toward the fire.

Her mom exhaled slowly as she pushed a marshmallow onto her fork and held it over the flames. "I'm going to miss it here."

Her dad held out the bag, and Allison snagged one for herself. As usual, her dad loaded his roasting stick with two per tine and settled down to intently watch the fire.

Finally, he broke the silence. "I'm not sure how to say this, so I'll be blunt," her dad told her. "We're sorry that we were both so caught up in our own lives that we didn't hear what you were trying to tell us, Allie."

Her mom nodded, biting her lip. "We both have some pretty painful memories of Family Court," she said. She reached out, brushing a stray hair behind Allison's ear like she used to when she was little. "I'm so sorry that you had to go through that by yourself. It was an incredibly brave thing to do."

Allison nodded, letting the words sink in. She thought about how strange religious rhetoric kept creeping into places where it didn't belong. About the pin that Michelle and other women wore in Manhattan.

"How did you—" Her voice faltered, but she forced herself to continue. "How did you live with it?"

Her mom turned to her. "With what?"

"The laws." There was a pop, and glowing embers drifted into the air. "You were detained." Allison hesitated, trying to find the right words. "You didn't get to choose."

Her dad looked down at the fire, poking at the embers. Mom sighed and set her marshmallow aside. "We didn't have many choices back then," she said quietly. "But we found a way to take back what we could. That's what people do. We adapt."

Allison's fingers tightened around her stick. "But it's not over," she told them. Her voice broke slightly, but she swallowed hard, pressing forward. "I left Manhattan, and it triggered an emergency lock-down. A full security sweep. People got detained because of me."

Her mother's expression softened, but her tone stayed firm. "The Council has already called for a full investigation. What happened was a clear overreach—and it will be dealt with."

Another silence stretched between them.

Finally, her mother reached out and took her hand. "My pregnancy was a very confusing time for us. Those journals only gave you a small fraction of what actually happened," she said. "Why didn't you bring them to me, sweetie? I could have answered your questions."

Allison hesitated. "Maybe I was afraid of what you'd say." *That you didn't want me. Either of you.*

Her mom's lips pressed into a sad smile. "I wouldn't have been angry," she said. "I would have tried to explain things that weren't in those pages."

"Like what?"

Her mom hesitated, her expression unreadable as she looked over at Dad. "Like the fact that I spend most of my pregnancy afraid that I'd do something wrong," she admitted. "That your dad and I weren't on the same page about a lot of things. That I felt like I was drowning, and journaling was the only way I could make sense of it."

Allison swallowed hard. "Was I a mistake?"

Her mom's eyes widened. "Never." She moved to kneel next to Allison's chair. "You are a gift from God, one I have been thankful for since before you were born."

Allison leaned forward, hugging her mom, trying not to sob as tears streamed down her face.

Her dad reached over and rescued her roasting stick. "Careful, Allie." He set it down on the table, her burnt marshmallow nearly dropping onto the patio.

Her mom pulled back, holding her by her shoulders. "I shared my journals with your dad." She glanced at him, and something unspoken passed between them. "We both needed a reminder of what that time was like."

He nodded and slowly pulled some of the roasted marshmallows from his fork to eat. "It was a very strange time in our lives, Allie," he told her. He popped a small piece into his mouth. "The new laws had just taken effect, and we honestly had no idea how to navigate them."

Allison swallowed hard, staring at the flames as they licked at the edge of the burning wood.

"I'm sorry," her dad said, his voice quiet. "Sorry about how you found out . . . how difficult your mom's pregnancy was for us." He paused. "I was quite the asshole, wasn't I?"

"Dad!" Allison gasped. She'd heard him swear at work, but never at home.

She looked up at her dad, searching for something in his hazel eyes that might loosen the knot in her throat. "Did you really not want me?" she asked, not sure if she wanted to know the answer or not.

Dad pursed his lips as he shook his head for a moment. "I'm not going to lie, Allie," he finally told her. "Younger me was pretty overwhelmed by just the idea of being a father. I was too young. Too immature to understand what was happening."

He leaned back in his chair, his roasted marshmallows forgotten. "When I first found out that your mom was pregnant, I wanted her to have an abortion. Later, I even talked about adoption." He hesitated. "Your mom shut me down both times."

She stiffened, her heart racing. He admitted it. He hadn't wanted her. "And?" she asked angrily.

"And then I held you," he told her. "All six pounds and ten ounces of you!" He leaned forward. "In that moment, I knew that I would do whatever it took to be there for you. To make you happy. Even if that means sending you to a boarding school in the middle of the icy Midwest."

"Oh, Dad . . . !" she softly wailed as she slipped off her chair and onto his lap. She'd spent so much time thinking her parents hadn't wanted her, especially her dad. But now, with his arms around her, rocking her gently like he used to when she was little, she could feel it again. His love. Steady and real.

Her mom came over and hugged both of them. "We weren't supposed to make it," she said to Allison. "We were young. Incredibly immature, both of us. But we built a life together, not because the law forced us to, but because at some point, we chose each other. We chose you."

Her dad pulled back to look at Allison. "You weren't planned. But you were never, ever a mistake."

The fire crackled softly, and in that quiet moment, something inside her shifted. They loved her. Both of them. And maybe that was enough.

The playground was as loud and chaotic as ever, filled with shrieks of younger kids echoing between the swings and slides. The creak of the old seesaw punctuated the air, and the occasional thud of a ball bounced off the pavement. The warm summer air carried the buttery scent of fresh pastries from a nearby Bäckerei stand.

Allison sat on the edge of the climbing frame, her feet dangling just above the ground. Her friends stood in a loose circle around her. But the usual teasing and gossip were missing. They were trying too hard to act normal, like this was just another afternoon at their favorite hangout.

But it wasn't.

"You're still coming back next summer, right?" Greta asked, scuffing her shoe against a loose pebble.

Allison forced a nod. "Absolutely." Her parents hadn't sold the Hamburg house. They'd kept it for her. And even if she couldn't find the words, she was deeply grateful.

Clara gave her a playful nudge. "Better not forget your German," she said. "If you come back talking like an American, we'll make fun of you."

Allison laughed despite the sadness she felt. "Then I guess we need to have weekly calls so I don't slack off, right?"

The words hung in the air, heavy and final. They'd all known this was coming. She was leaving, heading back to the U.S. after school. But now that it was real, no one seemed ready.

Greta dug into her backpack and pulled out a small box. "We got you something."

Carefully, Allison peeled back the tissue paper inside. A collection of tiny treasures was nestled in the box: photos of their group stuffed into a makeshift album, a charm bracelet with a tiny silver airplane, and, at the bottom, a can of Spezi.

"In case you get homesick," Lena said, her smile a bit forced.

Allison blinked hard, pressing her lips together before she could say something embarrassing. "You guys are the best."

They sat in the fading afternoon light, stretching out the moment as long as they could, talking about everything and nothing at all. It felt as if they just stayed there, she wouldn't have to go.

Mila was the first to break the spell, sighing heavily. "You should get going before we all start crying." She turned away to wipe a tear from her cheek.

Allison stood, the tiny box in her hands feeling heavier than it should. One by one, they hugged her. Each of them held on a little too tightly, like they could keep her from leaving if they didn't let go.

She turned toward the path leading back to her dad's house, her heart hammering as she forced herself to walk away.

She didn't look back. She couldn't.

Behind her, the playground still buzzed with life, as kids ran, laughed, and played, as if nothing had changed. But everything had.

Of course, she'd be back. They were her friends, and no matter where she lived, that wouldn't change.

The heat was suffocating, thick, and relentless as the afternoon sun bore down on them. Minnesota wasn't supposed to be this hot. It was known for its brutal winters, not stifling humidity. The air clung to Allison's skin, sticky, making every breath feel heavier. She wiped the sweat from her forehead with the back of her hand, looking around as her dad hauled another suitcase out of the trunk. The pavement beneath her shoes radiated heat, adding to her discomfort.

Oakmere Academy sat just outside Rochester, Minnesota. Allison took in the rows of red brick buildings, all lined up like they were trying to impress someone. Ivy crawled up the walls. Huge trees cast long shadows across the grass, and students and parents moved in clusters toward the dorms. It looked more like a university than a high school, with its towering windows and sprawling pathways that wound between the buildings.

"This place is huge," her dad muttered, adjusting his grip on her oversized suitcase. His shirt was already sticking to his back, but he didn't complain.

Allison nodded, barely hearing him over the dull hum of voices, the quiet whir of electric cars pulling in and out, and the rhythmic crunch of footsteps on the gravel pathways. The whole campus felt alive with movement, with upperclassmen and faculty guiding new students and overwhelmed parents toward the residential dorm.

Her mom stood a few steps away, watching the scene unfold. A few strands of her long black hair had slipped free from her French braid. When she finally spoke, her voice was softer than usual, but filled with pride.

"I was prepared for your first day of kindergarten, for your first science project, for so many firsts," she told her. "I always knew you'd do amazing things, and I can't wait to see what you create here."

Allison smiled. The nervousness hadn't quite disappeared but was overshadowed by something bigger—the thrill of something new.

The entrance to the dorm was crowded. Staff in matching polos smiled warmly as they directed families up the steps into the air-conditioned lobby. The cool air hit Allison like a wave, offering relief from the suffocating heat outside. The walls were lined with large digital directories, their glowing screens a sharp contrast to the grand wooden staircases that twisted up to the upper floors.

Her dad grunted as he hefted the last suitcase up the stairs. The halls were loud, filled with the sounds of doors opening and closing, voices echoing off high ceilings, and bursts of laughter from girls already forming friendships.

They stopped in front of her new room; the number was etched into a small digital plaque that softly glowed. The door unlocked with a quiet beep as she tapped her new key card against the panel. Inside, the space was simple but modern. A twin bed with crisp white sheets, the desk with a sleek, built-in smart board, a small closet, a dresser, and a window that overlooked the quad below.

Her mom walked toward the window, running a finger along the sill as she looked outside. From up here, the campus seemed even bigger, the neatly manicured lawns stretching out between the stately brick buildings.

Down below, a group of girls stood in the middle of the quad, their heads tilted upward as they guided small drones through the air, weaving them effortlessly between the trees. The tiny machines buzzed, dipping and soaring as if performing a choreographed dance.

Her dad watched them for a moment. "This place is a great fit for you, Allie," he finally said. "I can tell."

Allison raised an eyebrow. "Because of the brick and ivy?"

He chuckled, shaking his head. "Because of everything," he told her. "The tech here is cutting-edge." He gestured to the smart board. "It's built for kids who want to push themselves. You'll have access to real challenges, not just busywork."

A WARD OF THE STATE

Her mom was still watching the drones. "And it's not just about school, Sam," she said with a smile. "Look at them." She nodded toward the girls in the quad, their laughter floating up to the third-floor window. "It's a community. You're not just getting an education here—you're going to make friends with people who love the same things you do."

Allison was so happy. She was stepping into something meant for her. She grinned. "I know."

Her mom chuckled, despite the tears in her eyes. She came over and brushed a hand lightly over Allison's hair. "That's my baby girl!" she told her. "I'm so damn proud of you!"

Her dad pulled them both into a strong hug. "You're going to be amazing," he said.

Allison walked them downstairs, where other parents were getting final hugs. Some students waved them off impatiently, others held on just a little longer. Her mom and dad were somewhere in between, stepping back but reluctant to leave.

Her mom nodded at her. "I expect the weekly video calls to continue," she told Allison. "Friday evenings with both of us."

Her dad gave her a last, easy smile. "And we expect stories. Lots of them."

Allison nodded, standing a little taller. "Deal!"

They got into their car, and she watched them go, waving until they disappeared around the bend. The moment they were gone, she turned back toward the dorm, already looking forward to her new life. The sun was still high overhead and it cast a golden light over the entire quad. She looked back up at the drones soaring through the air.

She was home.

Epilogue

Allison stood by the hors d'oeuvres table, absently twirling the stem of her champagne flute as she surveyed the spread of seafood laid out on polished silver trays. Smoked trout croquettes, pickled shrimp, clams with bacon, and red bell pepper. Every bite was a quiet flex of wealth, sourced from expensive aquaculture tanks instead of the nearly empty oceans.

She ran a finger along the rim of her flute, the cool glass a steady contrast to the warmth of the room. Around her, familiar voices droned on in hushed tones, the cadence of polite sorrow punctuated by the clink of crystal and the low hum of business deals disguised as condolences. For most, it was a momentary inconvenience before everyone went back to their acquisitions, investments, and carefully orchestrated power plays.

If someone had bothered to look closely enough, they would see that the grief of her grandmother's passing wasn't the headliner of this gathering. It was just another accessory, worn like an appropriate piece of jewelry, acknowledged and ignored in equal measure.

Across the room, her cousin Patrick was in full salesman mode, his easy grin in place as he spun his latest project. His tone, just the right mix of charm and authority, tried to convey the same underlying message that The Firm lived by: The game never stopped. Not for grief, not for family, not even for death.

Typical.

Allison took a slow sip of champagne, her gaze trailing over the room. Her mom's side of the family had never been great with genuine emotion.

Maybe that's what bugged her the most. She had expected them to feel something, anything. The matriarch of their extended family had died. And yet, here they were, barely pausing before recalibrating their social chessboards.

She lifted her glass again and caught the quick glint of her ring. The smooth cut of the sapphire. Four carats, platinum band. Nothing gaudy. Just enough to remind her what she'd built, the choices she'd made, and the fact that they had been hers and hers alone.

Princesses slay their own damn dragons. Why wait for the prince when you can build your own empire? Her mom had told her that when she was little. It had been the best advice she'd ever gotten.

A hush rippled through the muted conversations. She knew before she even turned around who had just walked in.

"Oh my God," Patrick blurted, his voice cutting through the noise. "It's him."

Allison slowly turned around. Her cousin was practically vibrating with excitement, his usual cocky confidence taking a backseat to awe.

Ethan lingered in the doorway, his gaze cool and assessing. His sharp cheekbones, defined jawline, and dark brown eyes reflected his Chinese heritage, but it was the effortless elegance that set him apart. The custom-tailored black suit. The subtle sheen of expensive fabric. A sleek watch, understated but unmistakably expensive, glinted at his wrist, a quiet testament to old money and influence. No need for flash. His presence alone was enough.

Their eyes met across the room, and just like that, the tension in her shoulders loosened.

Patrick, oblivious, was already moving, practically shoving people aside in his eagerness to reach him. "Mr. Guo, it's an honor! Your company's expansion into lunar mining is legendary."

Allison fought the urge to roll her eyes.

Ethan barely acknowledged Patrick, his gaze settling on Allison as he stepped around her cousin. He rapidly closed the distance between them with the quiet confidence of someone always in control.

She took another sip of champagne, stretching the moment out just a little longer to let the anticipation build. And then, as Ethan reached her, his fingers slid easily into hers, their matching sapphire rings glinting under the soft lighting. He lifted her hand and pressed a gentle kiss onto her knuckles.

A few whispers flickered around them, a ripple of surprise spreading throughout the room. Allison barely noticed. Ah, my love, she thought.

Patrick, still hovering around them awkwardly, like a lost puppy, finally seemed to catch on. His eyes darted between them, visibly struggling to catch up with what he was seeing.

"Allison," Ethan said, his voice warm. "I've missed you."

Patrick let out a nervous laugh. "Ah, yeah, so this is my cousin, Allison."

Ethan didn't hesitate. "My fiancée, actually."

Patrick's expression froze, his entire posture shifting like someone had just yanked the floor out from under him. Allison turned to watch as the realization dawned—slow, painful, and entirely satisfying.

Ethan, ever the businessman, didn't let him off the hook. He turned to face her cousin, tucking Allison under his arm with quiet possessiveness. "Patrick Williams, right?" he asked. "You own a controlling interest in Ascendex." He turned back to Allison. "Aren't you considering angel funding for that company?" he asked rather innocently. As if he didn't know!

Allison nodded. "It's just one of a handful of companies I'm looking into."

Patrick blinked, rapidly looking back and forth between them. He coughed, his confident facade cracking just a little. "Ah. Uh, th-th-the automated launch vehicle we're hoping to roll out in 2063," he said, stammering just a bit.

Ethan nodded, thoughtful. "That explains why Mira has been reviewing data on near-orbit launches with you," he said as an aside to Allison.

She swirled her champagne, watching Patrick scramble to recover. He opened his mouth, then shut it again.

"I may be able to lower the cost per launch with a slight redesign of the model," she said smoothly, her tone cool enough to let Patrick know she wasn't just making conversation. "That would make Ascendex actually profitable." She paused to look up at Ethan. "Hopefully, Mira will have answers for me before we get back to Shenzhen."

Patrick exhaled sharply, forcing a tight smile as he straightened his jacket. "Well," he said, regaining some of his composure, "I'll let you two get back to it. Plenty to discuss, I'm sure." He lifted his glass in a small, measured toast. "Congratulations on your engagement." Then, without another word, he turned and walked away.

Around them, the conversations started up again; the moment dissolving into background noise. But, for Allison, something important had already changed. This part of her life, the need to prove herself to people who had never seen her as more than an afterthought, felt like a closed chapter.

She was already focused on the future. The nanobot lenses that she'd championed were launching next week. Augmented reality and vision correction in one simple package. After that, who knew? Interactive hologram rooms, maybe? The future wasn't slowing down, and neither was she.

She squeezed Ethan's hand, feeling the steady reassurance in his touch. Patrick was staring at them from across the room. He looked lost. For a split second, she almost felt bad.

Almost.

Allison let out a slow breath, her smile small but certain. She owned her own kingdom now. And she wasn't done building it.

Every dystopia starts with a single law. The Unborn Child Protection Act is more than fiction. It's a glimpse into a future shaped by today's choices.

This companion site uncovers the path from our present to 2042, one decision at a time. Subscribe for regular updates, exclusive content, and insights directly from the author.

Scan the QR code to join the Substack community and explore:

- Behind-the-scenes commentary

- First dibs on deleted scenes and bonus content

- Real-world context that inspired the novel

- Early previews of what's coming next

Prefer email updates outside of Substack? Join the full newsletter at: https://www.mewright.com/

The future is coming. Don't just read the story—follow the threads that lead us there.

The Fatherhood Mandate Preview

Curious about Sam's experience with the Wisconsin Individual Family Education program and Rylee's pregnancy? Here's the first chapter of **The Fatherhood Mandate**.

Sam stood on the rocky beach, watching the small waves lap against the monochrome shoreline. It was late August, but the wind coming off Lake Michigan was a bit chilly. *Probably should have brought a jacket*, he thought as he shoved his hands deep into his front pockets.

He kicked at the pebbles that littered the beach, then pulled his phone out of his back pocket to check the time. 8:10 am. It was too early for this shit.

Sam shaded his eyes as the sun momentarily poked through the somber clouds, then slid the phone back into his pocket and glared at the horizon. Of course, Rylee was late. She was always late.

He sighed. Rylee was the kind of girl that you could love one minute and hate the next. Bright blue eyes that just drew you in.

Long black hair and a saucy smile. Curves in all the right places. She knew what to say, when to say it, and what it took to get her way.

And that was the problem. Rylee always got her way.

Not this time, Sam thought as he kicked at the sandy pebbles at his feet. No more meaningless late night texts. No more screaming fights over some imagined insult. No more scheduling and rescheduling his life around her ever-changing wants and needs. It was over. Done.

He heard her cuss as she stumbled across the damp rocks and pieces of driftwood that littered the beach, her complaints almost lost in the mindless hiss of the surf as she slowly made her way across the deserted beach. He ignored her.

"Sam, I'm cold," Rylee said when she finally reached him. That telltale whine warned him she was already in a mood. "Can't we go someplace else?"

Sam felt her tentatively reach for him. He pulled away and shoved his hands into his front pockets again. "Just tell me what you want, Rylee," he said, eyeing the darkening clouds that threatened rain out over the lake. "We broke up. It's over. There's nothing more to say."

"It's really chilly out here," she whimpered. "I can't talk when I'm freezing to death!"

She sniffed as if she was holding back tears. He turned and one look was enough. Melodramatic expression. Bloodshot eyes. Blotchy skin from crying.

That was the last thing he needed that morning. "Let's go," he muttered. He grabbed her arm and forced her to walk toward the trail that threaded its way through the woods surrounding the beach behind them.

Sam felt her stumble over a small piece of driftwood and glanced down. Soft leather flats peeked out beneath a long dress that were more at home on a riverboat cruise than on sandy terrain. No matter how many times they'd been to Tietjen Beach, she just couldn't take the hint and wear sensible clothes.

He released her arm as they slowly made their way through the overgrown trail to the stairs. Wild grapevines, goldenrod, and assorted weeds crowded the entrance to the limestone steps and made it almost impossible to reach the rough, wooden handrails as they climbed.

They approached the top of the bluff. Sam headed for one of the benches that used to overlook the beach below. Now, trees and small brush huddled against the hill, creating an almost impenetrable view.

He sat down. "Tell me what's going on," he asked as gently as he could. Sometimes it was easier to just go with it.

Rylee slumped onto a nearby bench. Almost on cue, tears started rolling down her cheeks. "We can't break up, Sam," she whispered. She brushed her long, black hair away from her face. "I need you."

Sam turned away, staring at the clouds that randomly filtered through the foliage around him. It was definitely going to rain. He could smell it in the air.

"Rylee, it's over." Sam ducked his head, staring at the sandy ground. "You broke up with *me*. We're done."

"No!" Rylee stood, fists clenched, as she screamed at him. "You don't understand. We made a mistake!"

Sam leaned back and wearily looked up at her. "How many times do we need to break up before you finally accept that it's over, Rylee?" he asked, lightly mocking her. "Two more times? Five?" He searched her face for any bit of understanding. "Breaking up was your idea." He paused for emphasis. "Both times!"

Rylee screwed her eyes shut and turned her face to the sky. "I was wrong," she whispered. She opened her eyes and wiped her face with both hands. "Things have changed, Sam."

"What things?" Sam demanded. "I'm really tired of this, Rylee! Tell me what's going on!"

She sat down and slumped against the bench, covering her eyes with one hand. "It doesn't matter, Sam," she told him. "I'm probably worried about nothing."

Sam sighed as he stood up. "Fine," he growled. And, with that, he walked away, trying to ignore the quiet sobs behind him. He had better things to do than to deal with the drama queen.

Don't miss out on the next chapter of The Unborn Child Protection Act series. Get your copy of *The Fatherhood Mandate* today!

Author's Note

History used to be written by the victors. Now it's just data, shaped by whoever controls the system. With a few keystrokes, words can be reshaped. Events can be erased. Or worse, rewritten.

The truth doesn't vanish all at once. It's edited, versioned, and quietly replaced. Or, in some cases, deleted altogether—like the purge of educational materials and the removal of information about 'Notable Graves' from Arlington National Cemetery's website in early 2025 . Just another casualty in the culture war, buried beneath the compost heap of the so-called 'woke agenda.'

In the aftermath of the Supreme Court's decision in Dobbs v. Jackson Women's Health Organization, women began to die in 2022 because doctors were afraid to do anything as long as there was a fetal heartbeat. Since then, women across the United States have bled to death, succumbed to fatal infections, and wound up in morgues with what medical examiners recorded were 'products of conception' still in their bodies.

'Removing waste and fraud' became a euphemism for deepening economic inequality. And the closure of entire federal agencies, like the Department of Education, left the nation less competitive, less prepared, and more divided than ever.

In the early 2020s, ultra-wealthy individuals dramatically increased their financial support for far-right political movements around the world, leveraging their wealth to sway elections and shape policy in their favor. In the United States, figures like Elon Musk openly supported right-wing causes, including a campaign in which he pledged $1 million per day leading up to the 2024 election. Across Europe, Russian oligarch Viktor Medvedchuk was linked to covert funding of far-right, anti-EU politicians through platforms like Voice of Europe. These moves marked a global trend in which billionaires increasingly used their resources to tilt democratic systems toward nationalist and authoritarian agendas.

These events are the bedrock of *A Ward of the State*. From here, all that remains is a history as it was written for students in 2040, and for the ones who never thought to question the chaos that our country descended into.

A History of the Republic's Return to Order

As we stand in 2040, one thing seems clear to many: history has shown us that peace and stability come from a strong government rooted in traditional values. After years of unrest, uncertainty, and cultural drift, the Republic is returning to principles that once bound us together: unity, moral clarity, and a shared sense of purpose.

The roots of this return stretch back centuries. In the colonial era, early settlers brought with them firm beliefs about faith, family, and responsibility. Households were built around clear roles: fathers as leaders and protectors, mothers as caretakers and moral guides. These roles, supported by biblical teachings, helped create a society built on structure and trust.

For a long time, this way of life held firm. But in the 20th century, things began to shift. Movements like women's suffrage challenged old traditions. More women entered the workforce and called for independence, which many saw as progress. Others saw it as the beginning of a cultural unraveling.

By the 1960s and 70s, that foundation was shaken again. Feminism, civil rights activism, and LGBTQ movements pushed the boundaries even further. For some, it was a new era of freedom. For others, it was the beginning of confusion and decline.

In the 1980s, leaders like Jerry Falwell and Pat Robertson pushed back. They called for a return to moral certainty—faith, family, and clear gender roles. The Religious Right gained ground, and for a time, it looked like the tide might turn.

But the changes kept coming. Abortion access expanded. 'Reproductive rights' became a rallying cry. By 2015, same-sex marriage became legal. Many celebrated these milestones. Others warned that something fundamental was being lost.

In the years that followed, conservative leaders took action. With Project 2025 and Agenda 47, they set out to undo decades of policy that had, in their view, undermined the family and weakened national character. These plans replaced progressive programs with ones that emphasized faith, family, and duty.

Surprisingly, social media played a part too. A new wave of influencers—"trad wives" and "trad girlfriends"—used their platforms to promote homemaking, loyalty, and the joy of supporting a husband and raising a family. In a culture that had long pushed women toward careers and independence, these women offered something different: a return to roots.

In 2027, **The Media Accountability and Integrity Act** reshaped how the public accessed information. News outlets and publishers were required to get a license. Anonymous social media accounts were banned. Algorithms were rewritten to prioritize verified sources. Critics called it censorship. Supporters said it protected the truth and restored trust in public discourse.

Marriage, too, was redefined as a return to tradition. **The Marriage Protection and Unity Act of 2031** recognized only unions between one man and one woman of the same race. That same year, **The Family Incentive Program** provided tax breaks, housing support, and parenting stipends to couples in these approved marriages—solidifying the family as the cornerstone of national policy. Other households were no longer eligible for most public aid.

In 2032, **The Family Stability Act** brought back divorce laws that hadn't been seen since the 1950s. No-fault divorce was eliminated, and courts required proof of serious harm, like abuse or abandonment, before granting separation. The idea was simple: protect marriage, protect our children, protect our Republic.

In 2033, **The Faith Recognition and Religious Unity Initiative** made it official: faith would once again guide public life. Christian values returned to school events and civic rituals. Faith-based organizations were given more influence, and public officials were encouraged to lead with conviction and moral clarity.

A WARD OF THE STATE

Then came 2035. **The National Service and Readiness Act** made service to the Republic mandatory for citizens between the ages of 18 to 21. Young men served in the military or civil defense. Young women were placed in an all-female division focused on domestic logistics and community care. This became a rite of passage, a way to build discipline, loyalty, and a common identity.

Now, in 2040, as the world faces climate disruption, global instability, and economic strain, the Republic has chosen a path: strength through structure, freedom through duty. The government has made hard choices, limited some freedoms, and demanded more from its citizens—not to punish them, but to preserve them.

By reclaiming what was lost, the Republic has found its footing. What once felt like decline now looks like rebirth. Freedom, it turns out, means little without responsibility. And in the eyes of many, the Republic's strength today proves that tradition, order, and shared values still matter.

Acknowledgements

To my loving husband and daughter, thank you for your unwavering support. Your belief in me kept me going through the long hours of drafting and editing. I am grateful for your patience, understanding, and unconditional love.

Dave, your insight didn't just shape this book. It gave it clarity where it mattered most. Sam's growth as a father and husband wouldn't be nearly as grounded or pronounced without your influence. Your voice is in the silences he holds, the choices he makes, and the man he becomes. I'm grateful beyond words.

Jeff, you are more than a just a friend. For the past three years, I've known I could find you working away in Immersed VR. You've been a steady presence and a reliable collaborator. Whether verifying translations, broadcasting my VR book launches via LinkedIn or simply showing up to share the space, your insight and consistency made a lasting impact. This book is better because of you, and I'm grateful to have had you alongside me the whole way.

Alex, Gabriel, Janusz, James, and Miguel, thank you for showing up in all the best ways. Whether it was a quick game of mini golf, a Friday Watch Party, or just hanging out on Discord, your presence made a difference. I truly appreciate spending quality time with me in VR and bring fun, focus, and friendship to the process. Your group patience, encouragement and good humor helped tremendously.

And to #TeamWright, thank you all for providing feedback on that crucial first draft. You guys rock!

About the author

M.E. Wright is a writer, social scientist, and Midwest native with a keen interest in exploring the intersections of power, ideology, and human resilience. She crafts thought-provoking dystopian and speculative fiction that challenges societal norms while keeping readers engaged with complex characters and immersive storytelling.

When she's not writing, M.E. enjoys analyzing cultural shifts, exploring historical narratives, and engaging in spirited debates about the future of humanity. She measures distance in time, not miles, and—despite living deep in Packer country—has been known to secretly root for the Bears.

Also by M.E. Wright

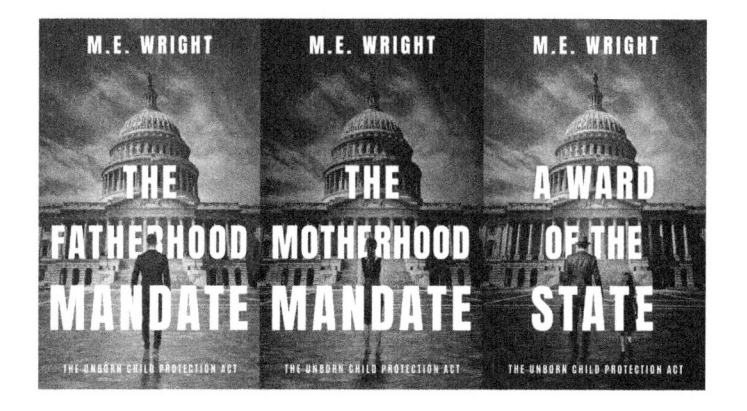

The Unborn Child Protection Act

The Fatherhood Mandate
The Motherhood Mandate
Thin Blue Lines

Order now at https://www.mewright.com/store/books to save and access exclusive signed editions and special offers.